高等学校商务英语规划教材

最新实用商务英语教程

"中国公司走出去"篇

主　编　杨祖宪

副主编　韩文进　谢　晴

朱敏华　朱义华

南京大学出版社

图书在版编目(CIP)数据

最新实用商务英语教程："中国公司走出去"篇/杨祖宪主编. —南京：南京大学出版社，2009. 9

ISBN 978-7-305-06240-7

Ⅰ. 实… Ⅱ. 杨… Ⅲ. 商务-英语-教材 Ⅳ. H31

中国版本图书馆 CIP 数据核字(2009)第 103779 号

出 版 者　南京大学出版社
社　　址　南京市汉口路 22 号　　　邮　编　210093
网　　址　http://www.NjupCo.com
出 版 人　左　健

丛 书 名　高等学校商务英语规划教材
书　　名　最新实用商务英语教程："中国公司走出去"篇
主　　编　杨祖宪
责任编辑　夏振邦　裴维维　李海霞　　　编辑热线　025-83686029

照　　排　南京南琳图文制作有限公司
印　　刷　南京大学印刷厂
开　　本　787×1092　1/16　印张 13　字数 332 千
版　　次　2009 年 9 月第 1 版　2009 年 9 月第 1 次印刷
ISBN 978-7-305-06240-7
定　　价　27.00 元

发行热线　025-83594756
电子邮箱　Press@NjupCo.com
　　　　　Sales@NjupCo.com(市场部)

Foreword

About China Inc.

Thirty years of phenomenal growth since 1978 has propelled China to become the world's third largest economy, the second biggest trader and exporter. One powerful engine driven this unprecedented growth is China Inc. , especially those companies that "go global. "

These Chinese firms conduct and expand their business globally by exporting their products or services, importing the raw materials or machinery they need. They also build factories and R&D centers abroad or engage in overseas mergers and acquisitions.

Every year a torrent of products surging out of these firms are finding their way into billions of homes and offices throughout the world. They are no longer just labor-intensive footwear or furniture, but now also include high-tech products such as PV solar panels and semiconductor devices. It is this trillion dollars worth of annual exports that helps China to leapfrog Germany to become the world's largest exporting nation soon.

China's insatiable need for natural resources and luxury goods, ranging from iron ores to commercial airplanes, from Rolls Royce vehicles to Louis Vuitton purses, is being felt around the world. China now is world's second largest crude oil importer and the third biggest consumer of luxury goods, accounting for 12 percent of sales worldwide.

The world community is also witnessing the fast growing presence and increasing power of Chinese firms almost everywhere—a Chinese auto plant popping up in Latin America, a refrigerator factory humming in the US and a high-tech firm erecting telecommunication networks in Europe. By the end of 2008, China's total stock of FDI outflows exceeded US $ 100 billion.

As these Chinese companies become increasingly internationally focused, they also venture into cross-border M&A transactions. Lenovo's takeover of IBM's PC division for US$1. 25bn in 2004 was widely hailed as the beginning of a wave of big acquisitions abroad by Chinese firms. Chinalco's move to inject $19. 5 billion into Rio Tinto Ltd—the world's third largest iron ore miner was considered another milestone of China's desire to invest large sums overseas though the deal was finally scrapped.

Thirty years ago, virtually every business in China was called a "factory" or "plant. " Being small and weak, hardly any of them operated competitively in global business. Today, many Chinese firms operate globally and some of them such as Lenovo, Haier and Huawei are beginning to compete with leading multinationals. It will not be another 30 years long before many more local companies become Chinese versions of GE or Nokia, Toyota or Samsung.

About the Course

Chinese Companies Going Global is a case-based business English reader, a companion to *MNCs Doing Business in China*. Catering for both academic and practical needs, this reader is intended for students at both intermediate and advanced levels, who desire to further improve their language proficiency or broaden their business knowledge. Those who are already in the business community will also find the case studies in the textbook helpful in their daily business decision-making process.

The book with 46 texts is organized into five parts with each centered on a different topic. Chapter One describes China emerging as a powerful economy. Chapter Two depicts the new boundaries of Chinese firms as a whole. Chapter Three hails the popularity of made-in-China products with end-users around the world while Chapter Four and Five mainly focus on Chinese firms engaged in purchasing overseas commodities and assets.

The texts written in genres of reports or editorials, commentaries or features are carefully selected from internationally well-known publications or academically recognized sources. They are also sufficiently annotated with introductory remarks, business tips, review questions, and supplemented by vocabulary and translation exercises. Instructors using this textbook are encouraged to design their own alternative tasks in an attempt to maximize the good effect derived from interaction between the text knowledge and their real-life experiences, between the language learning and business skill acquisition.

The Business English Reader *Chinese Companies Going Global* features an integration of BEC, an acronym for Business, English and Culture. Therefore, the textbook can be used in either a language class or a business studies class, and for an independent course or as a supplementary reader for a business course. As a matter of fact, its forerunner *MNCs Doing Business in China* has been extensively used ever since its début in 2006 in both language and business classes at hundreds of universities throughout China. This textbook, it is hoped, will be just as intellectually appealing and practically useful to both language and business students, and to learners both on campus and in the workplace.

Acknowledgements

I wish to express my warm thanks to the faculty and students at the School of Foreign Studies as well as students at MBA Educational Center of Jiangnan University, who field-tested some of the texts from the book.

Meanwhile, I am deeply grateful to David Scott, Ruth Anderson and Dr. LUO Jian for their professional insight and comments on particular business concepts and terms.

My special gratitude also goes to Professor YANG Jin-rong and his assistants at Nanjing University Press for their specialist advice and moral support.

Simon Yang
Jiangnan University

序 言

自1978年改革开放以来，中国经过30多年的惊人快速发展已成为世界级经济大国，GDP有望今年超越日本成为全球第二经济大国，进出口总量也将名列世界第二。中国取得如此令人骄傲的成绩，其“中国公司”功不可没，尤其是几十年来开展全球性经营活动“走出去”的公司更值得称颂赞扬。

中国公司走出去从事国际经营活动的形式多样，有的出口其产品与服务或进口其所需商品与设备，有的在海外建厂、设立研发中心，或并购海外资产。

每年来自中国制造的产品进入世界千家万户与数以千计的办公室，这些产品不仅仅是劳动密集型的鞋靴与家具，还有高科技的太阳能光伏组件与半导体器件。正是这些每年价值数万亿美元的出口产品使中国终将超越德国登上世界第一大出口国的王座。

中国经济的快速发展对全球资源和高档奢侈品的需求也是逐年攀升，铁矿石、商用飞机、劳斯莱斯高档汽车、路易威登箱包一一耀眼登上了中国进口采购单榜首。中国曾一举签下了价值174亿美元的空中客车，2008年世界顶级高档轿车宾利在中国销售超500辆，从而取代日本跃升至亚洲第一。同年中国已成为全球高档奢侈品第三大消费国，占全球销售额百分之十二。

十多年来中国公司走出去在海外投资建厂、开设研发中心也是与年俱增。自1999年以来，海尔公司在美国相继建立了设计中心在洛杉矶、生产基地在南卡罗来纳州、营销中心在纽约“三位一体本土化”的海外基地，为当地开发并生产了冰箱、冷柜、酒柜等能与美国本土主流品牌竞争的庞大白色家电产品群，并创下了7小时内销售7000台海尔空调的惊人纪录。华为技术公司自1996年起就在全球与美国3Com公司、英国电信、Telefonica等世界顶尖电讯公司建立了合作伙伴关系，并在印度、美国、瑞典、俄罗斯等国建立了研究中心，2008年其专利申请量排名为全球第一。目前，华为的产品和解决方案已经应用于全球100多个国家，以及35个全球前50强的运营商。中国工程机械制造之王三一重工在全球有12个海外子公司，产品批量出口到110多个国家和地区，继在印度、美国投资建成工程机械研发制造基地后又斥资1亿欧元在德国建设研发中心及机械制造基地。

随着中国公司全球化经营意识日益增强，越来越多的国内公司尝试并购海外企业。如果说2004年联想以12.5亿美元成功收购IBM个人电脑事业部是中国大型企业海外并购浪潮第一潮的话，那么2007年中投公司以30亿美元购买与2008年又增持美国第二大私募基金公司黑石股份的举措，2009年中铝公司出手195亿美元增资世界矿业巨头力拓（Rio Tinto）公司的尝试则仅是中国2万亿美元外汇储备在海外寻觅多元化长期投资浪潮中迭起的一朵朵浪花而已。

30多年前，中国的企业几乎都被称呼为“工厂”，无论是国营企业还是集体企业既小又弱，具有海外经营竞争力的企业更是寥若星晨。如今中国公司实力今非昔比，2008年一度在全球市值最高的十大上市公司中中国公司占了五席，中石化进入财富世界10强，联想、海尔、华为等公司在各自行业中已经可与世界顶尖对手不相上下、势均力敌。再过30年，坚信中国会涌现出更多自己的通用电气、爱立信、丰田、三星等享誉全球的世界级跨国公司。

《最新实用商务英语教程:"中国公司走出去"篇》(以下简称《中国公司走出去》)为数年前南京大学出版社出版的《跨国公司在中国——最新实用商务英语教程》(以下简称《跨国公司在中国》)一书的姐妹篇,同为实用商务英语案例类读本。全书精选来自国际英文主流媒体的46篇文章,共分五章:第一章为"盛世中国",描述改革开放30多年来中国取得了引人瞩目的辉煌成就;第二章为"中国公司",整体描绘中国公司的新面貌;第三章为"中国制造",探究中国产品走红全球的缘由;第四章为"中国采购",展现了中国公司和中国消费者全球采购与全球消费的惊人实力;第五章为"中国并购",精选了中国公司近年来在海外并购和尝试并购的案例,记载了他们成功的喜悦与失败的苦涩。

本书精选的46篇文章,内容时新、文字地道、文体多样。同时,每一课配有导读、注释与练习,旨在让读者看作结合、学练同步、学有所得、无师自通。本书既可单独用作商务英语专用教程,也可用于财经类专业课程的补充教材;既适用于商务英语专业学生和财经类专业学生,也适用于立志于进入或已经从事国际经营业务的白领阶层或招商引资的经理们。

《中国公司走出去》集语言水平提高、商务知识更新、跨文化意识提升于一体的特色教材。在校学生学好此书能同时让你的英语更加"洋味"十足,使你在课堂内就能品尝到中国公司闯荡海外市场的甜酸苦辣、在步入商界前就能辨别"蓝海"与"红海"的差异、在踏入异国他乡前就能了解当地风土人情、商业习俗。从商人士学透此教程,能有益提高你的国际沟通能力、增强你的招商引资力度,为你企业开辟更多的海外市场、为你公司海外经营带来更佳的辉煌业绩。

《中国公司走出去》一书的姐妹篇《跨国公司在中国》自2006年上市以来,已被国内数以百计的大学、公司、图书馆使用或收藏。不但外语学院的英语专业学生使用此教材,商学院的本科生与MBA学生也选用该教材。我有同样的信心,《中国公司走出去》如同她的姐妹篇也能走进数以百计的校园和公司,令莘莘学子与白领经理们都爱不释手。

在编写此书过程中,承蒙江南大学加籍David Scott与Ruth Anderson两位外教与南大同窗罗健博士在百忙中拨冗审阅该书文稿,也承蒙北京外国语大学中国外语教育研究中心第四批中国外语教育基金以及江南大学省级质量工程培育项目"EBC复合型英语人才培养模式创新实验基地"基金的资助,更感谢对外经贸大学施建军校长对此书的赞美与推荐。

由于编者水平与经验有限,难免不当之处,谨请使用本教材的同行与同学或其他读者及时指正,不胜感谢!

江南大学 杨祖宪

2009年盛夏写于江南大学蠡湖校区

Contents

目　录

Chapter One　Stronger China

盛世中国

Text 1　A Less Fiery Dragon

东方巨龙　依旧强大

导读　通常各国经济总量排位以美元计算，但一些国际组织如世界银行、国际货币基金组织却以PPP(购买力平价指数)来计算。他们的排位一时无比夸大了中国的经济实力，引得一些西方人终日诚惶诚恐。但根据世行最新数据统计，中国GDP“缩水”了40%，相比前几年按PPP计算的10万亿美元，如今中国GDP仅为6万亿美元，着实让那些“恐惧中国”的政治家或经济学家可以入眠安睡了。但源自华尔街的全球金融海啸也许又要让一些人重估中国经济赶超美国的日期，依旧强大的东方巨龙恐怕也许会使他们“今夜无眠”啦！

China may be a smaller economic giant than previously thought.

Americans who spend their time fretting about when their economy will be overtaken by China will have gleefully leapt upon new numbers suggesting that China's economy may in fact be 40 percent smaller than current estimates. However, the new figures, if confirmed, would also mean that the world economy has been growing rather more slowly in recent years than officially reported by the IMF[①], which is less salutary for everyone.

It is not the Chinese government that has been exaggerating the size of its GDP[②], but

---

① IMF: International Monetary Fund 国际货币基金组织，政府间的国际金融组织。基金组织设5个地区部门(非洲、亚洲、欧洲、中东、西半球)和12个职能部门(行政管理、中央银行业务、汇兑和贸易关系、对外关系、财政事务、国际货币基金学院等)。

② GDP: gross domestic product 国内生产总值。它是以国土原则计算的，指一定时期内一国所生产的产品和所提供的服务按现行市价计的总价值，但它不包括海外净收入，而国民生产总值(GNP)则包括海外净收入。

international organizations, such as the World Bank[①] and the IMF, which measure each nation's output in terms of purchasing-power parity (PPP)[②]. If China's GDP is converted into dollars using market exchange rates, it amounted to $2.7 trillion last year, only one-fifth of America's $13.2 trillion, and the fourth-largest in the world. But a dollar buys a lot more in China than in America because prices of many non-traded goods and services tend to be much lower in poor economies. Converting a poor country's GDP into dollars at market exchange rates therefore understates the true size of its economy.

Instead, many economists prefer to convert GDPs into dollars using PPPs, which take account of price differences between countries. *The Economist's* Big Mac index[③] is a crude measure of PPP. Much more sophisticated estimates are produced by the International Comparison Programme[④], co-ordinated by the World Bank, which gathers prices for more than 800 goods and services in countries around the globe. On a PPP basis, the World Bank ranks China as the world's second-biggest economy, with a GDP of $10 trillion last year. At its recent pace of growth, China's GDP could overtake America's by 2010.

The World Bank's estimate for China is widely used by economists. Yet few realize that it is based on a lot of guesswork, as the bank's previous international price surveys have not included China. Instead, it extrapolated from a study of prices in America and China that dates all the way back to the 1980s. The bank's latest price-comparison study, due to be published in mid-December, does include China for the first time, and preliminary evidence indicates that its GDP has been overstated in the past. In a recent article in the *Financial Times*, Albert Keidel, an economist at the Carnegie Endowment for Interna-

---

① 世界银行。联合国的专门机构之一,拥有 184 个成员国。其使命是消除贫困、提高发展中国家人民的生活水平。世界银行是为中、低收入国家消除贫困而提供贷款、政策咨询、技术援助以及技术分享服务的国际性金融机构。

② 购买力平价。它是表现人均购买力的一个指标。在经济学上,是一种根据各国不同的价格水平计算出来的货币之间的等值系数,使我们能够对各国的国内生产总值进行合理比较。

③ Big Mac index 巨无霸指数。购买力平价理论(PPP)就考虑到同一种商品在不同国家的售价,着重考察不同货币的实际购买力。购买力平价理论认为,从长期趋势看来,在任何两个国家间,购买同一组的商品和服务所花费的货币价值是一样的,而不同货币的兑换比率会朝着这个方向逼近,最终使购买者付出同样的代价。根据这一思想,《经济学人》杂志自 1986 年编制了"巨无霸指数",以麦当劳行销全球 120 个国家的汉堡包——巨无霸为标的,考察用当地货币购买这同一产品需要多少钱,来衡量这些国家的汇率是否处在"合理"水平。

④ 国际比较项目。它是世界银行开始的一项持续多年的经济统计项目,1993 年在实行的国民账户体系(System of National Accounts)中引入了购买力平价(PPPs)的概念。ICP 将近一千种产品和服务的价格作为比价样品,所以这种一篮子的产品购买力比较,可以比较客观全面地反映一个经济体的基本状况,相对于按现行汇率计算的 GDP 更能反映一国的经济力。

tional Peace, noted that PPP figures published by the Asian Development Bank (ADB)[①], as part of its input into the World Bank's International Comparison Programme, implied that China's GDP was 40 percent smaller than the number reported by the World Bank. Interestingly, the new figure is very close to what the Big Mac index has indicated all along.

Assume for a moment that Mr Keidel's figure of 40 percent is correct, then China's GDP in PPP terms is slashed from $ 10 trillion to $ 6 trillion. That would still leave it as the world's second-largest economy, but it would not overtake America for at least another ten years. India, on the other hand, would drop from third to fifth place in the world ranking.

Adjusting the Global Speedometer

China would probably be quite happy to see its GDP revised down, hoping that America might stop picking on a smaller, poorer economy. But revised PPPs would not only change international rankings, they would also affect the pace of global growth. To calculate world GDP growth, individual countries' growth rates are weighed by their share of world output. Using PPP weights, as the IMF does, the world economy has grown by an average of 5 percent over the past five years, its strongest pace since the early 1970s. This is largely because emerging economies have been growing by 7.5 percent a year (compared with only 2.3 percent in the G7 developed economies), and they account for around half of world GDP. But if China and India are 40 percent smaller than previously thought, world growth would be trimmed to 4.5 percent.

The difficulty of measuring PPP is one reason why some economists prefer to compare the sizes of economies using market exchange rates. After all, it is argued, countries trade with each other at market rates, so these provide the best basis for comparison. Measured this way, world growth over the past five years has been a still more modest 3.4 percent. Far from being the fastest pace for decades, that is slower than in the 1980s. So has the global boom been a mirage? A closer look at the numbers shows that this cannot be right. Measured at market exchange rates, emerging economies' share of global output last year was less than in 1980, even though they have been growing more than twice as fast as the rich economies. The increase in their share of global energy consumption, from 43 percent in 1980 to 55 percent in 2006, also confirms that their weight in the world economy has surely risen.

The raw dollar numbers are distorted by big currency swings. For instance, the de-

---

① 亚洲开发银行。它包括来自亚洲和太平洋地区的区域成员,和来自欧洲和北美洲的非区域成员。目前它共有成员 60 个,其中 43 个来自亚洲地区。年会一般在 5 月份召开。它的主要议题是探讨亚太地区的经济金融形势、发展趋势和面临的挑战,推动亚行作为地区性开发机构在促进本地区社会经济发展方面发挥作用。

valuations in East Asian economies in 1997-98[①] grossly exaggerated the drop in their output. Measured at PPP, emerging economies' share of world output has more realistically risen since 1980—and even if China's economy is smaller than thought, it is still a mighty beast. PPP data may be imperfect, but they give a better picture of the relative size of economies than market exchange rates do. In the words of John Maynard Keynes[②], "It is better to be roughly right than precisely wrong."

Words and Expressions

fiery [ˈfaɪərɪ] *adj.*	充满激情的，火热的
fret [fret] *v.*	苦恼，烦躁，焦躁不安
gleefully [ˈgliːfʊlɪ] *adv.*	欢喜地，高兴地，幸灾乐祸地
salutary [ˈsæljʊtərɪ] *adj.*	有益的
understate [ˌʌndəˈsteɪt] *v.*	轻描淡写，避重就轻
sophisticated [səˈfɪstɪkeɪtɪd] *adj.*	在行的，精确的
extrapolate [ɪkˈstræpəleɪt] *v.*	推知，推断
slash [slæʃ] *v.*	大幅度下降
speedometer [spɪˈdɒmɪtə] *n.*	（车辆等的）计速器
mirage [ˈmɪrɑːʒ] *n.*	幻景，海市蜃楼
distort [dɪsˈtɔːt] *v.*	歪曲，失真
mighty [ˈmaɪtɪ] *adj.*	强而有力的
in terms of	就……而言，以……的形式
pick on	挑剔，挑选

Exercises

Exercise 1 Choose the best answer for each of the following questions.

1. According to the writer, which of the followings can best reflect the relative size of economies?

   A. Big Mac index. B. ICP.

   C. Market exchange rates. D. GDP.

2. If China and India are 40 percent smaller than previously thought, world growth would be reduced to ______.

---

① 20世纪90年代晚期，东亚和东南亚的货币价值急剧下跌，严重影响了某些政府、银行和企业偿还外债的能力。有些国家，特别是印尼、泰国和韩国，从国际货币基金组织获取了大量贷款来偿还其债务。

② 现代西方经济学最有影响的经济学家之一。凯恩斯一生致力于研究货币理论，对经济学作出了极大的贡献，一度被誉为资本主义的"救星"、"战后繁荣之父"等美称。凯恩斯认同借助于市场供求力量自动地达到充分就业的状态就能维持资本主义的观点。

A. 7.5 percent B. 3.4 percent C. 2.3 percent D. 4.5 percent

3. The fact(s) that ______ can undermine the reliability of the PPP figures.
   A. prices of many non-traded goods and services tend to be much cheaper in poor economies
   B. converting a poor country's GDP into dollars at market exchange rates understates the true size of its economies
   C. much of the calculation is conducted on guesswork due to the lack of sufficient historical data
   D. all the above

Exercise 2 Fill in each of the blanks with the appropriate words given. Change the form of the word when necessary.

extrapolate revise slash account for swing

1. The IEA (国际能源署) estimated that the world oil demand next year will be million barrels a day, but it said that this estimate is subject to ________ due to recent economic indices(指数).
2. We can ________ the economic conditions from the description of purchasing-power parity.
3. Investment from other economic sectors developed from scratch, hitting 458.1 billion *yuan* in 1997 and ________ 18.2 percent of the national total.
4. The proposal would ________ federal tax rates across all levels of income, eliminate the so called marriage penalty and phase out estate taxes.
5. The economy ________ forward in the last decade.

Exercise 3 Translate the following sentences into English.

1. 购买力平价,而非市场汇率,被视为衡量相对生活成本的更好尺度,因为它的衡量基础是各个家庭用本国货币所能购买的商品和服务。(PPP)
2. 国家统计局宣布,2007 年中国出口额占全世界的 8.8%,为世界第二大出口国。
3. 为防止通缩持续,欧洲中央银行上月将利息降至 3.25%。(deflation, the European Central Bank, slash)

Text 2 Unstoppable yet Unsustainable
中国飞速发展的强势经济:难以阻挡,粗放型模式

导读 20世纪末与21世纪初世界危机四起,1997年东南亚的金融危机,2001年美国互联网泡沫破灭,2003年SARS疫情肆虐中国大江南北。然而,这一波又一波的国内外挑战,无法阻挡中国经济快速发展的步伐。在高投资、大出口与稳步增长的内需三驾马车驱动下,中国经济一路凯歌猛进,发展强势难以阻挡。但如此势如破竹的高速增长能否持久?又有哪些难以预测的国内外不利因素来制约中国经济的强劲发展?

China has barely paused for breath this year in its jet-propelled rise into a global power, returning the country to a position its leaders and people think it rightfully occupies.

For the third year in succession, the economy is on track to grow by more than 10 percent, according to Chinese statistics, a figure that many foreign investment bank economists think understates the true pace of development.

The leadership team of Hu Jintao, the president, and Wen Jiabao, the premier, has complemented the powerful economic re-emergence with a packed diplomatic schedule reflecting the new pressures, and interests, the country's growth has delivered it.

In a single week in November, it hosted 10 south-east Asian leaders in southern China, senior leaders from 48 African countries at a summit in Beijing and pulled together top envoys from six countries, including Japan and the US, to mediate North Korea's nuclear programme.

These separate events encapsulated China's paramount security interests, a need for stability in Asia, more raw materials—especially oil that Africa can provide— and good relations with the US.

At home, China has spawned a new caste of millionaires, an emerging middle-class centred in large cities on the coast, alongside a struggling rural class and urban poor. ①

The country has shown extraordinary resilience in the face of a wave of challenges since the late 1990s, successfully sailing through the Asian financial crisis, the bursting of the internet bubble and the recession in the US② and its own home-grown health crisis,

---

① 在中国,国内孕育了一个新的富豪阶层,一个集中在沿海城市的新兴中产阶层,以及一个苦苦挣扎的农村阶层和城市贫民阶层。

② 2001年网络泡沫,数以百计的.com公司在宣布破产之列,网络初创公司纷纷倒闭之余,导致美国经济低迷。

with the SARS virus in 2003.

Much underestimated, too, has been the stability that the relative maturity in the political system has provided.

But for all of this, China's rapid development remains a curious mixture of the unstoppable and the unsustainable.

The unstoppable part of the equation is increasingly apparent to most close observers of the country. In the short to medium term, the rapid growth will in all likelihood continue, driven by a high investment rate, swelling exports and healthy local consumption.

The threat of a financial crisis has receded with the reform of the banking sector in recent years. And in any case, the $1,000bn-plus in foreign reserves① means that the country has more than enough funds should they be needed in any financial emergency.

The sheer drive and ambition of the Chinese people is the X-factor often left out of the economic equation. ②

The pace of economic growth might ease slightly next year, to about 9.5 percent or so, but that is the kind of slowdown that China could manage with ease, and might even welcome.

China's growth has continued to bring down the poverty rate③, from 16 to 10 percent in the three years from 2001, according to the World Bank's measure of $1 a day in consumption using global prices.

But at the same time, the poverty dynamic has changed in a way that worries the leadership.

In the two years from 2001, according to a World Bank study, the income of the poorest 10 percent of Chinese actually fell by about 2.5 percent, despite rapid economic growth.

More than half of these new poor do not live in villages and about 70 percent of them had suffered an "income shock," as a result of health problems, crop loss or injury.

"This suggests that further poverty reduction in China will require measures that reach households with different types of safety nets or insurance, for example health insurance, crop insurance—but also welfare programmes recognizing that some households have

---

① foreign reserves 外汇储备，即一国货币当局所持有的、可以用于对外支付的国外可兑换货币。并非所有国家的货币都能充当国际储备资产，只有那些在国际货币体系中占有重要地位，且能自由兑换其他储备资产的货币才能充当国际储备资产。

② 中国人的万丈干劲与雄心，是常常被经济方程式遗漏的未知因素。

③ 贫困率。即收入低于贫困线的人口占总人口的比率，这是最为常用的指标。贫困指数是指用贫困人口规模标准化的累积贫困距(即贫困人口的收入和贫困线之差与贫困线的比率)，也称为贫困深度指数，反映了贫困人口的贫困程度。

no adult who can work,[①]" says David Dollar, the World Bank's country head for China.

Messrs Hu and Wen have made tackling the rich-poor gap a priority of their economic programme, but the corruption, in some local political authorities, make it difficult to proceed quickly on the issue.

...

The other big issue, the impact of which is more difficult to calibrate, is environmental degradation. The government has vowed to address this issue by forcing higher environmental standards and more efficient use of energy.

In part, this is a product of China's success. The desire for development means that governments at both a central and local level are reluctant to rein in economic growth.

China's economic structure faces global risks as well. The country's current account surplus has swollen to about 8 percent of gross domestic product and shows little sign of slowing.[②]

Does such a system have the flexibility to manage the country's myriad challenges, both of a prosperous and increasingly demanding urban middle class, and a large, poor farming community?

Amid China's uneven, 21st century boom, that remains an open and, for the moment, unanswerable question.

Words and Expressions

jet-propelled *adj.*	喷气发动机推动的
complement [ˈkɒmplɪment] *v.*	补足,补充,与……相配
re-emergence *n.*	复兴
envoy [ˈenvɒɪ] *n.*	使者,使节
mediate [ˈmiːdɪeɪt] *v.*	调停
encapsulate [ɪnˈkæpsjuleɪt] *v.*	简述,归纳
paramount [ˈpærəmaʊnt] *adj.*	最高的
spawn [spɔːn] *v.*	引发,引起
caste [kɑːst] *n.*	社会等级
resilience [rɪˈzɪlɪəns] *n.*	(活力,精神等的)恢复力,适应力;复原力

---

① 中国政府总理温家宝在上海召开的世界银行全球扶贫大会讲话中指出,中国是人口众多的发展中大国,是全球减贫事业的重要实践者,中国政府将继续积极参与全球的减贫事业。2005 年 3 月,温家宝总理在第十届全国人民代表大会第三次会议的工作报告中提出,要完善企业职工基本养老保险制度,坚持社会统筹个人账户相结合,扩大做实个人账户试点。要推进国有企业下岗职工基本生活保障向失业保险并轨。要依法扩大养老、失业、医疗、工伤等社会保险覆盖面,提高个体、私营和外资企业的参保率,完善灵活就业人员的参保办法。有条件的地方可探索建立农村居民最低生活保障制度。

② 中国的经济结构还面临全球风险。中国的现金账户盈余已经增至 GDP 的 8%左右,而且丝毫没有减缓的迹象。

swell [swel] *v.* 增大，扩大
mete [miːt] *v.* 惩罚
emulate ['emjuleɪt] *v.* 效仿
dynamic [daɪ'næmɪk] *n.* 动态，力度，强度
calibrate ['kælɪbreɪt] *v.* 划刻度，测定
vow [vaʊ] *v.* 发誓
mandate ['mændeɪt] *n.* 命令，指令
myriad ['mɪrɪəd] *adj.* 无数的
in succession 连续
for all 尽管
make for 有助于造成(某种关系、情况等)

Exercises

Exercise 1　Choose the best answer for each of the following questions.

1. In China's economic program, what has been given priority by Chinese leaders according to the article?
   A. Protecting the environment.
   B. Dealing with the corruption of the government.
   C. Developing the insurance industry.
   D. Tackling the rich-poor gap.
2. What has prevented the central government from increasing the outlays on health and education?
   A. The corruption in the provincial and city leaders.
   B. The fact that they had increased dramatically with the economic development.
   C. The government's lack of fund.
   D. The fact that the service provision provided by the cities and provinces have been sufficient.

Exercise 2　Fill in each of the blanks with the appropriate words given. Change the form of the word when necessary.

mete out　make for　be reluctant to　leave out of　confer to

1. Creditors will ________ invest their money into the companies that are likely to go bankrupt.
2. As a technical adviser to the project, Mr Zhang's income is up to 10,000 dollars every month, ________ bonus and other subsidies.
3. If the advertising agents run false advertisements, the consumers may request administrative departments to ________ punishment.
4. In 1998, an MBA degree ________ him by Oxford University.

5. Conduct of that kind hardly ________ a harmonious atmosphere in the company.

Exercise 3 Translate the following sentences into English.

1. 我们忠诚地希望贵公司能有足够的适应力，来应对未来的一波又一波的困难和挑战。(show extraordinary resilience)
2. 跨国公司都把扩大在当地的市场作为发展计划中的头等大事。(make sth. a priority)
3. 改善企业的内部环境，有利于遏制腐败。(stem ... through, ameliorate)

Text 3 As China Grows, So Do America's Woes

中国发展:几家欢喜几家忧

导读 随着全球经济一体化进程的加速,中国凭借其丰富的廉价劳力资源与巨大的消费市场磁力,吸引了来自全球各国数以万计的公司来投资设厂。美国许多跨国公司也纷纷仿效把生产车间迁移到中国,并把价廉物美的商品返销到美国本土市场。如此让美国消费者着实得到了实惠。

What's more important to you: American factory jobs or cheap stuff? As America's factory-based industries move production lines to China, American workers lose tens of thousands of jobs but the rest of us gain the ability to buy some of our favorite items at all-time low prices.

The switch that really brought the whole issue to the forefront for me was when my beloved (and the all-American best-selling shoe in world history) Chuck Taylor Converse All-Stars[①] production line was closed in Pennsylvania and moved to Asia. The shoe quality didn't go down so much as it simply changed. American Chuck Taylor's would wear out where the toe area connected to the laces part of the shoe—forgive my lack of correct technical shoe jargon—and also in the back. But the new Chinese Chucks were wearing out a little more quickly, but from the sides. One day my entire right foot slipped out of the left side of my shoe.

But let's step back. Where did this new manufacturing trend come from? Why is China so popular for manufacturing the world's goods? In 1972 President Richard Nixon was the first US president to visit the People's Republic of China and lay the foundation for trade relations. Since then, the United States has been continually working with China to increase free trade. Bill Clinton was instrumental in getting China into the World Trade Organization[②]. In 2005, spurred on by the US Congress, China tacked the worth of their Chinese *yuan* to the worth of the US dollar.[③] By doing this, China made free trade be-

---

① 1917年,第一双Converse All Star鞋诞生,自其问世至今,Converse已成为全世界家喻户晓的帆布鞋代名词,同麦当劳快餐、可口可乐饮料、Levi's牛仔裤一道,成为美国文化精神的象征。

② 世界贸易组织(WTO)。它成立于1995年1月1日,其前身是关税和贸易总协定(GATT)。WTO总部在瑞士日内瓦,是世界上最大的多边贸易组织,目前已经拥有137个成员,成员的贸易量占世界贸易的95%以上。WTO与世界银行、国际货币基金组织并称为当今世界经济体制的"三大支柱"。

③ 自2005年7月21日起,我国开始实行以市场供求为基础、参考一篮子货币进行调节、有管理的浮动汇率制度。人民币汇率不再盯住单一美元,形成更富弹性的人民币汇率机制。

tween the two superpowers much simpler. As we buy more, China produces more and prospers.

This seems pretty good, right? American-owned companies, in order to save money and work in the interest of their shareholders, move production to China. In China, their production costs are fractions of what they previously were in the United States, and profits grow. In turn, Wal-Mart, among others, can offer you the same products at lower prices all the time.

But here is where it begins to get a bit more interesting. Some American companies don't want to move their production lines to Asia. They're loyal to their American workers and don't want to compromise American jobs for bigger profits. But large corporate chain retailers, specifically Wal-Mart, have contracts with their product suppliers. These contracts are quite lucrative for the companies that land them, and competition for these contracts is stiff among producers because they guarantee high sales worldwide. In these contracts, Wal-Mart is allowed to set the price they are willing to pay for each item, like television sets, for instance.

Let's say an American-based dealer has a contract with Wal-Mart to sell them each television for \$55. Wal-Mart is able to turn to that company and tell them they won't pay more than \$40 per unit and if this company can't meet their requirements, they'll turn to one of their competitors. The television company, which cannot make a profit by producing their televisions in the United States and selling them for \$40, is faced with losing their contract with Wal-Mart and in turn a large portion of their market share, or lowering production costs. In order to keep their contract the company will move their production plant to China in order to produce their product at the demanded price.

It is things like this that increase America's trade deficit and in turn lower the worth of the US dollar, sending the United States into a downward spiral. The US trade deficit, which began in the 1970s, is the difference between what goods the United States produces and the domestic demand or the worth of our exports versus our imports. Historically, the US currency was backed by a gold standard[①], which allowed us, in the case of a trade imbalance, to send gold to make up for the imbalance. But since the US abandoned the gold standard in 1933 and is able to print as much money as it would like, the reversal of the trade deficit is more difficult.

In August 2006, based upon the rapid growth of the twin debts (US trade deficit and

---

① 金本位制就是以黄金为本位币的货币制度。在金本位制下，每单位的货币价值等同于若干重量的黄金(即货币含金量)；当不同国家使用金本位时，国家之间的汇率由它们各自货币的含金量之比——金平价(Gold Parity)来决定。金本位制于19世纪中期开始盛行。在历史上，曾有过三种形式的金本位制：金币本位制、金块本位制、金汇兑本位制。其中金币本位制是最典型的形式，就狭义来说，金本位制即指该种货币制度。西方国家于第一次世界大战爆发后，宣告金币本位制破产，并在1929—1933年世界经济危机之后，宣布放弃金块本位制。

national debt), Italy decided to sell a large portion of its US dollar holdings and purchase, instead, British pound sterling, causing the worth of the US dollar to drop. Shortly after Italy's move, many other countries followed suit.

The national debt, which is money owed by the government to creditors, i. e., foreign governments, began early in our country's history during the Revolutionary War[①] when we borrowed money from countries to help fight the English. The debt has existed and has fluctuated greatly in our country's 231 years of existence. It was at its highest, as compared to the gross domestic product (GDP), during the 1940s due to our involvement in World War Ⅱ. The GDP is essentially the market value of every final product or service the country produces. Currently, China holds $339 billion in US Treasury securities.

Here's something else to keep in mind: Chinese cities continue to grow at astonishing rates. In 1952 there were approximately 72 million Chinese people living in cities and urban areas; by 2004 that had jumped to 540 million people. It is estimated that, with a 1 percent increase per year, by 2020 900 million Chinese will live in cities. Bringing former rural and farm populations into the urban and industrial centers enlarges the need for energy production. With every new factory or housing complex constructed the increase of energy needed for heating, electricity, et cetera rises exponentially. The United States is currently the world's single largest consumer of energy and China is quickly catching up. Soon there will be a huge struggle between the two superpowers for oil and other abundant sources of energy, which, no pun intended, drive our country forward. If you think energy costs are up now, wait until we have to fight China to get our hands on resources.

In the end, companies like Wal-Mart constantly require lower prices from their dealers. In order to remain competitive, American companies are forced to move their plants to China. This grows the US trade deficit along with our ever-growing national debt and lowers our dollar's worth. In the end, China and companies like Wal-Mart make out like bandits while America slowly begins to sink under the weight of our own consumerism. But, hey, we can get cheap flat-screen TVs. That's something.

Words and Expressions

instrumental [ɪnstrʊˈmentl] *adj.* 起重要作用的
tack [tæk] *v.* 以大头针钉住，附加，跟随
fraction [ˈfrækʃən] *n.* 少量，一点儿
lucrative [ˈluːkrətiv] *adj.* 获利多的，赚大钱的
reversal [rɪˈvɜːsl] *n.* 颠倒，反转，扭转
fluctuate [ˈflʌktʃʊeɪt] *v.* 波动，起伏不定
exponentially [ˌekspəˈnenʃəlɪ] *adv.* 成倍地，幂地，指数地

---

① 美国独立战争。1775—1783年，为脱离英国的殖民统治而进行的战争。

bandit [ˈbændɪt] *n.*	土匪
consumerism [kənˈsjuːmərɪzəm] *n.*	用户至上主义
to the forefront	处于最前列;进入重要地位
trade deficit	贸易逆差
spur on	驱使,鼓舞,激励,刺激
a downward spiral	日益下降

Exercises

Exercise 1 Choose the best answer for each of the following questions.

1. Which of the following is not instrumental in promoting China's export to America?
   A. President Nixon's visiting China in 1972.
   B. China's entry into the WTO.
   C. China's tacking of the worth of Chinese *yuan* to the worth of the US dollars.
   D. The appreciation of Chinese *yuan*.
2. Some Americans believe that many American companies have moved their factories to China has contributed to all the following except ________.
   A. the shortage of energy in America
   B. the increase of American national debt
   C. the depreciation of the US dollar
   D. the increase of American trade deficit
3. According to the writer, ______ will push the demand of energy to soar in China.
   A. the increasing FDI
   B. the increasing number of private cars
   C. the urbanization process
   D. the development of infrastructure

Exercise 2 Fill in each of the blanks with the appropriate words given. Change the form of the word when necessary.

to the forefront tack on stuff fraction reversal spiral fluctuate

1. If you are really something, you should do your ________.
2. The poems were ________ at the end of the book.
3. Only a ________ of the students understand what the teacher said.
4. The new product took the company ________ of the computer software field.
5. The prices of vegetables and fruits ________ with the seasons.
6. The company's financial problems were only a temporary ________.
7. The destructive ________ of violence in the inner cities has become a serious problem.

Exercise 3 Translate the following sentences into English.

1. 经济的快速发展使得中国在国际上的地位变得日益重要。(upward,spiral)
2. 大学里几年的刻苦学习和丰富的工作经验帮助他顺利地完成了在财务委员会的工作。(assiduous study)
3. 因投资者将金融领域的裁员视为经济不景气的征兆,华尔街股市今日震荡。(layoff, fluctuate)

Text 4 Get Ready for the Next Big China Effect
着手准备:又一个"中国效应"

导读 2007年,中国证券市场基本上延续了2006年的走势,股指和股价持续上行,是一个快速上行的牛市。在全球其他市场因美国次级抵押贷款风波进行抛售的时候,中国股市却几乎每个交易日都在创造着历史新高,甚至有人预测上证指数将达8000点。中国股市风景这边独好的根源在于中国的金融史,而银行的大量放贷、贸易顺差导致外汇的大量流动性,来自全球的"热钱"也一起为此推波助澜。随着人民币的升值,投资于房地产与股市的资产大大增值,中国资本日后必将走出国门,购买海外资产。全世界才体验了一次波澜壮阔的"中国制造"效应,现在得着手准备应对又一场席卷全球的"中国购买"效应。

As global markets freeze, fret and fall, there is an island of bullish sentiment way out east. Welcome to China's stock market, 75 percent up on the year, which is building historical highs on an almost daily basis while the rest of the world watches America's subprime① troubles and sells off.

China's market has come a long way in a short time. From kerb trading on the back streets of Shanghai in 1984, the market's official capitalization is now $2,700bn. It has been one of the world's best-performing markets over the past 12 months. Average prices are some 50 times historical earnings, with a number of companies having price/earnings ratios② of more than 1,000. Risk aversion? There is no easy Mandarin translation.

One is tempted to write this bullish sentiment off as unsustainable exuberance that will fade once fundamentals reassert themselves. The truth is more complicated. Massive liquidity—and wealth—have been accumulated in China over the past two decades and it is currently locked up in mainland equities and real estate. In less than five years that wealth is going to flood out of the country, causing huge tremors in overseas asset markets.

The future did not always look thus. During 2002-04 China's stock market looked sick, crippled by slow profit growth. The Shanghai composite briefly fell below 1,000 and

① 次级房贷危机。次级抵押贷款是指一些贷款机构向信用程度较差和收入不高的借款人提供的贷款。在前几年美国住房市场高度繁荣时,次级抵押贷款市场迅速发展。但随着美国住房市场大幅降温,加上利率上升,很多次级抵押贷款市场的借款人无法按期偿还借款,导致一些放贷机构遭受严重损失甚至破产。

② 市价盈利比率(简称市盈率),也称"股价收益比率"。它是最常用来评估股价水平是否合理的指标之一,由股价除以年度每股盈余(EPS)得出(以公司市值除以年度股东应占溢利亦可得出相同结果)。

many thought its pulse would stop soon afterwards. In recent days, however, the index has exceeded 4,800; 5,000 looks reachable and some boosters are looking for 8,000 before the Beijing Olympics kicks off in August 2008.

To some this looks like a bubble. In May, Beijing hit the market with a series of measures, including an increase in the trading tax, to damp sentiment and prevent a bigger bubble. But those measures were no match for corporate profit growth, low interest rates and all that liquidity.

Today's boom has its roots in China's financial history. Even before 2004, the amount of money sloshing around China's economy (and stored under beds) was massive relative to the scale of goods and services produced. By 2004 the ratio of M2[①], the broad indicator of money supply, to gross domestic product had reached 160 percent, much higher than in most other economies. China had got to this point by stimulating its economy in slow times, by either massive bank lending or budgetary stimulus packages. In recent years, more liquidity has been imported via huge trade surpluses[②](running at \$20bn a month), plus foreign investment and "hot" money inflows.

The People's Bank of China, the central bank, has kept much of this liquidity at bay via sterilization operations[③], but pressures are immense and interest rates remain suppressed. In 2003, these funds began to slosh into property and then, in mid-2006, into equities, monetizing them. But this will change in the next three to five years as China's wealth gets more adventurous and starts to travel. Many routes for taking out funds have been opened up already. The mainland's high-net-worth investors are active in the H-share[④] market in Hong Kong and QDII[⑤], the scheme where retail investors give their money to banks to manage offshore, is becoming more popular. The all-but-certain appreciation of the *renminbi* keeps the wealth locked up at home.

But given a 5 percent or so appreciation each year, the *renminbi* will soon become more fairly valued. China's household and corporate wealth becoming footloose presages

---

① M2货币供应量之二,指广义货币。广义货币是一个经济学概念,和狭义货币相对应。在经济学中以M2来表示,其计算方法是社会流通货币总量加上活期存款以及定期存款等储蓄存款。

② 贸易顺差,也就是在一定的单位时间里(通常按年度计算),贸易的双方互相买卖各种货物,互相进口与出口,甲方的出口金额大过乙方的出口金额,或甲方的进口金额少于乙方的进口金额,其中的差额,对甲方来说,就叫做贸易顺差。

③ 冲销性操作。它是指当汇率出现不恰当波动时,中央银行一方面进入外汇市场抛出或补进外汇使汇率达到适当水平;与之同时,则通过购买或出售政府债券等国内资产来抵消干预汇率而释放或回笼本国货币的影响,以维持国内货币供应量的不变。

④ H股,即注册地在内地、上市地在香港的外资股。在纽约和新加坡上市的股票分别叫做N股和S股,均取自第一个英文字母。

⑤ QDII是一项投资制度,设立该制度的直接目的是为了"进一步开放资本账户,以创造更多外汇需求,使人民币汇率更加平衡、更加市场化,并鼓励国内更多企业走出国门,从而减少贸易顺差和资本项目盈余",直接表现为让国内投资者直接参与国外的市场,并获取全球市场收益。

an important change. We are all familiar with one of the effects of a globalizing China: the relative price of labor falls, meaning cheaper "stuff". The second-round effect will be very different. As China's wealth globalizes, the relative price of assets bought by private China is going to rise. Residential land in Hong Kong and Vancouver, farmland in Africa and natural resources in Asia will bear the first brunt of these outflows. The second wave could be companies with big and successful operations in China itself, where local consumers are witnessing the successful growth of many global companies themselves.

The "China price" will no longer be the cheapest world price for a commodity. It will be the hefty premium paid for assets in which private China has invested. Do not think about the Shanghai stock exchange as an anomaly. Think about it as the future.

Words and Expressions

bullish [ˈbʊlɪʃ] *adj.*	似公牛的，看涨的，上扬的
kerb [kɜːb] *n.*	街头的边石
capitalization [ˌkæpɪtəlaɪˈzeɪʃən] *n.*	资本化，股本，资本总额
Mandarin [ˈmændərɪn] *n.*	中国官话，普通话
exuberance [ɪgˈzjuːbərəns] *n.*	茂盛，丰富，健康
reassert [ˈriːəˈsɜːt] *v.*	再断言，重复主张
tremor [ˈtremə] *n.*	震动，颤动
overhang [ˌəʊvəˈhæŋ] *v.*	悬于……之上，悬垂
booster [ˈbuːstə] *n.*	〈美俚〉热心的拥护者，支持者
damp [dæmp] *v.*	抑制
slosh [slɒʃ] *v.*	(液体)(在一容器)流动；溅，泼
budgetary [ˈbʌdʒɪtərɪ] *adj.*	预算的
sterilization [ˌsterɪlaɪˈzeɪʃən] *n.*	冲销操作；灭菌，消毒
all-but-certain *adj.*	确然无疑的
footloose [ˈfʊtˌluːs] *adj.*	自由自在的，到处走动的
presage [ˈpresɪdʒ] *v.*	成为……的前兆，预示，预言
Vancouver	温哥华市
brunt [brʌnt] *n.*	冲击，冲势
commodity [kəˈmɒdɪtɪ] *n.*	日用品
hefty [ˈheftɪ] *adj.*	很大的，超出一般的，可观的
premium [ˈpriːmɪəm] *n.*	额外费用，奖金，保险费
anomaly [əˈnɒməlɪ] *n.*	不规则，异常的人或物
sell off	廉价卖清
write off	认为……是失败[没有希望]，认为……不行；报废，注销
lock up	把(钱)搁死(成为不易兑现的资本)

kick off	开始
keep ... at bay	控制

Exercises

Exercise 1　Choose the best answer for each of the following questions.

1. When China's stock market looked sick during 2002-04, what did the investors worry about?

   A. The huge overhang of state-owned shares might one day flood the market.

   B. Massive liquidity had been accumulated in China over the past two decades.

   C. America's subprime troubles.

   D. The possible flooding out of China's wealth.

2. According to the writer, what keeps the wealth locked up in China?

   A. The depreciation of the *renminbi*.

   B. The appreciation of the *renminbi*.

   C. The prosperous real estate industry.

   D. Chinese government's stimulus packages.

3. In recent years, the increasing liquidity imported to China can be attributed to ______.

   A. China's huge trade surpluses　　B. foreign investment

   C. "hot" money inflows　　D. all the above

Exercise 2　Fill in each of the blanks with the appropriate words given. Change the form of the word when necessary.

capitalization　write off　overhang　hefty　slosh

1. The team failed to ________ on their early lead.
2. The path was cool and dark with ________ trees.
3. They sold it easily and made a ________ profit.
4. There is a lot of money ________ around in professional tennis.
5. He has ________ two cars this year.

Exercise 3　Translate the following sentences into English.

1. 传统价值再次得到肯定。(reassert)
2. 不言而喻,随着版权法得到很好的贯彻,软件市场得以较规范的管理,盗版问题必将得到解决。(piracy problem)
3. 近年来,更多流动性通过巨额贸易顺差(每月200亿美元)流入中国,还有外国投资和"热钱"的流入。("hot" money inflows)

Text 5 China Economy: Breathing Fire
中国经济如火如荼

导读 21世纪是不分国家、只追求和使用高效生产要素的全球化经济时代。中国以其独特的发展模式,占据对外贸易优势,使其经济发展速度遥遥领先于各国。但过度快速发展的负面现象也日渐显露:国内由于信贷过多,出现了投资过剩、通货膨胀等严峻问题;国外由于与美国贸易摩擦所引发人民币升值的压力也日益增大。人民币升值对中国企业影响较大,因为好多企业仅是组装厂家而已,利润微薄,升值过快会导致企业亏损或倒闭,而升值速度过慢又会面临美国保护主义的惩罚。如火如荼的中国经济面临"快慢"两难的棘手选择。

One would think that Asian equity markets[①] would be happy at the news that China's economy, the regional powerhouse, is growing even faster than expected. But that's not the way it turned out. Shortly before China's government said, late last week, that the economy grew at an annualized pace of 11.1 percent in the first three months of 2007, and as forecasts rose for the year's overall growth, traders on the region's big exchanges briefly took fright. The next day markets rebounded.

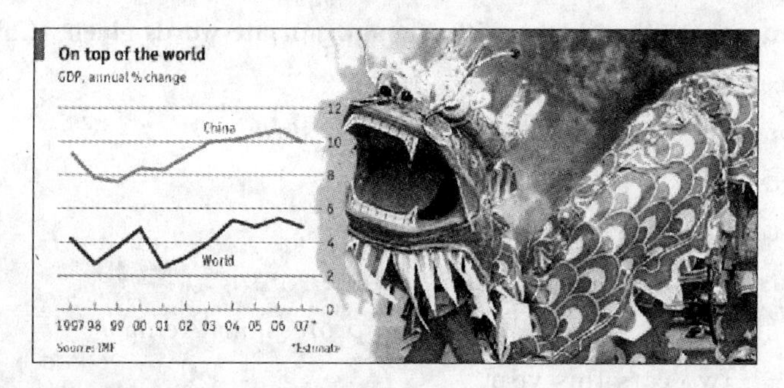

Nobody is jumpy about growth, of course, but of the government's reaction to it. Chinese officials are getting worried that a meltdown may be pending, and have been intervening to dampen things down. But over the past few years tighter interest rates, lending restrictions and heavier bank regulation have failed to cool the economy.

China's fairly primitive financial infrastructure makes it difficult to fine-tune credit

① 股票市场

kick off 开始
keep ... at bay 控制

Exercises

Exercise 1 Choose the best answer for each of the following questions.

1. When China's stock market looked sick during 2002-04, what did the investors worry about?
   A. The huge overhang of state-owned shares might one day flood the market.
   B. Massive liquidity had been accumulated in China over the past two decades.
   C. America's subprime troubles.
   D. The possible flooding out of China's wealth.
2. According to the writer, what keeps the wealth locked up in China?
   A. The depreciation of the *renminbi*.
   B. The appreciation of the *renminbi*.
   C. The prosperous real estate industry.
   D. Chinese government's stimulus packages.
3. In recent years, the increasing liquidity imported to China can be attributed to ______.
   A. China's huge trade surpluses B. foreign investment
   C. "hot" money inflows D. all the above

Exercise 2 Fill in each of the blanks with the appropriate words given. Change the form of the word when necessary.

capitalization write off overhang hefty slosh

1. The team failed to ________ on their early lead.
2. The path was cool and dark with ________ trees.
3. They sold it easily and made a ________ profit.
4. There is a lot of money ________ around in professional tennis.
5. He has ________ two cars this year.

Exercise 3 Translate the following sentences into English.

1. 传统价值再次得到肯定。(reassert)
2. 不言而喻,随着版权法得到很好的贯彻,软件市场得以较规范的管理,盗版问题必将得到解决。(piracy problem)
3. 近年来,更多流动性通过巨额贸易顺差(每月 200 亿美元)流入中国,还有外国投资和"热钱"的流入。("hot" money inflows)

Text 5 China Economy: Breathing Fire
中国经济如火如荼

导读 21世纪是不分国家、只追求和使用高效生产要素的全球化经济时代。中国以其独特的发展模式，占据对外贸易优势，使其经济发展速度遥遥领先于各国。但过度快速发展的负面现象也日渐显露：国内由于信贷过多，出现了投资过剩、通货膨胀等严峻问题；国外由于与美国贸易摩擦所引发人民币升值的压力也日益增大。人民币升值对中国企业影响较大，因为好多企业仅是组装厂家而已，利润微薄，升值过快会导致企业亏损或倒闭，而升值速度过慢又会面临美国保护主义的惩罚。如火如荼的中国经济面临"快慢"两难的棘手选择。

One would think that Asian equity markets[1] would be happy at the news that China's economy, the regional powerhouse, is growing even faster than expected. But that's not the way it turned out. Shortly before China's government said, late last week, that the economy grew at an annualized pace of 11.1 percent in the first three months of 2007, and as forecasts rose for the year's overall growth, traders on the region's big exchanges briefly took fright. The next day markets rebounded.

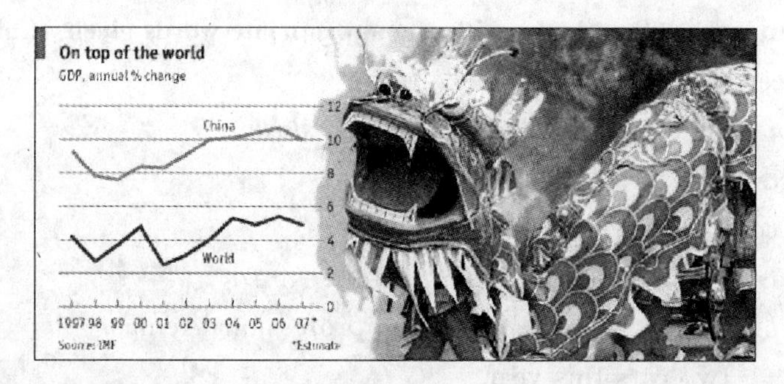

Nobody is jumpy about growth, of course, but of the government's reaction to it. Chinese officials are getting worried that a meltdown may be pending, and have been intervening to dampen things down. But over the past few years tighter interest rates, lending restrictions and heavier bank regulation have failed to cool the economy.

China's fairly primitive financial infrastructure makes it difficult to fine-tune credit

---

① 股票市场

kick off 开始
keep ... at bay 控制

Exercises

Exercise 1 Choose the best answer for each of the following questions.

1. When China's stock market looked sick during 2002-04, what did the investors worry about?
   A. The huge overhang of state-owned shares might one day flood the market.
   B. Massive liquidity had been accumulated in China over the past two decades.
   C. America's subprime troubles.
   D. The possible flooding out of China's wealth.
2. According to the writer, what keeps the wealth locked up in China?
   A. The depreciation of the *renminbi*.
   B. The appreciation of the *renminbi*.
   C. The prosperous real estate industry.
   D. Chinese government's stimulus packages.
3. In recent years, the increasing liquidity imported to China can be attributed to ______.
   A. China's huge trade surpluses B. foreign investment
   C. "hot" money inflows D. all the above

Exercise 2 Fill in each of the blanks with the appropriate words given. Change the form of the word when necessary.

capitalization write off overhang hefty slosh

1. The team failed to ________ on their early lead.
2. The path was cool and dark with ________ trees.
3. They sold it easily and made a ________ profit.
4. There is a lot of money ________ around in professional tennis.
5. He has ________ two cars this year.

Exercise 3 Translate the following sentences into English.

1. 传统价值再次得到肯定。(reassert)
2. 不言而喻,随着版权法得到很好的贯彻,软件市场得以较规范的管理,盗版问题必将得到解决。(piracy problem)
3. 近年来,更多流动性通过巨额贸易顺差(每月 200 亿美元)流入中国,还有外国投资和"热钱"的流入。("hot" money inflows)

Text 5　China Economy: Breathing Fire

中国经济如火如荼

导读　21世纪是不分国家、只追求和使用高效生产要素的全球化经济时代。中国以其独特的发展模式，占据对外贸易优势，使其经济发展速度遥遥领先于各国。但过度快速发展的负面现象也日渐显露：国内由于信贷过多，出现了投资过剩、通货膨胀等严峻问题；国外由于与美国贸易摩擦所引发人民币升值的压力也日益增大。人民币升值对中国企业影响较大，因为好多企业仅是组装厂家而已，利润微薄，升值过快会导致企业亏损或倒闭，而升值速度过慢又会面临美国保护主义的惩罚。如火如荼的中国经济面临"快慢"两难的棘手选择。

One would think that Asian equity markets[①] would be happy at the news that China's economy, the regional powerhouse, is growing even faster than expected. But that's not the way it turned out. Shortly before China's government said, late last week, that the economy grew at an annualized pace of 11.1 percent in the first three months of 2007, and as forecasts rose for the year's overall growth, traders on the region's big exchanges briefly took fright. The next day markets rebounded.

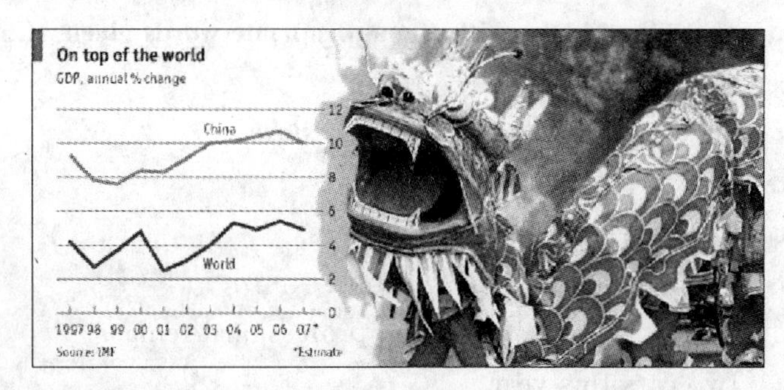

Nobody is jumpy about growth, of course, but of the government's reaction to it. Chinese officials are getting worried that a meltdown may be pending, and have been intervening to dampen things down. But over the past few years tighter interest rates, lending restrictions and heavier bank regulation have failed to cool the economy.

China's fairly primitive financial infrastructure makes it difficult to fine-tune credit

① 股票市场

kick off 开始

keep ... at bay 控制

Exercises

Exercise 1 Choose the best answer for each of the following questions.

1. When China's stock market looked sick during 2002-04, what did the investors worry about?

   A. The huge overhang of state-owned shares might one day flood the market.

   B. Massive liquidity had been accumulated in China over the past two decades.

   C. America's subprime troubles.

   D. The possible flooding out of China's wealth.

2. According to the writer, what keeps the wealth locked up in China?

   A. The depreciation of the *renminbi*.

   B. The appreciation of the *renminbi*.

   C. The prosperous real estate industry.

   D. Chinese government's stimulus packages.

3. In recent years, the increasing liquidity imported to China can be attributed to ______.

   A. China's huge trade surpluses B. foreign investment

   C. "hot" money inflows D. all the above

Exercise 2 Fill in each of the blanks with the appropriate words given. Change the form of the word when necessary.

capitalization write off overhang hefty slosh

1. The team failed to ________ on their early lead.
2. The path was cool and dark with ________ trees.
3. They sold it easily and made a ________ profit.
4. There is a lot of money ________ around in professional tennis.
5. He has ________ two cars this year.

Exercise 3 Translate the following sentences into English.

1. 传统价值再次得到肯定。(reassert)
2. 不言而喻，随着版权法得到很好的贯彻，软件市场得以较规范的管理，盗版问题必将得到解决。(piracy problem)
3. 近年来，更多流动性通过巨额贸易顺差(每月 200 亿美元)流入中国，还有外国投资和“热钱”的流入。(“hot” money inflows)

Text 5　China Economy: Breathing Fire
中国经济如火如荼

导读　21世纪是不分国家、只追求和使用高效生产要素的全球化经济时代。中国以其独特的发展模式，占据对外贸易优势，使其经济发展速度遥遥领先于各国。但过度快速发展的负面现象也日渐显露：国内由于信贷过多，出现了投资过剩、通货膨胀等严峻问题；国外由于与美国贸易摩擦所引发人民币升值的压力也日益增大。人民币升值对中国企业影响较大，因为好多企业仅是组装厂家而已，利润微薄，升值过快会导致企业亏损或倒闭，而升值速度过慢又会面临美国保护主义的惩罚。如火如荼的中国经济面临"快慢"两难的棘手选择。

One would think that Asian equity markets① would be happy at the news that China's economy, the regional powerhouse, is growing even faster than expected. But that's not the way it turned out. Shortly before China's government said, late last week, that the economy grew at an annualized pace of 11.1 percent in the first three months of 2007, and as forecasts rose for the year's overall growth, traders on the region's big exchanges briefly took fright. The next day markets rebounded.

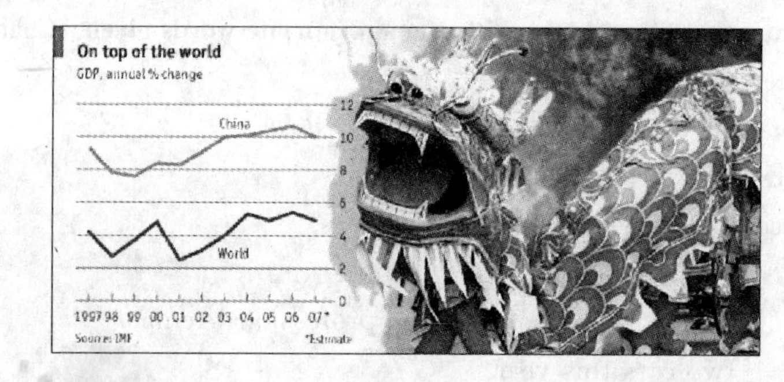

Nobody is jumpy about growth, of course, but of the government's reaction to it. Chinese officials are getting worried that a meltdown may be pending, and have been intervening to dampen things down. But over the past few years tighter interest rates, lending restrictions and heavier bank regulation have failed to cool the economy.

China's fairly primitive financial infrastructure makes it difficult to fine-tune credit

① 股票市场

through monetary and fiscal policy.[①]

As worries grow about credit bubbles and overinvestment,[②] no one knows quite how hard the government may need to step on the brakes. All this makes investors, who should be bullish, uncertain about what the near future may bring.

Across the Pacific, protectionists in America, who should be displeased to hear of even faster Chinese growth, may have found a note of cheer. If the Chinese government wants to get runaway growth under control, it may allow faster appreciation of the *yuan*.

Relations between China and America have been getting tense, thanks to the growing flow of cheap Chinese goods into American markets. But the Bush administration has so far stayed relatively friendly towards its trading partner. China has not been called a currency manipulator[③], despite domestic American pressure over the controlled currency. The *yuan* is now trading at about 7.7 to the dollar, up by a little over 7 percent since the Chinese currency went off its fixed peg in mid-2005[④]. More vocal critics[⑤] would like to see appreciation well into double digits, and have threatened sanctions if that does not happen. Until now, the administration has managed to stall such drastic moves with soothing talk about gradual increases.

That may be changing, however. China's trade surplus with America and its foreign-exchange reserves continue to grow, making economists fidgety and protectionist politicians livid. In the first three months of this year alone, China added $135.7-billion worth of foreign currency to its reserves, compared with $247.3 billion for all of 2006. This coincides with the lame duck phase[⑥] of the Bush administration, hamstrung by a newly Democratic congress, and politically crippled by the debacle in Iraq. With the 2008 presidential campaign getting into full swing, the administration is rapidly losing the will and strength to fight the protectionists.

On Friday April 20th Hank Paulson, America's treasury secretary[⑦], said that Chinese officials "are not moving, in my judgment, quickly enough" to loosen restrictions on the *yuan*. In the past Mr Paulson has been rather sympathetic to the Chinese on their currency conundrum[⑧], so this does not bode well for relations between the two. Some now

---

① 中国的金融体系相对稚嫩，使得很难有效运用财政和货币政策来调节信贷。我国货币政策工具和财政政策工具的协调配合主要表现为财政投资项目中的银行配套贷款。货币政策与财政政策的协调配合还要求国债发行与中央银行公开市场的反向操作相结合。

② 经济泡沫和过度投资

③ 货币操控者

④ 2005 年 7 月 21 日起，人民币汇率不再盯住单一美元，而是开始实行以市场供求为基础、参考一篮子货币进行调节、有管理的浮动汇率制度。

⑤ 畅言无忌的评论家

⑥ 一个不可能继任的官员的最后在职阶段

⑦ 美国财政部长

⑧ 货币难题

reckon that trade sanctions against China are on their way.

Indeed, they have already started. Last month, America slapped anti-dumping duties on imports of high-gloss paper from China, in response to a complaint from domestic manufacturers. It has also filed a complaint at the World Trade Organization against Chinese copyright violations.

If the Chinese government were to let off some economic steam by allowing the *yuan* to appreciate more, this might—temporarily, at least—appease some of America's "fair traders". It also makes some economic sense for China. Because its financial infrastructure is a little shaky, the central bank is not completely able to "sterilize" its foreign-currency transactions. The massive reserves it is accumulating could therefore translate into inflationary pressure, forcing it to clamp down on growth. A more freely floating currency would ease this stop-and-go cycle.

However, it's not clear how much impact this would really have on exports. For many of the products it exports, China is merely an assembler of parts made elsewhere, which is why its trade surplus with the rest of the world is less impressive than its bilateral one with America. Should the *yuan* rise, it will make those inputs cheaper for Chinese firms, so export prices will rise less than the *yuan*-bashers might hope.

Words and Expressions

equity [ˈekwɪtɪ] *n.* (无固定利息的股票);(公司发行的)股票的值,股本

annualized [ˈænjʊəˌlaɪzd] *adj.* (利率、通货膨胀率等)按全年计算的

rebound [rɪˈbaʊnd] *v.* 反弹

jumpy [ˈdʒʌmpɪ] *adj.* 易受惊吓的,神经质的;跳跃的

meltdown [ˈmeltdaʊn] *n.* 熔融

pending [ˈpendɪŋ] *adj.* 行将发生的,迫近的

dampen [ˈdæmpən] *v.* 抑制;减少

fine-tune *v.* 调节,调整(经济等)

runaway [ˈrʌnəweɪ] *adj.* 摆脱控制的,失控的;物价飞涨的

appreciation [əˌpriːʃɪˈeɪʃən] *n.* 上涨,升值

manipulator [məˈnɪpjuleɪtə] *n.* 操控者,操纵者

vocal [ˈvəʊkəl] *adj.* 畅所欲言的;畅言无忌的

sanction [ˈsæŋkʃən] *n.* [常作~s]国际制裁

stall [stɔːl] *v.* 拖延,推迟

soothing [ˈsuːðɪŋ] *adj.* 抚慰的,使人宽心的

fidgety [ˈfɪdʒɪtɪ] *adj.* 坐立不安的,过分注意细节的

protectionist [prəˈtekʃənɪst] *n.* 保护贸易论者

livid [ˈlɪvɪd] *adj.* 铅色的,大怒的

hamstring [ˈhæmstrɪŋ] *v.* 使瘫痪,使寸步难行

cripple ['krɪpl] *v.*	严重影响,削弱经济
debacle [deɪ'bɑːkl] *n.*	崩溃
appease [ə'piːz] *v.*	安抚,缓和,平息
basher ['bæʃə] *n.*	攻击者
clamp down	施加压力(钳制,制止,强制执行)
bode well	主吉;是好兆头
copyright violation	版权侵犯

Exercises

Exercise 1　Choose the best answer for each of the following questions.

1. After the news that China's economy grew faster than expected in the first quarter of 2007 was announced, the Asian stock markets ______.
   A. went up slightly　　B. roared
   C. remained stable　　D. dipped
2. What were Chinese investors worried about in the face of the economic growth?
   A. The economy might have been overheated.
   B. The possible American sanctions on China.
   C. Chinese government might take some measures to cool down the economy.
   D. China's fledgling financial markets could hardly withstand international risks.
3. Why does the Chinese government's intention to slow down the overheated economy appease American protectionists?
   A. Chinese government might allow faster appreciation of the *renminbi*.
   B. It will hinder the flow of American investment into China.
   C. It might make Chinese economic development more sustainable.
   D. It can let off some bubbles in Chinese economy.

Exercise 2　Fill in each of the blanks with the appropriate words given. Change the form of the word when necessary.

trade surplus with　dampen ... down　get runaway　bullish

1. Chinese officials are getting worried that a meltdown may be pending, and have been intervening to ________ things ________.
2. For many of the products it exports, China is merely an assembler of parts made elsewhere, which is why its ________ the rest of the world is less impressive than its bilateral one with America.
3. If the Chinese government wants to ________ growth under control, it may allow faster appreciation of the *yuan*.
4. All this makes investors, who should be ________, uncertain about what the near future may bring.

Exercise 3 Translate the following sentences into English.

1. 由于中国廉价商品持续流入美国市场，中美关系日益紧张。(the growing flow of)
2. 中国的外汇储备世界第一，2004 年为 6099.32 亿美元，至 2008 年 9 月已增长三倍达 19055 亿美元。(foreign exchange reserves, triple)

Text 6 The Rural Roots of China's Economic Miracle
为中国经济的奇迹寻根求源

导读 中国经济延续30年的两位数增长,这是西方经济原理所无法解释的经济奇迹。1978年中国GDP约为455.7亿美元,2008年经济总量接近4万亿美元,进出口贸易2008年突破2.5亿万美元,双双进入全球三甲。中国30年的改革开放源自1978年安徽凤阳小岗村的家庭联产承包责任制。20世纪80年代中期贫困人群大大下降,农村家庭收入年增长高于10%。90年代中国城市进入一个快速发展期,而农村变化缓慢,农民年收入增加跌入低谷,仅4%,数以万计的农民进城打工以维持生计。在过去的5年中,中国领导人胡锦涛先生倡导了一系列惠民、利民的发展新目标,如和谐社会、提高普通老百姓收入,而不是一味追求GDP,回归到30年前万里等老一代领导人倡导的农村改革。因此,中国经济高速发展的奇迹渊源来自于30年前的农村变革。

For years China's economy has been rapidly developed. Under the surface of "miracle," agriculture has become the great barriers in the way of developing.

In designing his economic policy program for the next five years, President Hu Jintao is well advised to seek counsel from someone virtually unknown to those Chinese who came of age in the 1990s. He is Wan Li①, 91 years old and still intellectually alert.

Mr Wan was a special guest at the opening session of the 17th Communist Party Congress in Beijing last week. It was he, more than anyone else there, who put China on the right track. In the 1980s he was a vice-premier in charge of agriculture, and before that he was the party secretary of the impoverished Anhui Province.

It was in Anhui that the true Chinese miracle began. In December 1978, 18 households in Xiaogang Village made a secret decision to privatize their rural output. Fearing reprisals, the households entered into a pledge—written in blood—to support the families of their leaders should they be arrested. ②

Mr Wan did not arrest them. On the contrary, he endorsed the experiment and bravely defended it in the face of withering attacks from conservatives.

The experiment, which became known as the household responsibility system③, was

---

① 万里,1980年4月到1988年4月任国务院副总理。

② 1978年12月,安徽凤阳小岗村18户不想饿死的农民在一起写下血书,签下分田到户"生死契约",成为中国改革的一个起点。

③ 家庭联产承包责任制。农户以家庭为单位向集体组织承包土地等生产资料和生产任务的农业生产责任制形式。

adopted by 90 percent of villages in Anhui within a year and by the rest of the country a few years later.

Mr Wan was then promoted to vice-premier. In that position, he worked tirelessly to support rural financial liberalization, lengthening the leasehold of farmland, removing employment restrictions on private businesses, deregulating rural-urban trade, curtailing the power of party officials in the countryside and introducing grassroots democracy to village governance.

The result was that rural household income per capita galloped ahead at more than 10 percent a year in the 1980s. Western economists may tout foreign direct investment and global-isolation as the reasons for China's poverty reduction. But the true credit lies with the rural reforms.

The vast majority of China's poverty reduction came in the first half of the 1980s. Also during that period, income distribution improved.

A defining characteristic of Mr Wan and other leaders of the 1980s was that they respected the inclinations and actions of farmers rather than imposing their own visions. The 1980s reforms were a classic example of a bottom-up, wisdom-of-the-crowd success story. A market economy, in essence, is an economic democracy. Mr Wan once told his subordinates always to assume that they were in the wrong if the farmers wanted to do something different from them.

It is truly unfortunate that China in the 1990s deviated from these market-conforming policy principles. In the 1990s, rural China was starved of financial resources in order to support industrial development in the cities. The effect of the urban policy bias was dramatic. Rural income growth collapsed from double-digit annual increases in the 1980s to about 4 percent a year in the 1990s. Since then, under the leadership of Mr Hu, it has recovered to 6 percent.

China will succeed or fail not because of how many skyscrapers Beijing and Shanghai have but as a result of the economic fortunes of its vast countryside. Domestic consumption will not grow if rural incomes do not improve and if rural residents are forced to save for their medical and educational expenses.

It may be counter-intuitive to think that China's high-technology future depends on its countryside—but not if you believe in market principles. The success of low-tech businesses in rural China will force urban companies to innovate in their production and technology to maintain their competitive edge. The rural stagnation of the 1990s sent millions of migrants to the cities in search of jobs. Urban companies, never short of labor, were flooded with tens of millions of eager job-seekers and they did what any rational owners and managers would do in similar circumstances—they favored labor-intensive production at the expense of research and development.

In the past five years, Mr Hu has formulated many worthy objectives, such as creating a harmonious society and raising the living standards of average people above gross domestic product growth.

Words and Expressions

counsel ['kaʊnsəl] *n.*	商议，评议
impoverished [ɪm'pɒvərɪʃt] *adj.*	贫穷的，无力的
privatize ['praɪvətaɪz] *v.*	使归私有，私营化
reprisal [rɪ'praɪzəl] *n.*	报复
endorse [ɪn'dɔːs] *v.*	认可，支持
deregulate [dɪ'regjʊˌleɪt] *v.*	解除，管制
curtail [kɜː'teɪl] *v.*	缩减限制
grassroots [ˌgrɑːs'ruːts] *v.*	基层
tout [taʊt] *v.*	吹捧
entrepreneur [ˌɒntrəprə'nɜː] *n.*	企业家，主办人
intuitive [ɪn'tjʊɪtɪv] *adj.*	直觉的
stagnation [stæg'neɪʃən] *n.*	停滞，淤害
Communist Party Congress	中国共产党代表大会

Exercises

Exercise 1 Choose the best answer for each of the following questions.

1. After Mr Wan was promoted to be vice-premier, what contribution did he make on this position?
   A. Supporting rural financial liberalization.
   B. Lengthening the leasehold of farmland.
   C. Removing employment restrictions on private businesses.
   D. All the above.
2. When did China's rural household income gallop?
   A. 1990s.　　B. 1980s.　　C. 1978.　　D. 2008.

Exercise 2 Fill in each of the blanks with the appropriate words given. Change the form of the word when necessary.

counsel　deviate　privatize　intuitive　endorse　tout

1. I had to ________ my painting about for months before I got any buyer.
2. Some former state-owned enterprises have been ________.
3. The bus had to ________ from its usual route because of a road closure.
4. He had an ________ sense of what the readers wanted.
5. I whole-heartedly ________ his remarks.
6. We'd better listen to the ________ of our elders.

Exercise 3　Translate the following sentences into English.

1. 中国的成败并不取决于北京和上海拥有多少座高楼大厦，而在于广大农村地区的经济命运。(as the result of)
2. 基层民主是农村治理的有效手段。(grassroots)
3. 在中国农村地区，科技含量较低的企业取得成功，将迫使城市企业在生产和科技方面创新，以保持其竞争优势。(maintain)

Text 7 Chinese Market Economy Puzzle

中国"市场经济"地位的困惑

导读 经历了近30年的改革，中国排除了数以万计的障碍，其私人企业的产值占全国GDP 50%之多，中国也成为了世界第三大出口市场。可是包括美国、欧盟在内的主要西方国家和组织至今尚未正式承认中国为市场经济国家。自中国2001年加入WTO以来，"非市场经济地位"成了西方发达国家针对中国产品反倾销调查中惯用的一个法宝，而且屡用不弃。而令人感到蹊跷的是他们在数年前就承认俄罗斯为市场经济国家，尽管后者还不是WTO的成员。很明显，承认市场经济地位关键不是一个国家的市场自由度，而是出口到西方的产品结构，中国出口的产品是与西方国家本土公司的产品相竞争，而俄罗斯出口的是西方国家稀缺的大宗商品。

Is China a market economy? After a quarter-century of reforms that have bulldozed market barriers, made the country the world's third-largest export market and, by some estimates, shifted more than half its output into private hands, it is clearly moving in that direction. But not nearly far enough to suit western politicians.

China's economic status is far more than an academic debating point. How it is defined shapes global trade flows worth hundreds of billions of dollars a year and directly affects the prices of the clothes you wear, of many of the electronic gadgets you use at home and at work and quite soon, probably, of the car you drive.

The reason is that when China joined the World Trade Organization in 2001 it reluctantly agreed, under international pressure, to be treated for 15 years as a "non-market economy" (NME) in anti-dumping cases against its exports. As the world's most popular anti-dumping target, facing hundreds of such cases, China has lived to regret the decision.

Anti-dumping is the great legal let-out from the non-discrimination principles on which multilateral trade rules are founded.

It entitles WTO members unilaterally and selectively to slap high tariffs on imports they consider injuriously cheap, using methodology that independent economists and importers have long criticized as flawed and opaque. ①

The odds are stacked more heavily still against the dozen or so countries that the US and European Union treat as NMEs. In judging the "fairness" of their export prices, western authorities may and often do disregard their producers' actual costs and use instead

---

① 它使世贸成员单方面享有选择性地运用被独立经济学家和进口商长期以来批评为有缺陷和不透明的方法——反倾销高额关税，来打击他们认为价格便宜得有威胁性的进口商品。

estimates based on the costs of producers elsewhere. In China's case, a favorite proxy is India, even though it has a far less developed manufacturing sector that barely exports some goods of which China is a volume producer.

The US and EU each have their own, different, checklists for designating countries as NMEs. They cover such things as the extent of government controls, operation of supply and demand, private property rights, foreign ownership curbs and, in the case of the US, currency convertibility and labor rights.

No one can seriously argue that China meets all the criteria of a fully-fledged market economy (though Beijing claims it meets 70 percent of them). But the same standards could as easily be used to disqualify as market economies many of the WTO's 149 members, which include a fair share of economic basket cases, autarkies, kleptocracies and failed states. It is also debatable whether Britain or France, in their industry nationalization heydays less than 30 years ago, would have passed the test.

The crowning inconsistency is the US and EU decision four years ago to recognize Russia as a market economy. Not only has Russia yet to qualify for WTO membership, its rule of law is shaky, its state has engaged in large-scale confiscation of private property and its massive energy industry, by far its largest exporter, is answerable to the Kremlin.

Western recognition was supposed to reward Moscow for economic reforms and to encourage it to go further. But why Russia, why not China, which has done vastly more to liberalize its economy?

The answer, of course, has little or nothing to do with market freedom①. It is that Russia exports relatively few goods to the west, most of them scarce commodities; while China is all too good at selling things that compete with western manufactured products.

Beijing, meanwhile, uses NME status as a bargaining chip② with other governments, insisting they recognize it as a market economy in return for development aid and the preferential trade deals③ its Asian neighbors are eager to sign. More than 50 countries have obliged so far, proving that even cherished economic principles are for sale if the price is right.

Words and Expressions

bulldoze ['buldəuz] *v.* 推倒,推平,强迫
gadget ['gædʒɪt] *n.* 家用小机械,小配件
let-out *n.* 可钻空子的机会
injuriously [ɪn'dʒuərɪəslɪ] *adv.* 有害地,伤害地

① 市场自由度
② 谈判筹码
③ 优惠贸易待遇

proxy ['prɒksɪ] *n.*	代用品，代表者
autarky ['ɔːtɑːkɪ] *n.*	自给自足政策，经济独立政策
kleptocracy [klep'tɒkrəsɪ] *n.*	盗贼统治(的国家)
heyday ['heɪdeɪ] *n.*	全盛时期，最高潮
confiscation [ˌkɒnfɪs'keɪʃən] *n.*	没收，充公，征用
realpolitik [reɪ'ɑːlpəʊlɪ'tiːk] *n.*	实力政治，权利政治
sop [sɒp] *n.*	安抚物，取悦物
fully-fledged *adj.*	羽毛丰满的，成熟的
basket case	完全没有希望的人

Exercises

Exercise 1 Choose the best answer for each of the following questions.

1. China was forced to accept being treated as a Non-market Economy in the WTO for ______ years.

   A. 10 B. 15 C. 20 D. 15

2. Which of the following is not a standard of the WTO to disqualify a member as a market economy?

   A. The extent of government controls.

   B. Operation of supply and demand.

   C. Foreign ownership curbs.

   D. The preferential trade deals.

3. Why was Russia labelled as a market economy by the US and the EU?

   A. Because of its export of bulk competitive goods.

   B. Because of its export of scare commodities.

   C. Because of its military power.

   D. Because of its close diplomatic relationship with the other two parties.

Exercise 2 Fill in each of the blanks with the appropriate words given. Change the form of the word when necessary.

electronic gadget liberalize qualify for economic reforms oblige

1. Talks have continued late into the night in Geneva in an attempt to avoid a break-down in negotiations to ________ world trade.
2. An ________ is a small technological object that has a particular function, but is often thought of as a novelty.
3. World Bank's Board of Executive Directors Tuesday approved a US$20 million loan to support China's ________.
4. My graduate school training combined with my internship should ________ me ________ this particular job.

5. I felt ________ to leave after such an unpleasant quarrel.

Exercise 3　Translate the following sentences into English.

1. 中国的经济状况远超过学术界所预期的。(economic status)
2. 莫斯科的经济改革应该得到奖励。(reward)
3. 中国满足所有成熟市场经济体所应有的标准。(fully-fledged)

Text 8 Bringing Best Practice to China
中国经验全球共享

导读 如今中国已融入国际经济，中国的成功经验也可为全球共享：在中国研发的产品可以成为全球产品，在中国开发的工业流程也可成为全球流程。至今全球500强公司中已有460多家来到中国经营业务，成功者居多。如果你在中国的企业尚未成为你公司全球经营浩瀚天空中的明星，你公司的全球型业务，也许已陷入困境。学会如何在中国经营，把握世界上竞争最激烈的市场，将会指导你如何在全球其他市场更好地胜人一筹。

As the country merges into the world economy, best practice in China will become best practice globally, products developed in China will become global products, and industrial processes developed in China will become global processes.

How do your operations in China stack up, measure by operating measure, against what your company is doing in Europe, Japan, and the United States? This may be a more critical question than you realize: Within a decade, if your organization in China isn't a star in your company's performance firmament, you may be in trouble—globally.

This question is also a very complex one to answer. Thousands of multinational companies of all sizes, including more than 460 Fortune 500 companies, now operate in China, and many are doing just fine. The American Chamber of Commerce in China conducts an annual business climate survey, and in its most recent one (which took place in 2006) 64 percent of the member companies reported that business in China was profitable or very profitable. One out of three said that their operations in China had higher margins than their worldwide organizations did, and another third reported margins on par with the global average.

But the conditions for success in China have been changing. Many multinational companies are expanding across the country to ever-smaller cities and towns, establishing positions to serve fast-growing segments of the Chinese middle class and small- and medium-sized businesses. In the process, they frequently incur greater sales, marketing, and distribution costs and take on new organizational challenges as they try to understand—and meet—the needs of customers in such markets. Moreover, they're encountering stiff competition from regional and national domestic Chinese rivals, which frequently know these customers better, have long-established business relationships in local markets, and compete relentlessly on price in places where consumers typically have much less money to spend than those in the big cities.

What's worse, today's sunny numbers mask underlying performance shortfalls. Because manufacturing-labor costs in China are a fifth of their levels in Europe and the United States, for instance, many multinationals have been running plants in China less efficiently than at home, and are still coming out way ahead. A recent McKinsey① study of 30 multinational-owned factories in China found that waste reduced profits by 20 to 40 percent. Similarly, though several multinational retailers that source goods in China save as much as 20 percent compared with costs elsewhere, we've studied many of the goods they buy and found that they could realize far greater savings—often double what they achieve today—if they managed procurement processes as rigorously as they do in more established markets.

Managers don't underperform in China intentionally. Waste is endemic to manufacturing plants there partly because some multinationals have inherited, through partnerships or acquisitions, legacy processes, employee mind-sets, and manufacturing approaches. A chaotic environment, changing regulation, and a red-hot talent market all do not help either. Waste in production plants, inefficient distribution networks, underleveraged procurement processes, and lackluster market research are hard to change, and if margins are good and business is growing, managers focus on growth, not operational improvements. But "good-enough" execution isn't sufficient any more as businesses expand in China and competition stiffens. Companies such as Danfoss②, GE, KFC, Johnson & Johnson③, and Nokia are showing that execution counts in China. They took a different approach, with a far greater emphasis on high performance standards and operating rigor, and are beating domestic and global competitors in China's smaller cities. In essence, these high-performing companies took best practices from operations elsewhere and adapted them—sometimes a little, sometimes a lot—to the realities of China.

This is the gold standard for how multinationals will raise the bar for execution in China over the next decade.

First Came Emerging Market Strategies

Fifteen years ago, multinational companies won in China by developing strategies to create privileged or first-mover access within highly focused markets. They secured government permission to enter, partnered with Chinese companies, and sold existing brands—from cars to cosmetics, hearing aids to handbags, skis to scarves—at premium prices to affluent buyers and large companies in China's four or five largest cities. One European automaker, for example, moved quickly during the 1980s to secure preferential treatment for sales in Shanghai: the right location, the right government relationships,

① 国际咨询公司麦肯锡，世界级领先的全球管理咨询公司。

② 丹佛斯集团，是机械、电子产品和控制领域研发及生产的领先者。

③ 美国强生公司，成立于1887年，是世界上规模大、产品多元化的医疗、卫生保健品及消费者护理产品公司。

the right joint ventures. It then shut out other global OEMs from this market for nearly a decade. Industrial companies lined up in Beijing to sell their existing catalogs, with little adaptation to local circumstances. Simply showing up in China was a strategy that paid dividends.

Making the right strategic choices was critical; execution was another matter. Superb operating performance on the level that multinationals expect of their managers in competitive developed markets has been hard to achieve—even to define. Reliable data on markets and customers are rare, so it is difficult for managers to make decisions with as much clarity and confidence as they would in Europe or the United States. Managers in developed markets have access to a wealth of information, from point-of-sale data to reports on segments, products, and markets from third-party research firms. Not so in China. The managers of multinational companies thus found that they couldn't replicate the marketing and product-development processes they had honed in developed markets, using information obtained there.

Similarly, multinational companies in China have had to work within logistics and distribution structures dating back to the days of the planned economy. What's more, building a reliable base of high-quality suppliers has been a constant challenge. Even recently, some multinational companies have suffered high-profile setbacks because of problems with Chinese suppliers. In response to the seemingly unique situations encountered in China, multinational managers often created made-to-order processes and systems.

Many multinationals, for instance, designed custom HR systems and management-development processes, separate from their global systems, for organizations in China. A number of companies coped with the variability of manufacturing there by adding more people and machines—a solution they would never have adopted at plants in Brazil or Germany. Others dealt with unreliable suppliers by double- and triple-sourcing components and carrying more inventory.

As these examples suggest, the China-specific practices companies have created might be judged subpar elsewhere. But operations in China reflect market entry strategies and a high-growth environment that gave companies a lot of breathing room: Competition held at bay, influential partners, pricing power, and affluent buyers hungry for global brands. Such systems, processes, and functions got the job done and were often good enough to accept.

Say goodbye to that era. Today China is open for business, and competition from both multinationals and local companies is increasing. Strategies based on creating and sustaining privileged access look more and more outdated. Joint-venture partners and acquisition targets are available to the highest (or at least most suitable) bidder. Business licenses are readily available. Particularly since joining the World Trade Organization, in December 2001, China has changed many of its rules and procedures governing business. It is beginning to resemble the rest of the world.

In other words, China has turned a corner, from an emerging market, where local context drives most strategic and operating decisions, to a maturing one, with world-class execution a cornerstone for success. As multinationals expand beyond the big cities and Chinese companies become more competitive, executives will need to ensure that their organizations develop, produce, sell, market, and distribute goods to customers as effectively and efficiently as possible.

Who's Getting It Right?

A few successful multinationals in China already understand this. Their managers ran against the grain by rejecting the idea that China required unique operating approaches and performance standards. Instead, these managers focused on implementing top global processes in China, tuning them locally as needed, and linking them globally at every opportunity.

Alcoa, for instance, introduced its highly successful Alcoa Business System at its Shanghai manufacturing plant in 1998. Modeled on Toyota's integrated lean operations, the system helped boost the company to a global leadership position in its sector during the 1990s. This approach to lean operations, with some adaptations, is working in China. Within six years of beginning to transform the Shanghai plant, Alcoa shortened lead times by 30 to 50 percent, doubled sales volumes (for domestic sales and exports alike), and greatly reduced inventories.

Other companies have also brought global systems and practices to China. GE has introduced, to great effect, its Six Sigma quality control standards at its lighting division's plants there. To lower procurement costs, the company has implemented a version of the sophisticated online bidding system it uses in more mature markets. Citigroup and HSBC have extended their finely honed leadership-training and -development processes and systems to China. Each year, HSBC puts 400 managers from around the world, including China, through a global-rotation program that trains them in world standards and practices.

Cleveland-based Preformed Line Products① (PLP), a telecommunications hardware supplier, is another company that has introduced world-class lean techniques in its manufacturing operations in China. Adherence to hierarchy has a very long history there, however, so line workers tend to seek answers from bosses rather than solve problems as teams, though team-based problem solving is a cornerstone of lean manufacturing. PLP therefore adapted its problem-solving meetings to the cultural realities of China—holding shorter, more focused gatherings, for instance—to achieve the results that might come out of lean initiatives in Brazil or the United States.

---

① 帕尔普线路器材公司，设在美国克里夫兰，是一家市值2亿美元的公司，生产电缆和电信企业所用的电缆夹具。

Rethinking Your China Operations

Transforming Chinese operations from good enough to world class isn't easy. It can be vexing even to decide where to begin. Should marketing improvements come before manufacturing ones? What roles should senior executives from the home office and in China assume? And of course, no single solution is common to all companies in all industries, nor would a single answer handle all the complexities and uncertainties of the Chinese market.

Yet our work in China with the multinational and domestic companies getting things done very well there shows that executives can use a single approach to sort through the choices and trade-offs. A sequence of steps can help managers move through a complex agenda, from redefining a global corporation's goals in China to defining its impact on global strategies.

Elevate Your Aspirations

For most companies, the first step in improving a Chinese operation will be to reexamine their goals and, possibly, hit the reset button. China's economy is changing at an unprecedented pace. Business goals set a decade ago are likely to be out of date. And before raising the bar on execution, some companies may need to rethink the strategies they are executing against.

That's what Danfoss, a $3 billion global manufacturer headquartered in Denmark, discovered in 2005. At the time, its business in China was thriving—growing by around 35 percent a year, primarily by making and selling components and devices designed in Europe to Chinese manufacturers. But when the company conducted a review of its products and markets, it realized that despite growth rates a Silicon Valley entrepreneur might envy, it was losing market share in China.

Danfoss aimed its products primarily at the market's high end. A Danfoss motor-speed control used in commercial refrigerators, for instance, appealed to Chinese makers of costly appliances, but manufacturers selling midpriced or inexpensive commercial refrigerators needed controls that were less pricey, saved energy, and better withstood dust—a need in China but not Europe. The company's managers realized that these less-than-premium markets were staggeringly large, so even if Danfoss sustained its double-digit growth, higher-volume competitors would soon eclipse it. The upshot: Danfoss refocused its metrics from revenue to market share growth.

To meet these new goals, Danfoss overhauled its operations in China. It expanded its distribution network from the big cities to nearly 40 urban markets across the country, opened R&D centers there, dramatically expanded its Chinese employee base (from 700 in 2004 to almost 4,000 projected by 2008), and shifted to China much of the responsibility for developing new products for Chinese markets.

Once companies change or ratify their business goals and operating plans, managers should raise the bar on execution—across every function, from marketing to sourcing, manufacturing to product development, talent management to M&A. In our experience, many multinational executives in China settle for the performance they have rather than the performance they could get. Top- and bottom-line numbers may look great, but they could look a lot better if companies started to reduce waste and inefficiency. Multinationals can realistically cut their operating costs in China by around 15 percent annually and expect their revenues to rise by 30 percent as well. In fact, we know of several multinationals in China that should regard these as their minimum targets.

Setting new goals in China is a top-down process involving the CEO and, typically, the board as well. Danfoss reset its goals there at the behest of its chief executive, Jorgen Clausen, who had traveled the Silk Road while on vacation in 2004 and saw first hand the potential for his company in the smaller cities and towns.

Companies also need top-down support to raise the bar on execution; high aspirations demand effective blocking and tackling. Getting this job done may require top executives to remove barriers and create space for experimentation. In a survey we conducted recently with CEOs at 40 multinationals, most said that they supported the efforts of their organizations to develop a China strategy. But the CEOs whose companies are winning there reported that they have been personally involved in resolving issues (such as legal problems, budgeting challenges, and HR concerns) that impeded the creation or growth of the China business.

Face Trade-offs Realistically

The crux of the transformation must be importing world-class global processes and adapting them to Chinese realities when necessary or overhauling current China processes by raising performance to the level of a company's best global processes. This means upgrading its manufacturing quality and productivity, as well as the effectiveness of sales and marketing, to achieve global standards and realize this huge market's full potential. Knowing what practices to take from the global tool chest and how to adapt them to China requires both a good understanding of world-class management techniques and a practical sense of how the country operates.

Frequently, managers must make trade-offs. Some innovations developed in China, for example, should be designed to meet local needs and take advantage of low-cost supply or capital-expenditure opportunities. But sometimes global consistency can be equally important—for instance, if an innovation designed and made in China goes global.

Companies should base such strategic choices on local realities, not popular myths. To take advantage of differences in capital and labor costs, for example, Honda built its factory in China with substantially less automation than it had in plants in Japan or the United States. But in the steel industry, shop floor labor is a much less important factor. That helps to explain why Capital Steel has built a vertically integrated automated plant at an astonishing pace and scale.

Globalize from China

Finally, winning companies will leverage their local success by globalizing their China operations. They will rethink China's role in worldwide strategy, organization, and operations and integrate that role globally wherever possible. As competition in China's markets intensifies, managers at domestic companies are rapidly learning how to adopt best practices from around the world. Chinese companies recognize that they must step onto the global stage before the multinationals lock them out. The best of both domestic and foreign companies in China are working to apply global standards.

In such a competitive hothouse, adapted practices will evolve quickly, and as China merges into the world economy best practice there will become best practice globally. More products developed in China will become global products; more industrial processes developed in China will become global processes. The ability to develop a Chinese talent pool will therefore be critical across all functions. Learning how to execute in China—the world's most competitive market—will teach companies how to compete more aggressively elsewhere.

Words and Expressions

firmament [ˈfɜːməmənt] *n.*	穹苍，苍天
incur [ɪnˈkɜː] *v.*	招致，承受，遭遇
relentlessly [rɪˈlentlɪslɪ] *adv.*	无情地，残酷地
procurement [prəˈkjʊəment] *n.*	获得，(政府的)收买，斡旋，促成
underperform [ˌʌndəpəˈfɔːm] *v.*	表现不佳，工作不如预期(或同行)
endemic [enˈdemɪk] *adj.*	地方性的，某地[某民族]特有的
red-hot *adj.*	炽热的，灼热的
leverage [ˈliːvərɪdʒ] *n.*	杠杆作用
lackluster [ˈlækˌlʌstə] *adj.*	无光泽的（暗淡的，无生气的，平凡的）
point-of-sale	销售点系统
replicate [ˈreplɪkeɪt] *v.*	折叠，复制，摹写
hone [həʊn] *v.*	用磨刀石磨，磨练
inventory [ˈɪnvəntərɪ] *n.*	清单，目录，存货，总值，详细记载
subpar [ˈsʌbˈpɑː] *adj.*	欠佳
vexing [ˈveksɪŋ] *adj.*	使人烦恼的，使人恼火的
pricey [ˈpraɪsɪ] *adj.*	昂贵的，过分昂贵的
upshot [ˈʌpʃɒt] *n.*	结果，结局，结尾
behest [bɪˈhest] *n.*	命令
impede [ɪmˈpiːd] *v.*	妨碍，阻碍，阻止
crux [krʌks] *n.*	十字形，关键
tool chest(=toolbox)	工具箱

Exercises

Exercise 1 Choose the best answer for each of the following questions.

1. Which of the following is not a difficulty facing foreign multinationals in China?
   A. Higher margins in China than in more established markets.
   B. Stiff competition from regional and national domestic Chinese rivals.
   C. A chaotic environment, changing regulation, and a red-hot talent market.
   D. Waste, inefficient distribution networks, underleveraged procurement process, and lackluster market research.
2. Which one of the following is not a reason why multinationals are difficult to make right strategic choices?
   A. Reliable data on markets and customers are unavailable.
   B. It's hard to build a reliable base of high-quality suppliers.
   C. Logistics and distribution structures in China date back to the planned economy.
   D. Preferential accesses are hard to find.
3. Which of the following company does not adopt lean techniques in its business practices?
   A. Alcoa. B. Toyota.
   C. Citigroup and HSBC. D. PLP.
4. When Danfoss elevated its aspiration, which of the following statements is not true?
   A. Though Danfoss' growth rates were high, its market share in China was shrinking.
   B. Danfoss shifted its focus from revenue to market share.
   C. Danfoss expanded its business scope.
   D. Danfoss was more responsible for Chinese market.
5. To face trade-offs realistically, multinationals should ______.
   A. lay more emphasis on global standards
   B. focus more on Chinese realities
   C. strike a balance between global standards and local needs
   D. base strategic choices on popular myths

Exercise 2 Fill in each of the blanks with the appropriate words given. Change the form of the word when necessary.

impede incur endemic procurement inventory

1. Any expenses you may ________ will be chargeable to the company.
2. Since then, she has extended her yogurt-buying strategy to the ________ of other basic necessities.
3. Admittedly, bribery and corruption are ________ to our political and economic systems, but it doesn't necessarily follow that all politicians and business people resort to illicit behavior.

4. We would like to know if you have any interests in our ________ of products.
5. The development of the project was seriously ________ by a reduction in funds.

Exercise 3 Translate the following sentences into English.

1. 为了维持营业，一家企业必须担负起一定的费用和开支。(incur)
2. 该国劳工市场缺乏灵活性，这严重阻碍了它的经济恢复。(impede)
3. 他们又想出一个增加收入的办法。(hit upon)
4. 在商品价格下跌时，海琴能够帮助他们抵补存货价跌的损失。(hedge, offset)

Text 9 Spending Time

中国经济将依旧后劲十足

导读 在过去的5个年头中，中国经济尤为动力十足，年增长保持在10%左右。源自美国次贷危机的全球金融危机使中国经济也不能独善其身，房价跳水、出口下滑、工厂减产、企业裁员、备受看好的消费也呈现疲软。面对这突如其来的经济骤然走弱态势，中国政府频频出手，打出一系列如减税、减息，调高出口退税，万亿巨资投入基础设施建设的组合拳。另外，连续数月CPI与海外大宗商品价格的回落也将有助中国经济率先走出全球经济衰退阴影。一旦雨过天晴，经过结构调整，脱胎换骨的中国经济将会依旧动力十足。

For the past five years, China has enjoyed what can only be called turbo-charged growth. In each year, the economy not only expanded by more than 10 percent but in each year the growth rate also accelerated.

Such a rapid pace of expansion could not continue forever and this period is now clearly coming to an end. But what sort of slowdown China experiences during the next few years remains unclear.

The government is hoping for a gradual decline in growth to more sustainable levels which will take some of the steam out of property markets, but without damaging employment too much. The performance of the economy in the first half of the year, when it expanded by 10.4 percent, appeared to indicate this was happening. "The slowdown has only been gradual and will likely remain so for the rest of the year," says Qu Hongbin, economist at HSBC in Hong Kong[①].

However, there is an increasing amount of evidence that China might suffer a much sharper slowdown that would include a sharp drop in property prices, a decline in exports and problems in the banking system. Stephen Green, economist at Standard Chartered Bank[②] in Shanghai, has one of the more pessimistic outlooks for China, predicting 7.9 percent growth next year and 7.1 percent the year after.

While most other countries would be happy for such a forecast, slower growth would have big implications for many of the UK groups that have invested heavily in China, such

---

① 香港上海汇丰银行有限公司(即汇丰银行)于1865年在香港和上海成立。汇丰银行在亚太地区的20多个国家和地区设有600多家分行和办事处并在亚太地区外的8个国家设立了23家分行和代表处。

② 英国渣打银行，总部位于伦敦，全球有60,000名员工。1858年在上海成立第一间分行。

as HSBC and Standard Chartered and retailers Tesco[①] and Marks & Spencer[②]—which opened its first store in China earlier this month.

The sector of the economy that will inevitably suffer is exports, which have been one of the principal drivers of economic growth in recent years. To the surprise of many economists, China's exports have grown more than 20 percent this year, despite the slowdown in the US. In part, this is because exporters have managed to find new markets for their products in booming emerging economies, such as Brazil and Russia[③], and in the Middle East.

But the problem for China's exporters is that two of their other biggest markets—the European Union and Japan—are also now suffering real economic problems, which will make it much harder for companies in China to keep expanding exports.

Indeed, there are already signs of real distress from parts of the export sector. According to the National Development and Reform Commission, China's main economic planning body, 67,000 small companies have closed down so far this year, most of which are likely to be in the export sector.

The economy could cope with weaker exports. However, it will be much more vulnerable if there is also a big drop in investment, which has been one of the other main drivers of growth.

As a result, close attention is now being paid to the property sector, which is one of the most important components of overall investment, but which is looking extremely exposed. Data on house prices in China can be difficult to assess: While the government's main price index for 70 cities shows that prices fell modestly last month, the anecdotal information from a host of different cities suggests there have been big drops in prices.

There is more conclusive data of an impending slump in the market. Last year, the number of properties sold increased 26 percent, but in the first half of this year it fell by 11 percent. In August, the amount of floor space under construction fell—an indicator that was backed up by weak figures for steel and cement production. "The only real way out is for prices to fall sharply or for the government to bail out developers," says Shen Minggao, a former Citigroup economist now working at *Caijing* magazine.

The government has been actively trying to cool the property market, introducing a string of measures to limit credit to property developers and to make it harder to obtain a mortgage. However, the risk is that the slowdown in the housing market will go too far.

A property crash could cause a cascade of unwanted effects: If too many property

---

① Tesco乐购是英国领先的零售商，也是全球三大零售企业之一。Tesco在全世界拥有门店总数超过3,700家，员工总数达440,000多人。

② Marks & Spencer（马莎）是一家总部位于英国伦敦的零售企业。每周有超过2,100万名消费者光临门店。

③ 新兴经济体，代表国为金砖四国（BRIC），即Brazil，Russia，India，China.

developers went bankrupt, it would increase unemployment; and it would cause considerable pain to the banking sector, given that about 30 percent of all loans go to either developers or mortgages. "There is bound to be a big increase in non-performing loans[①] if property prices fall sharply," says one researcher at a government think-tank in Beijing.

With exports and investment both under large clouds in the next couple of years, the performance of Chinese consumers has become much more important. The headline news about consumption has been extremely positive: In the past two months, retail sales have risen 23 percent, which is close to the highest level in the past nine years. The buoyant figures have encouraged some economists to predict that the country's consumers could prevent the economy from slowing too sharply during the next year.

Yet beneath the surface, a number of questions have been raised about just how robust the retail sales really are. Several important industries have reported a very different situation—car sales, for example, have begun to decline during the past month and air travel slumped over the summer. Income figures also present a much less optimistic outlook, with the rate of growth in urban incomes dropping 50 percent in the first six months of the year. And if the housing market slumps, that will inevitably spill over into consumption as fewer people buy washing machines and sofas for new homes.

The good news is that the Chinese government has more room for maneuver than most others responding to a slowing economy. With consumer price inflation dropping in recent months, it has some space to cut interest rates, although inflation at the factory level remains high.

On the fiscal front, China could reap the benefit of the conservative budget policy it has been running in recent years. The authorities have plenty of scope to accelerate spending on railways, roads and metros to boost overall investment.

"If the economy slows much more sharply than we expect, we have no doubt that Beijing has the financial capacity and the political will step in quickly with fiscal and administrative measures designed to boost growth," says Andy Rothman, economist at the brokerage and investment house CLSA in Shanghai.

Yet if property woes cause a collapse in private investment, there is only so much the government can do to make up the gap. Given the big questions now hanging over the Chinese economy, many economists believe the government needs to accelerate a series of reforms it has already outlined that would shift the balance of the economy away from production and towards consumers.

For a number of years, China's leaders have understood that they cannot rely forever on large yearly increases in exports and rapid rates of domestic investment. If high rates of growth are to be sustained in the long-term, they concluded, then consumption has to play a larger role in the economy. In particular, to get Chinese to save less and consume more,

---

① 不良抵押贷款,简称 NPL。

the authorities need to expand a social security network. The prospect of a global recession and a local property crash have brought home the need to implement this agenda more forcefully.

Words and Expressions

indicator ['ɪndɪkeɪtə] *n.*	指标
slump [slʌmp] *n.*	衰退，(物价)暴跌
robust [rəʊ'bʌst] *adj.*	强势的
fiscal ['fɪskəl] *adj.*	财政的
maneuver [mə'nuːvə] *n.*	回旋
recession [rɪ'seʃən] *n.*	经济衰退
turbo-charged growth	涡轮式增长
budget policy	预算政策

Exercises

Exercise 1 Choose the best answer for each of the following questions.

1. Which of the following is not indicating the recent economic slowdown in China?
   A. A sharp drop in property prices.
   B. A decline in exports.
   C. Increase of employment opportunities.
   D. Problems in the banking system.
2. What is the percent of growth for Chinese economy the year after the next according to Standard Chartered Bank's economist?
   A. 7.1. B. 7.9. C. 11. D. 26.
3. What are not the unwanted effects of property breakdown?
   A. Increase of unemployment.
   B. Banking sector pain.
   C. Reliance on sales of land to finance spending.
   D. Increase of migrant labor.

Exercise 2 Fill in each of the blanks with the appropriate words given. Change the form of the word when necessary.

sharp drop pessimistic outlook market slump spill over implement

1. My wife and I are teachers, and our jobs often ________ into our family life.
2. Chinese companies recorded a ________ in both the number and value of domestic and overseas initial public offerings in the third quarter.
3. Forecasters predict further housing ________ in the third quarter.

4. The Ministry of Health has been working intensively to ________ a comprehensive epidemic curbing plan.

5. Survey offers ________ for workers in many large US corporations.

Exercise 3 Translate the following sentences into English.

1. 在未来几年中国将会经历何种形式的放缓，仍然很难讲。(slowdown)

2. 作为近年来经济增长的主要推动因素之一，出口部门不可避免地会受到影响。(driver)

3. 针对下滑的经济趋势，中国政府比大多数其他国家拥有更大的调控空间。(maneuver)

Chapter Two China, Inc.

中国公司

Text 10 China's Firms Set Sights on World

中国公司走向世界

导读 几百年以来，中国华侨足迹踏遍全球五洲，建起了一座座中国城或一条条唐人街，开起了一家家饭店或商店。如今，中国公司大踏步走向世界，无论在发达的北美或欧洲，还是在发展地区的南美与非洲，处处都有中国公司的厂房或车间、经销店或矿山。从1996年到2005年，中国公司海外投资共300亿美元之多，仅2007年一年在美国上市的中国公司就多达29家，中国公司的自主品牌产品也走入了海外市场千家万户，中国公司的经理们还走进了美国顶尖商学院的课堂，汲取先进管理知识与经验。中国万向集团在美国的公司还获得了当地政府的补贴，当地政府还宣布了特别的“万向日”来表彰公司给当地带来了就业机遇。全世界都感受到：中国公司正走向世界。

Amid the torrent of clothes, electronics and toys surging out of China comes a little-noticed export: international companies.

For centuries, individual Chinese have sought their fortunes abroad, creating Chinatowns around their restaurants and shops. Now, Chinese firms are going global, pushed by a government turned more pragmatic, pulled by untapped markets and armed with bundles of money from a thriving economy back home.

Auto plants are popping up in Latin America. A sprawling commodity bazaar promises a provincial Swedish city new life. A car parts distributor is snapping up ailing companies in the US Rust Belt①, a TV factory hums in South Africa and a high-tech firm is landing contracts to revamp the Persian Gulf's② telecommunication networks.

---

① 美国锈带，指中西部诸州，东起俄亥俄州，西至艾荷华州，北至密歇根州。这些地区曾经是美国传统制造业中心，现在衰退了。

② Persian Gulf 波斯湾。印度洋西北部边缘海，又名阿拉伯湾，通称海湾。位于阿拉伯半岛和伊朗高原之间。该地方拥有全世界最丰富的石油资源，储量约占全球63%。

Just as the earlier arrival of Japanese companies changed US manufacturing, over time Chinese companies could affect how their Western rivals approach innovation, competition and business itself.

"We not only consider ourselves pioneers," says Sean Chen, who at 26 is overseeing the construction of a $100 million electrical parts plant and industrial park in the American South. "We also consider ourselves explorers."

Chen and his fiancee, Joy Chen—both took American first names—moved from Shanghai to Atlanta to set up shop for General Protecht Group Inc., a company controlled by his father. While the goal is profits, Sean Chen and his father view the venture almost as a social experiment—its aim, he said through an interpreter, is to marry the best Chinese and American work practices.

"I want to have the efficiency and execution normally shown by the American employees and the brotherhood that a Chinese company normally shows," Sean Chen says. "There are capitalists and there are socialists and I want to see whether they can get along."

The Chinese corporate presence is still small overseas, but it's growing fast:

Chinese companies invested more than $30 billion in foreign firms from 1996 to 2005, nearly one-third in 2004-05 alone, according to an analysis by Usha Haley, a professor of international business at the University of New Haven. Computer maker Lenovo Group helped launch the frenzy in December 2004 by announcing it would acquire IBM Corp.'s personal computer unit for $1.75 billion.[①]

In the United States and Canada, Chinese firms now have about 3,500 investment projects, compared to 1,500 five years ago, according to an estimate by Maryville University Professor Ping Deng. Large state-owned companies jumped ahead; medium and small private firms are catching up. Total investment in the US is between $4 billion and $7 billion, Ping estimates. In Europe, Chinese acquisitions last year alone totaled $563.3 million, according to research company Dealogic.

Last year, 29 Chinese firms debuted on US stock exchanges[②], just two shy of the total for the previous three years combined, according to the Bank of New York Mellon Corp.

The number of US visas issued to Chinese executives and managers who transfer to US posts within their companies nearly doubled to 2,043 between fiscal years[③] 2004 and

---

① 电脑制造商联想集团在2004年12月宣布以17.5亿美元的价格购买IBM的个人电脑业务。其中6.5亿美元为现金,6亿为股票,完成交易后IBM占有联想股票18.5%,联想5年内有权使用IBM的ThinkPad品牌。

② 美国证券交易所,即NYSE(New York Stock Exchange)。

③ fiscal years财政年度,指公司因会计需要而制定的年度。财政年度可以是日历年度,也可以跟日历年不同,例如从2月份开始。

2007. The current fiscal year is on pace to top that, US State Department statistics show.

Chinese businesses are not just establishing offices and factories overseas. They are also developing and selling products under their own brands, rather than simply supplying Western firms in search of cheap manufacturing.

The competition may make it harder for American and European firms to milk early profits from cutting-edge products before reducing prices and releasing them to the mass market. Vulnerable sectors include high-definition TVs, portable DVD players, medical technology, and perhaps even cars, according to Peter Williamson, a professor of International Management at the University of Cambridge with extensive China experience.

At the Detroit Auto Show[①] in January, one mid-sized SUV from China with goodies including a leather interior was priced at just $14,000—less than half what many comparable cars cost. Models could be available by early next year in nine states.

Chinese firms can use their low-cost manufacturing advantage to pile on additional features. And they can do that by copying taste-making Western firms, circumventing the expense of product development. If the quality is high enough, the strategy can be highly effective.

"It will pull to pieces the profit models of their competitors," Williamson says. "It's a classic case of attacking your competitor where you know they're reluctant to respond, because it's very costly."

The dynamic recalls how Japanese auto makers forced their US competitors to make options such as power windows and air conditioning standard.

Unlike the Japanese, whose 1980s' arrival in the US was at first greeted as a threat, Chinese businesses are being courted by states including Michigan, California, Illinois and Georgia.

Chinese Investments Face Scrutiny

Not that all arms are open.

US congressional scrutiny has dogged several investments, including the billions of dollars that government-owned funds are investing in top Wall Street institutions[②]. National security concerns have scuttled several deals, including the attempted 2005 purchase of oil giant Unocal Corp. and a $2.2 billion bid to buy the tech company 3Com in February.

In the Swedish coastal city of Kalmar, labor union and media criticism has been the backdrop for delayed Chinese plans to open a hotel and wholesale warehouse for Chinese-made commodities. Project manager Angie Qian tramps around, trying to get things done at the speed she was used to in Shanghai.

"China is developing very quickly and so people work very fast and don't plan very far

---

① 底特律车展。底特律即密歇根州最大城市，世界著名的汽车城。

② 华尔街机构。它位于美国纽约(New York)曼哈顿岛南端，是当今世界上最大的资金市场和国际金融中心。

ahead," says Qian, herself a study in constant motion. "In Sweden everything takes a much longer time."

The $160 million project, going up on the site of a shuttered chocolate factory, could help revive a city abandoned by car maker Volvo and train maker Bombardier Transportation[①].

It wouldn't be the first project of its kind. Dubai boasts an enormous Dragon Mart shopping mall and residential complex; Chinese centers with other backers have opened in Eastern Europe, Italy, England and Russia.

But the Kalmar project faces problems.

Fanerdun Group, the company bankrolling the project, has reportedly not received Chinese government approval to transfer funding from China to Sweden. The company has said it will pay wages of Chinese workers into Chinese bank accounts instead of Swedish accounts.

The national construction workers' union and local media have criticized Fanerdun for not paying some of the Chinese workers who helped prepare the site at all. The issue has delayed construction.

Elsewhere, miscalculations have led to early, and sometimes spectacular, failures. There was the Splendid China theme park in Florida that no one really visited. A group of investors never recovered from the fiasco of trying to evict poor tenants from the downtown Los Angeles hotel they planned to refurbish.

Chinese companies that wither often see the first branch as a trophy, and neglect the long-term strategy that can lead to greater profits, according to business Professor Ping. He based his survey on 400 Chinese companies doing business in the US and Europe.

Drastic differences in business culture also can hobble a venture. Western managers can demand more authority than Chinese bosses are accustomed to, and official directives can alienate workers.

Playing Catch-up in Formal Training

For all their energy and drive, many Chinese managers and executives lack formal training. That is changing.

At UCLA's Anderson School of Management, for example, Chinese applications more than doubled from 87 in 2005 to 180 in 2007. The 2007 class had 14 Chinese students, the most in the school's history.

Wife and husband Stella Li and Steven Zhu quit high-profile careers in China to study in Los Angeles. Li is slated to graduate this spring—Zhu got his MBA last year and landed at Google doing data-driven sales analysis. Both see an opportunity to gain a sophistication in finance and strategy they couldn't get working back home.

"We definitely want to take all the experience and the things we learned in the US

---

① 汽车制造商沃尔沃和火车制造商庞巴迪运输公司

back to China," Li said. "But in short term, we would like to get more exposure in business here."

Chinese firms are still learning the kinds of data-driven market analysis, branding and other business practices that are commonplace in the West.

"What's scary to think of is when they marry cost consciousness with US-style just-in-time inventory management[①]," says Charles Freeman, a China specialist at the Washington-based Center for Strategic and International Studies, who recalls talking to a cell phone maker that was storing 100 million headsets behind its factory.

Few Chinese companies have been in the US longer than the American subsidiary of the auto parts giant Wanxiang Group, which incorporated in 1993. The founder of the home company is one of China's richest men. His son-in-law, Pin Ni, led the Chicago-area subsidiary from cheap parts supplier up the value chain by buying or working with companies that were distressed—owing to competition from China.

Wanxiang America Inc. has been welcomed for saving manufacturing jobs. Illinois has proclaimed a Wanxiang Day and Michigan offered the company subsidies.

Pin talks exactly like what he is—an executive who's part of a multinational. It's all about core competence and optimizing strength and horizontal integration[②]. He casts himself as a matchmaker who spots what disparate firms do best to create as efficient a manufacturing process as possible.

"Even today you want to say, is there enough Chinese companies in the United States?" Pin asks. "I would say no."

Words and Expressions

torrent [ˈtɒrənt] *n.* 急流
revamp [riːˈvæmp] *v.* 修补
distributor [dɪˈstrɪbjətə] *n.* 分销商
sprawling [ˈsprɔːliŋ] *adj.* 蔓延的
venture [ˈventʃə] *n.* 风险投资企业
cutting-edge *adj.* 先进的
SUV= sport utility van 越野车
circumvent [ˌsəːkəmˈvent] *v.* 围绕，包围
devastating [ˈdevəsteɪtiŋ] *adj.* 摧毁式的

① 即时库存管理。JIT 追求一种无库存或库存达到最小的生产系统。JIT 的基本思想是生产的计划和控制及库存的管理。

② 横向整合。指公司在价值链的同一层面上获取整合经营业务。包括生产同类产品，收购竞争产品等。与之相对的是纵向整合(vertical integration)，即价值链不同层面上的业务整合，包括兼并上游和下游价值链的供应商和零售商。

scrutiny ['skruːtɪnɪ] *n.* 详细审查
bankroll ['bæŋkrəʊl] *v.* 提供资金
hobble ['hɒbl] *v.* 蹒跚
subsidiary [səb'sɪdɪərɪ] *n.* 分支机构
disrupt [dɪs'rʌpt] *v.* 破坏
hammer ['hæmə] *v.* 捶打，捶击
wreck [rek] *n.* 破坏
untapped market 未开拓市场
state-owned company 国有企业
milk early profit 获取早期利润
data-driven market analysis 数据驱动的市场分析
core competence 核心竞争力

Exercises

Exercise 1 Choose the best answer for each of the following questions.

1. What is not a fundamental factor for more Chinese firms going global?
   A. Pushed by government.
   B. Pulled by untapped markets.
   C. Armed with bundles of money.
   D. Equipped with highly-advanced facilities.
2. Which of the following is not an example for Chinese corporate presence overseas growing fast?
   A. The investment in 2004-05 is one-third of that of the previous decade.
   B. The investment projects have over doubled over the past five years.
   C. The Chinese firms that debuted on US stock exchanges are more than the total for the previous three years.
   D. The number of Chinese executives and managers transferring to US is almost twice that between fiscal years 2004-07.
3. Chinese companies' cost advantage is described as ______.
   A. meaningless B. chronic C. devastating D. significant
4. All of the following but ______ show that not all arms are open.
   A. national security concerns
   B. labor union and media criticism
   C. drastic differences in business culture
   D. lack of long-term strategy for Chinese companies
5. So far as playing catch-up in formal training is concerned, which of the following statements is not true?
   A. There have been more and more applicants to international schools for formal training.

B. Li and Zhu will go back home once they gain a sophistication in finance and strategy.

C. It is scary to marry cost consciousness with JIT inventory management.

D. Wanxiang has been a headache for states like Illinois and Michigan.

Exercise 2 Fill in each of the blanks with the appropriate words given. Change the form of the word when necessary.

shortage sharp jump bankrolling wholesaling backdrop

1. By ________ the project the Council forgoes the opportunity to invest.
2. BP reports ________ in profits for the 3rd Quarter.
3. In its narrowest definition, a labor ________ is an economic condition in which there are insufficient qualified candidates to fill the position.
4. We cannot separate the company acts from the political ________.
5. The market for electronic product ________ is expanding.

Exercise 3 Translate the following sentences into English.

1. 因被公司派遣至美国而获得签证的中国高管和经理的数量几乎翻倍增长。
2. 中国领导者担心政治对于社会的影响，尤其是在这样一个家庭在食物上的花费占到收入的一半的社会里。
3. 中国公司仍在学习数据驱动的市场分析。

Text 11 Chinese Firms Make "Startling Progress" in Productivity
中国公司生产率的进步令人惊讶

导读 中国公司通过采用世界先进技术、采纳更高的质量管理理念变得更加具有竞争力，更加现代化，他们在生产率方面的进步着实让世界同行刮目相看、震惊万分。

Chinese firms have made "startling progress" in improving productivity levels this decade thanks to their adoption of advanced technologies, higher quality recruitment and their rapid transformation into competitive and modern businesses, the Conference Board[①] said.

While Chinese firms still operate at productivity levels well below their foreign counterparts, multinational businesses should be aware of the competitive challenges they will pose, a report by the Conference Board, a US-based international business organization, said.

"The pace of restructuring and the resulting rise in the productivity of Chinese firms should be a caution to multinational businesses that regard China solely as an untapped market opportunity," the report said.

"Chinese firms, including many of the lumbering and seemingly hopelessly out-dated and inefficient SOEs[②] are beginning to compete effectively with even the most advanced global companies," it said.

Citing an analysis from the US International Trade Commission[③], the report said private Chinese domestic firms have this year taken the lead from foreign firms as exporters to the rest of the world of "made in China" products.

"Interestingly, while foreign firms have high average productivity, domestic private Chinese firms and joint ventures exhibit productivity growth that outpaces foreign firms," the report said.

"This is consistent with foreign firms creating operations with state of the art technology that makes it difficult to push the productivity frontier rapidly while Chinese firms enjoy substantial restructuring benefits as they adopt new technology and processes," it added.

---

① 美国经济和市场调查研究组织。该组织主要负责测量美国经济的健康状况。

② SOE(state-owned enterprises)国有企业

③ the US International Trade Commission(USITC)美国国际贸易委员会。美国联邦政府下设的一个独立的、非党派性质的、准司法联邦机构。

Words and Expressions

restructure [ˌriːˈstrʌktʃə] *v.* 调整，改组，更改结构，重建构造

state of the art 技术发展水平

Exercises

Exercise 1 Choose the best answer for each of the following questions.

1. Chinese firms have made "startling progress" in improving productivity levels this decade thanks to the followings except ________.
   A. adoption of advanced technologies
   B. higher quality recruitment
   C. rapid transformation into competitive and modern businesses
   D. people were hard-working
2. Which of the following statements is true?
   A. The pace of restructuring and the resulting rise in the productivity of Chinese firms is satisfying.
   B. Multinational businesses regard China solely as an untapped market opportunity.
   C. The pace of restructuring and the resulting rise in the productivity of Chinese firms gives a caution to multinational businesses.
   D. Chinese firms are hopelessly out-dated and inefficient SOEs.
3. Who has exhibited productivity growth that outpaces foreign firms?
   A. Domestic private Chinese firms.
   B. Joint ventures.
   C. SOE (state-owned enterprises).
   D. Both A and B.
4. What do you think is the author's possible attitude towards productivity growth?
   A. Approving. B. Disapproving.
   C. Indifferent. D. Enthusiastic.

Exercise 2 Fill in each of the blanks with the appropriate words given. Change the form of the word when necessary.

startling adopt pose restructure lumber outpace

1. The spread of the prairie is indeed a ________ sight.
2. We can ________ the fastest of your boasted airplanes.
3. We should ________ flexible strategy and tactics in a war.
4. The carpenter trimmed the ________ with a plane.
5. Let's ________ for a group photo.

6. Continue to deepen cultural ________.

Exercise 3 Translate the following sentences into English.

1. 宝洁和沃尔玛的合作理念是“合作，规划，预测，补充”。（collaboration，planning，forecasting，replenishment）
2. 国内私有企业和合资企业生产力的增长展现出了超越外国公司的水平。（private Chinese firms，joint venture）
3. 丰田是一家具有很强国际竞争力的企业，其销售规模、营利能力等在世界主要汽车制造厂商中都处于领先地位。（sale scale，profit ability，take a leadership）

Text 12 China's Champions "Run Risks Overseas"

中国冠军企业闯荡海外市场

导读 但凡在国内成功的中国企业走出国门发展海外业务时，常常都准备不足，资金匮乏，或缺乏管理与品牌知名度。用世界标准来衡量，多数公司规模也较小，有些公司甚至派遣家属前往海外进行管理工作，缺乏培养与留住海外经理人员、开拓海外市场的策略。但近年来成功走出国门的国内冠军企业也逐渐显山露水，如国家石油公司中石化和中石油，通讯公司华为，家电业巨头海尔与格兰仕，汽车零部件与整车厂家万向、奇瑞与吉利。华为与海尔在海外已有巨大的需求，联想用17.5亿美元购买了IBM的个人电脑事业部与旗下的ThinkPad商标使用权。中国商务部将考虑推出优惠政策，鼓励中国公司走出国门去海外投资，预计中国海外投资在2010年前将每年增长22%。

Established Chinese enterprises expanding overseas are often poorly prepared, lacking sufficient finances, capable management and strong branding, a study released yesterday has found.

Joint research by IBM's[①] business unit and Shanghai's Fudan University concludes that even though many Chinese companies may prosper abroad within the next decade, most face serious risks as they lack a coherent expansion strategy.

The findings suggest several domestic companies, especially household appliance and electronic makers, are increasing in value but are unready to compete in mature markets such as the US and Europe. "Most Chinese companies remain small by global standards," says the report, based on dozens of interviews with company executives and experts.

"Many Chinese manufacturers still compete on low-cost labor and low-pricing, rather than on innovative, branded products and services with higher profit margins."

The report identified only 14 Chinese enterprises with annual revenues of more than $15bn, while the US has more than 10 times the number of companies with those sales.

"National champions" singled out as most likely to succeed in the near-term in developed markets include the main oil companies, telecommunications company Huawei, appliance manufacturers Haier and Galanz, auto parts company Wanxiang Group[②], and

---

① 国际商业机器公司。1914年创立于美国，是世界上最大的信息工业跨国公司。

② 万向集团。它创建于1987年，主导产品为东风系列轻型、中型、重型及工程车等变速箱壳体、箱盖及跃进汽车集团G427发动机飞轮壳。

carmakers Chery[1] and Geely[2].

Huawei[3] and Haier already rely heavily on overseas demand. Computer maker Lenovo acquired IBM's PC division, including its ThinkPad trademark, for $1.75bn in late 2004, the largest acquisition by a Chinese technology company to date. [4]

Beijing is to consider relaxing rules on direct outward investment, which the Ministry of Commerce forecasts will grow about 22 percent a year up to 2010. But China's outward investment is only a small fraction of its inward foreign direct investment. "It's a tiny player," said Alan Beebe, China director for IBM's business arm and one of the report's authors.

Mr Beebe argued many companies were underinvesting[5] in branding and R&D, failing to take advantage of opportunities to develop into world-class organizations.

He cited Hon Hai, Tai Wan Region's electronics company, as being a good model. "Our recommendation is to decide whether you need to have a consumer brand," he said.

The report also mentioned the problems Chinese companies had in choosing and retaining executives to carry out overseas strategies.

Executives at some Chinese companies even posted their own relatives overseas, said Chee Hew, an IBM consultant and another report co-author.

"You have to find someone who knows China and knows the foreign market," she said. "Many companies don't have a clear strategy when they go out ... it's rather opportunistic."

Words and Expressions

coherent [kəʊ'hɪərənt] *adj.*	一致的，连贯的
margin ['mɑːdʒɪn] *n.*	盈利，利润
household appliance	家用电器
single out	单独挑出
auto parts	汽车零部件

---

① 2006年，国际汽车制造商协会（OICA）发布的全球汽车企业产量排名中，奇瑞以30.72万辆的总产量位居第27位。

② 浙江吉利控股集团有限公司连续4年进入全国企业500强，跻身于国内汽车行业十强。

③ 华为技术有限公司。它从事通信网络技术与产品的研究、开发、生产与销售，是中国电信市场的主要供应商之一，并已成功进入全球电信市场。

④ 此次并购意味着联想的PC年出货量将达到1,190万台，销售额将达到120亿美元，形成遍及全球160多个国家和地区的庞大分销和销售网络和广泛的全球认知度。

⑤ 投资不足

Exercises

Exercise 1　Choose the best answer for each of the following questions.

1. Many Chinese companies face serious risks overseas because ________.
   A. they lack sufficient finances, capable management and strong branding
   B. by global standards, most Chinese companies remain small
   C. many Chinese manufacturers still compete on low-cost labor and low-pricing
   D. all the above
2. Many Chinese companies are facing the following problems except ________.
   A. they do not compete on innovative, branded products and services with higher profit margins
   B. foreign governments make regulations to limit companies' development
   C. they were underinvesting in branding and R&D
   D. they choose and retain unqualified executives in overseas markets
3. According to the passage, which of the following statement is not true?
   A. Chinese enterprises can not make a success abroad.
   B. More than 140 American enterprises have the annual revenues of over $15bn.
   C. The government is likely to reduce the limitation in direct outward investment.
   D. It is advisable to choose someone who knows markets of home and abroad as the executive in overseas investment.

Exercise 2　Fill in each of the blanks with the appropriate words given. Change the form of the word when necessary.

margin　single out　cite ... as　acquire　recommendation

1. What are your average operating ________?
2. He was ________ as the outstanding performer in the sports meeting.
3. She has ________ a good knowledge of this subject.
4. The teacher gave us some ________ on solving this problem.

Exercise 3　Translate the following sentences into English.

1. 今年，这个国家旅游业收入总额仅有 150 亿美元，而美国是这一数字的 10 倍多。
2. 中国的直接对外投资只是外国对华直接投资的一个零头。
3. 许多大学科研投资不足，未能充分利用机遇发展成为世界一流大学。

Text 13 Companies: Cultural Confusion
What Goes Around Comes Around. It's China's Turn.
文化差异——中国公司走出去的困惑
风水轮流转，这次轮到中国公司了

导读 当西方公司进入中国时，因不知东方文化的风俗习惯，付出了昂贵的学费。如今风水轮流转，当中国公司在海外狼吞虎咽般地并购西方公司时，连连吞下苦果，重蹈他人覆辙。在并购前他们往往准备仓促，超额支付并购费用，也不知如何整合统筹海外资源，结果是接二连三的亏损与灾难。明基在购买西门子手机业务一年后因大幅亏损不得不关闭工厂，TCL分别收购德国施耐德与法国汤姆森电视机业务后，虽然一时成为世界最大的电视生产厂家，但这两个品牌早已在西方消费者心中消失了，显然收购前的调研工作草率马虎。

When they first entered China, many Western companies made costly mistakes. Not knowing the ropes, they underestimated the complexity of operating in such a huge domestic market, were blissfully unaware of the nuances of Chinese bureaucracy and flew in Western bosses often accused of arrogance.[①]

What goes around comes around—and this time it's the Chinese who are getting burned. Now that they've begun gobbling up Western companies, it turns out they haven't learned much from others' mistakes. "Chinese companies investing in the West are not the turbo capitalists everyone expects them to be," says Wang Wee, M&A consultant with Deloitte & Touché in Düsseldorf[②]. They often arrive unprepared, overpay for acquisitions, fail to do their due diligence and aren't sure how their new Western holdings fit into their global strategies. The result: a recent series of nasty corporate disasters.

Exhibit A may be BenQ[③], the cell-phone maker that last week announced it would shut the struggling German plants it took over from Siemens[④] only last year. Despite in-

① 西方公司刚开始进入中国市场时，由于不了解行情诀窍和中国的商业习俗，碰了许多钉子。因为没有做好进入中国这个庞大市场的政治和经济方面的功课，他们常常被认为傲慢无礼。

② Deloitte&Touché 德勤会计公司，世界五大会计事务所之一。Deloitté Consulting 向来强调"经验重于培训"。

③ 明基 BenQ 成立于1984年。2001年12月，明基电通正式发表"BenQ"自有品牌，以"时尚产品网络化"为核心发展概念，涵盖液晶显示器、数码相机、移动电话、宽带网络等多元化产品线。

④ 西门子是世界上最大的电气和电子公司之一。西门子活跃在中国的信息与通讯、家用电器等各个行业中，其核心业务领域是基础设施建设和工业解决方案。

vesting in new models and assembly lines, the new brand has seen its worldwide market share plummet, from 5 percent in 2005 to just 3 percent today, leagues behind market leader Nokia's 33 percent. Last year BenQ CEO K. Y. Lee bragged that the Siemens purchase would help him catch up to the likes of Nokia or Motorola[①], the latter of which operates a profitable German plant to make its state-of-the-art multimedia cell phones. Consultant Wang says it is clear BenQ underestimated the costs and complexities involved.

The litany of Chinese mistakes eerily echoes Europe's own in the China market.[②] When consumer-electronics maker TCL[③] took over the defunct German TV brand Schneider[④], the Chinese thought it was their ticket to the lucrative Western market. After then buying France's Thomson, TCL was suddenly the world's largest maker of TVs. But TCL hadn't done its research: Schneider hadn't been anywhere on consumers' radar for years. New Chinese management also had zero experience operating in Europe's fragmented and cutthroat consumer markets.

Done right, Chinese investment is a win for both sides. Just a year after it was taken over by Beijing No. 1 Machine Tools, for instance, the once struggling Aldrich Co burg[⑤] has hired 30 new workers and is planning for 20 more. Thanks to the new parent company, the Bavarian maker of highly complex milling machines has improved its access to the Asian market—and Beijing No. 1 can now sell its machines in Europe. Chinese management has been hands-off, says finance director Owe Harold, with a clear division of labor between Bavaria and Beijing. Investor Kiang, too, is expanding operations at Wells. For neither company do High German wages seem to bean issue. "Quality production and access to markets is much more important," says Kiang. Too bad for BenQ.

Words and Expressions

blissful ['blɪsfʊl] *adj.*	极乐的,乐而忘忧的
nuance [njʊ'ɑːns] *n.*	细微差别,微妙之处
nasty ['nɑːstɪ] *adj.*	令人不快的,严重的
plummet ['plʌmɪt] *v.*	暴跌;笔直坠下
state-of-the-art *adj.*	当前水平,最新水平

① 诺基亚和摩托罗拉,移动通信的全球领先者。

② 当年欧洲公司进入中国市场所犯的错误和遇到的困难并未能给今天走出去的中国公司带来警告。他们没有从中吸取教训。

③ TCL集团股份有限公司创立于1981年,TCL集团旗下主力产业在中国、美国、法国、新加坡等国家,设有研发总部和十几个研发分部。在中国、波兰、墨西哥、泰国、越南等国家拥有近20个制造加工基地。

④ 施耐德电气的配电业务全球第一,自动化和控制业务居世界第二位。施耐德电气在全球范围内为能源和基础设施以及住宅等领域提供产品和服务,开发了全系列的集成化、智能型和通讯型等解决方案。

⑤ 2005年11月北京第一机床厂成功收购世界重型机床龙头企业:德国阿道夫·瓦德里希科堡机床联合公司。

litany [ˈlɪtənɪ] *n.* 连续，系列

eerily [ˈɪərɪlɪ] *adv.* 不安地，可怕地

defunct [dɪˈfʌŋkt] *adj.* 不再使用的，失效的

cutthroat [ˈkʌtθrəʊt] *adj.* 残酷的，无情的

hands-off 不干涉的，不插手的

assembly line 生产线，流水线

know the ropes 晓得诀窍，熟悉风土人情

gobble up 吞食，贪食

league behind 落后于

haggle with 争论不休，讨价还价

Exercises

Exercise 1 Choose the best answer for each of the following questions.

1. The western companies fell into many mistakes except ________ when they first entered China.

   A. they underestimated the complexity of Chinese market

   B. they knew little about the nuances of Chinese bureaucracy in China

   C. they were too arrogant

   D. they didn't realize cultural obstacles between Asian and western world

2. Which of the following is not a problem of Chinese companies when they go out, according to the passage?

   A. They underestimate the costs and complexities.

   B. They overpay for acquisition.

   C. Little market research has been done in order to get information abroad.

   D. They don't pay enough attention to the quality of products.

Exercise 2 Fill in each of the blanks with the appropriate words given. Change the form of the word when necessary.

hands-off nuance plummet haggle ... with gobble up

1. He watched her face intently to catch every ________ of expression.
2. Share prices ________ to an all time low.
3. The two parties have achieved a ________ treaty.
4. He ________ over the price of the horse ________ the dealer.
5. The children ________ their food and rushed out to play.

Exercise 3 Translate the following sentences into English.

1. 联想收购 IBM 个人电脑是一项暴利的投资。
2. 全球化的中国公司可以通过市场调查获取当地行情。
3. 这家国有企业因为经营不善面临破产。

Text 14 The Chinese Are Coming; Expanding Chinese Companies Have Finally Discovered the Old World.

中国人来了，不断扩张的中国公司终于发现了“旧大陆”

导读 走进位于意大利东部的城市普拉托，城内的城垛还是正宗的中世纪遗物，饭菜也是地道的当地托斯卡口味。可是当你步入该城的工业区，文化就骤然变化了，咖啡馆的店面不是意大利文，而是地地道道的中文，就连当地的街名、报纸也全是汉字，短短几年在普拉托的中国人从区区数百人猛增到一万多人。离普拉托1,000公里以外的北面，坐落着一座瑞典小镇，这个名叫Alvkarleby的小镇正在翘首企盼一个新地标的诞生，这个地标就是由中国创业家耗资1千万欧元建造的商业旅游中心，内有中式宝塔与特大菩萨，这一中心将成为华人进入欧洲的桥头堡。此外，还有数以万计的中国留学生在英国、爱尔兰等国攻读学位，中国的家庭作坊也开进了西班牙马德里的街坊里弄。如今，欧洲已经成为中国最大的贸易伙伴，同时新来的中国公司在欧洲也发现了两千年前的“新大陆”……

The battlements are authentically medieval, the food distinctively Tuscan. But wander into the industrial district of Prato and the culture switches abruptly. The language of the cafés isn't Italian, it's Chinese. So too for many street signs and newspapers. In the past few years, the city's Chinese population has surged from just a few hundred to some 10,000. More than 2,000 Chinese-owned enterprises have helped revive Prato's flagging textile industry.

A thousand or so kilometers north, the Swedish town of Alvkarleby awaits a new landmark. Near the main highway, a Chinese entrepreneur is building a 10 million business and tourism center, complete with pagoda and outsize Buddha. The purpose: to provide a meeting point for Swedes planning a foray into China, or a base for Chinese investors looking to launch in Europe. Smart idea. In the past four years, Chinese investments in Sweden have climbed from zero to more than 50. By the end of the year, China could overtake Germany as the country's largest investor.

In the latest twist to globalization, the Chinese are coming to Europe. Last year the European Union replaced the United States as China's largest trading partner, and business is often ready to overlook political differences as economic ties multiply. "It's been overwhelming, especially in the last 10 months," says London banker Ying Fang, who helps raise money for capital-hungry Chinese companies. "When I tried to start a Chinese economic association here 10 years ago, no one even seemed to know where China was.

Now everyone wants a slice."

Check out the investment figures. Sure, the absolute numbers remain small. But the growth curve tilts steeply upward. According to the consultants Ernst & Young[①], the total number of Chinese projects in its annual accounting of foreign investors in Europe has risen fivefold since 2000. Among recent announcements: everything from a joint venture to assemble bicycles in the Czech Republic to a first move into the European market by the giant China Telecom. Hamburg alone is now home to more than 350 Chinese companies, many of them representing larger concerns back home. Nigel Wilcock, an investment specialist at E&Y says, "If you follow the logic, you could expect Chinese investment in Europe to follow the same pattern as with Japan." That's some prospect. For the past 10 years, the Japanese have consistently rated among Europe's keenest outside investors, behind only the United States.

Europeans have worked hard to grab their share. Four years ago, only the British ran an office in China to lure investors. Today almost everyone does. Prime Minister Romano Prodi, who recently led a 700-strong delegation to Beijing, talks of making Italy "a gateway to the East." In London, the No. 1 destination for Chinese investment in Europe, city leaders talk of creating an entirely new Chinese business quarter just to the east of the capital's main financial district. In Austria, the government will help pay the €100 million needed to establish a new Chinese Technology Park outside Vienna.

The enthusiasm is clearly mutual. For the past five years, Beijing has been prodding its businessmen to look overseas, build global brands and tap into foreign know-how[②]. Last year China's outward investment climbed 25 percent. According to press accounts in Germany, the Chinese Trade Ministry has produced a country-by-country shopping list of promising markets. Europe tops the list. When Chinese Premier Wen Jiabao visited Europe last month, he was accompanied by a clutch of business dignitaries that included the chiefs of the FAW[③] group, China's leading automaker; Bao-steel, one of the world's largest steel concerns, and CNOOC[④], the fast-growing petroleum and gas company.

In some cases, the Chinese have targeted big-name enterprises that have fallen on hard times. The venerable Rover car company in Britain is now in the hands of the Nanjing Automobile Corp. China's Qianjiang Group, the country's largest motorcycle manufactur-

---

① Ernst & Young公司是20世纪50年代一系列兼并的产物。1989年,原八大会计事务所之中的Arthur Young及Ernst & Whinney之间的兼并造就了现在的Ernst & Young。

② 外国先进技术

③ 中国第一汽车集团公司(原第一汽车制造厂)简称"一汽"。1953年7月15日破土动工。1991年,与德国大众汽车公司合资建立15万辆轿车基地;2002年,与天津汽车工业(集团)有限公司联合重组;与日本丰田汽车公司实现合作。

④ 中国海洋石油总公司(以下简称中国海油)是中国最大的国家石油公司之一,负责在中国海域对外合作开采海洋石油及天然气资源,是中国最大的海上油气生产商。公司成立于1982年,注册资本949亿元人民币,总部位于北京,现有员工4.4万人。

er, last year took charge at Benelli, the 95-year-old Italian company famous for its distinctive scooters and motorcycles. Elsewhere, it's the smaller specialized businesses that appeal. In Germany, for example, the Chinese have been snapping up companies from the Mittelstand, the raft of smaller niche manufacturing businesses that have traditionally been the nation's economic mainstay. Small to medium-size Chinese companies are also getting into the act, according to Michael Charlton of Think London, the capital's foreign-investment agency. "The more Chinese companies establish offices here, the more they discover new markets," says Li Niu, business coordinator for Mindray, a Chinese medical-equipment company that this year set up its first European office in London.

Depending on the line of business and its markets, European countries each possess their own particular charms. Britain scores high for the English language, for example, and companies seeking to raise the big money needed for expansion are drawn to London's capital markets. In the past five years, six Chinese companies have chosen a listing on the London Stock Exchange, while an additional 42 have opted for the smaller Alternative Investment Market. Naturally the authorities are keen to smooth their path. A team from the City last month accompanied Lord Mayor David Brewer on a swing through China offering explanatory seminars on the intricacies of raising capital.

At the microlevel, Britain's allure is very different. It's easy enough for would-be settlers to hide from the tax or immigration authorities, say, in a Chinese community that ranks as the largest in Europe. According to official figures, the number of Londoners born in China has doubled in the past five years. Thousands of Chinese students are currently studying in Britain, and often they choose to stay on after graduation, finding work in the no-questions-asked economy even when their visas have lapsed. Ireland, too, appeals powerfully, thanks to a freewheeling business culture, low corporate taxes and a generous distribution of work permits. Result: a Chinese population that may have topped 150,000. "It's easy to make money here," says Paddy Song, originally from northern China, who arrived in Ireland six years ago after stints in France and Sweden. "It's easy to make money here." He should know. His own Shining Emerald Group includes property, an accounting service and a Chinese-community newspaper.

Elsewhere, the Chinese have flourished where they have found a familiar culture of family-run microbusinesses[①]. In practice, that often meant Spain—watch for the Chinese-run convenience stores of Madrid—or Italy. "The latest move is to see what we can offer China," says Romeo Orlandi of Osservatorio Asia, a Bologna-based think tank. Though most Chinese investors have stuck to the country's industrial north, many have headed to the less-developed south. Sicily alone is now home to more than 1,200 Chinese-run businesses, many of their small trading companies that have sprung up in the past two years.

The EU's new member states in Eastern Europe offer a cheap base and an easy route

---

① 中国人大量出现在他们熟悉的家族经营商业文化群体中，有自己的文化圈。

into the continent's markets. Take the case of Wei Xiang, who moved to Budapest in 1990, he says, in order to paint. Then came an opportunity to make money—designing shoes for Hungary's emerging consumer class and manufacturing them in China. Today he employs 70 people and sells 3 million pairs of Wink brand shoes a year across Eastern Europe. Like others, he's convinced that his future lies in Europe, not in America, once the magnet for Chinese emigration.① He is sending his teenage children to Budapest's American school and wants them to go on to study in the United States. But he himself is happy to stay in Hungary. "The US is far from here, and we know much more about the European customers and the shoes they want," he says.

Words and Expressions

flagging [ˈflæɡɪŋ] *adj.*	疲乏的,变弱的
pagoda [pəˈɡəʊdə] *n.*	塔,宝塔
foray [ˈfɒreɪ] *n.*	短暂访问
capital-hungry *adj.*	缺乏资金的
tilt [tɪlt] *v.*	倾斜,倾侧
prod [prɒd] *v.*	鼓励,鼓动
clutch [klʌtʃ] *n.*	一群(人或动物)
dignitary [ˈdɪɡnɪtərɪ] *n.*	显贵,要人
venerable [ˈvenərəbl] *adj.*	令人尊重的,值得尊重的
intricacy [ˈɪntrɪkəsɪ] *n.*	错综复杂
freewheeling [ˈfriːˈhwiːlɪŋ] *adj.*	随心所欲的,无拘无束的
spring up	迅速出现,突然兴起
snap up	抢购,抢先弄到手

Exercises

Exercise 1 Choose the best answer for each of the following questions.

1. Which of the following statement is not true according to the text?

A. In the past four years, Chinese investments in Sweden have climbed from zero to more than 50.

B. For the past five years, Beijing has been prodding its businessmen to look overseas, build global brands and tap into foreign know-how.

C. The venerable Rover car company in Britain is now in the hands of the Nanjing Automobile Corp.

---

① 跟其他人一样,他相信自己的未来在欧洲,而不是曾深受中国移民青睐的美国。

D. In the past five years, five Chinese companies have chosen a listing on the London Stock Exchange.

2. According to the consultants Ernst & Young, the total number of Chinese projects in its annual accounting of foreign investors in Europe has risen ________ since 2000.

   A. threefold　　　　B. fourfold

   C. fivefold　　　　D. sixfold

3. Who offer a cheap and convenient route into the continent's markets?

   A. The United States.　　　　B. Britain.

   C. France.　　　　D. EU's new member states.

Exercise 2　Fill in each of the blanks with the appropriate words given. Change the form of the word when necessary.

flagging　grab　foray　dignitary　snap up

1. Mutual funds ________ new investors in QDII products.
2. Domestic auto-makers ________ into overseas market.
3. Global business giants ________ market shares in Dongjiang Port Area of Tianjin Port.
4. ________ of the Soviet should maintain or control the existing system from which they derive private benefit. But they choose to convert the system to another. Because they will be better in the new one.
5. "Chinese demand for imports is showing no sign of ________," said Li Ling, a trader at Star Futures Co. in Shanghai. "As it's entering a peak consumption period, some processors increased purchases."

Exercise 3　Translate the following sentences into English.

1. 中国政府鼓励企业把目光投向海外，打造全球品牌、引进国外技术。(prod, foreign know-how)
2. 改革开放以来，中国的私营企业有如雨后春笋般的出现。(spring up)
3. 最近几年，这座城市的中国人从仅几百人猛增至1万人，超过2000家中国企业帮助复兴了普拉托正在衰退的纺织业。(flagging)

Text 15 Don't Know Li-Ning? Ask Shaq!

没听说过"李宁"？问一下NBA顶级中锋——"侠客"吧！

导读 体育服装品牌"李宁"虽然在国外鲜为人知，但在中国国内却家喻户晓，他的知名度可与耐克、阿迪达斯媲美，其市场份额占有率也紧随前者。李宁公司上半年销售收入猛涨近40%，达2.5亿美元，其在香港交易所的股价在过去几年中也飙升了300%。李宁品牌迅速蹿红的奥秘是该公司结盟了美国NBA大明星，他们包括骑士队的著名后卫达蒙·琼斯，原迈阿密热火队的顶级中锋沙奎尔·奥尼尔。假如老外至今还不知"李宁"，那就请他们去问问大"侠客"奥尼尔吧！

The Beijing sportswear company is giving Nike and Adidas a run for the money on the mainland, and its stock is up 300 percent over the past year.

Not many people outside of China have heard of Li-Ning, but in the country's fast-growing sportswear market, the Beijng company is proving a serious competitor for the likes of giants Nike[①] and Adidas[②]. While those two behemoths still dominate among Chinese consumers, Li-Ning is in the third place, with market share just below the roughly 17 percent to 18 percent that Nike and Adidas have. That makes Li-Ning the top Chinese sportswear brand, slightly ahead of domestic rival Anta. The Hong Kong-listed Li-Ning has turned in a strong first half year: Sales are up 39.2 percent, to $255 million, and net profits surged 52.6 percent, to $26.4 million. The stock price is up more than 300 percent over the past year.

While Li-Ning only came in 15th in the *Business Week*[③] Interbrand survey when it came to familiarity, it was rated 13th when marketing executives were asked which Chinese brands best serve "as an ambassador for China." (Fujian province-based Anta was not included among the 28 Chinese brands surveyed.) That put it ahead of car company Chery—rated a top brand that is already serious and recognizable—as well as telecom equipment maker ZTE, auto companies Geely and Brilliance, and air conditioner

① 耐克公司。正式成立于1972年，其前身是由现任总裁菲尔·奈特及比尔·鲍尔曼教练投资的蓝带体育公司。

② 阿迪达斯成立于1949年，主要生产运动鞋类，服饰以及包和球类用品。与耐克公司为两大海外体育用品零售巨头。

③ 《商业周刊》，全球销量第一的美国资讯和管理杂志。

manufacturers Midea and Gree[①], all rated as "contenders," and expected to become top brands over the next three to five years.

Teaming with NBA Stars

No doubt one reason for that good rating on "ambassadorship" is Li-Ning's successful marketing and branding efforts, mainly focused on sports sponsorship. Li-Ning spends about 17% of revenues on marketing annually, more than most Chinese companies. National Basketball Association's Miami Heat center Shaquille O'Neal[②] is the brand's top star, after having signed a five-year agreement in August, 2006.

While Li-Ning shoes aren't available in the US, the company figures that an alliance with Shaq helps to lure the growing number of NBA fans in China who follow the league. Li-Ning also has signed Damon Jones, a guard with the Cleveland Cavaliers. And while the company doesn't have Chinese superstar Yao Ming in its stable, it has signed Yao's Houston Rockets teammate, forward Chuck Hayes. And on Sept. 24, Li-Ning announced it will also sponsor top tennis player Ivan Ljubicic, the Croatian who was ranked No. 3 on the Association of Tennis Professionals tour last year and is now No. 12.

The Olympics figure prominently in Li-Ning's past and future. The Beijing sports company was founded in 1989 by former Olympics gold winner gymnast Li Ning, winner of three gold medals at the Los Angeles Olympics in 1984. Li, 44, continues to serve as chairman as well as head of business development, while 39-year-old Guanghua School of Management MBA holder Zhang Zhiyong now is CEO and runs the company's operations.

Riding the Wave of the Beijing Olympics

Investors include CDH China Holdings, a Beijing-based private-equity firm, and GIC Special Investments, the Singaporean government fund. Li-Ning now is counting on next year's 2008 Beijing Olympics to drive its branding efforts.

The company is sponsoring the medal-winning Chinese table tennis, diving, gymnastics, and shooting teams. And on June 7, 2007, Li-Ning and the Spanish government announced the company would be the official sportswear provider for the Spanish Olympic delegation at next year's games. The year-long run up to the world's biggest sporting event clearly is key for Li-Ning. The company plans to add 700 new retail outlets in 2007 to its existing 4,300, and by the opening of the Olympics next August Li-Ning will have 5,600 outlets spread across the mainland. Those include directly-managed shops, conces-

---

① ZTE 中兴通讯。它是中国最大的通信设备制造业上市公司,1985 年公司成立。中兴通讯是中国综合性电信设备及服务提供商,拥有无线产品、网络产品、终端产品三大产品系列。

Brilliance 新晨科技股份有限公司,是一家高新技术企业,总部设在北京。

Midea 美的集团,是一家以家电业为主,涉足房产、物流等大型综合性现代化企业,是中国最具规模的白色家电生产基地和出口基地。

Gree 珠海格力集团公司。珠海市规模最大的企业之一,拥有"格力"、"罗西尼"两个中国驰名商标。

② 现已转会至克利夫兰骑士队。

sion counters, and franchised outlets. And in April it rolled out a new, lower-end sports brand, Z-do, including shoes, apparel, and sports accessories that retail from around $13 to $40, or about half the cost of its flagship Li-Ning products.

Rounding out its brand offerings are products for its joint venture with French outdoor sports brand Aigle that the two companies launched in 2005.

While the Interbrand survey showed more international executives view Chinese brands as "cheap" and "a good value" than any other qualities, "youthful," "dynamic," and "smart" were the next three adjectives cited, all arguably well-suited for a sporting goods company. Indeed, the survey also showed that sporting goods, along with electronics, mobile phones, and automotive, was one of 10 categories where overseas marketing executives predict within five years "a Chinese brand will be a leader outside of China."

Credit Suisse Group analyst Catherine Lim cites in an Aug. 20 research report Li-Ning's "current portfolio of three brands, strong product development and research capabilities, continued enforcement of control over its franchisee distribution channel and supply chain management," in giving China's sports player an "outperform" rating. Expect to hear a lot more from the nation's scrappy domestic sports brand in the coming year before the world's biggest sporting event opens in Beijing.

Words and Expressions

franchise [ˈfræntʃaɪz] *n.*	特许经营权
lower-end *adj.*	低档的
apparel [əˈpærəl] *n.*	服饰;衣服
accessory [ækˈsesərɪ] *n.*	附件;装饰品
portfolio [pɔːtˈfəʊljəʊ] *n.*	有价证券财产目录
scrappy [ˈskræpɪ] *adj.*	散乱的
run up	(事情的)前奏,预备期
round out	圆满完成

Exercises

Exercise 1 Choose the best answer for each of the following questions.

1. The reason the passage has mentioned for Li-Ning's good rating on "ambassadorship" is ________.
   A. high quality and reasonable price
   B. friendly image in the foreign people's mind
   C. branding efforts and successful marketing
   D. a large market-share on the oversea market
2. What's the plan of Li-Ning in the year-long run up to the world's biggest

sporting event?

A. To add 700 new retail outlets in 2007.

B. To add more concession counters shops across the mainland.

C. To open more franchised outlets.

D. All the above.

3. Which of the following statement is not true according to the passage?

A. Li-Ning is the top Chinese sportswear brand ahead of Anta.

B. Li-Ning spends more of its revenues on marketing than most of the Chinese companies.

C. Li-Ning will be the official sportswear provider for the Spanish Olympic delegation at next year's games.

D. Li-Ning was one of the 10 categories which were predicted as a leader outside of China within 10 years.

Exercise 2 Fill in each of the blanks with the appropriate words given. Change the form of the word when necessary.

run up concession roll out lower-end accessory round out

1. The firm's promise to increase our pay was a ________ to union demands.
2. ________ for this car include a roof rack and a radio.
3. Many things needed to be dealt with during the ________ to an opening ceremony.
4. On the last year's trade fair, their company ________ a new economy type car.
5. The chairman ________ his speech by calling on all the employees to join in the project.
6. Our new brand is viewed not only to fit the taste of the upper-class, but also to offer ________ products for those young consumers.

Exercise 3 Translate the following sentences into English.

1. 他在故乡举行了一场音乐会,以此圆满结束了他的巡回演出。(round out)
2. 考虑到不同的消费阶层,今年他们推出了一款抵挡产品。(lower-end)
3. 随着中国成功申办 2008 年北京奥运会,体育用品商都期望能够进入中国市场。(count on)

Text 16 Chinese Bank Knocks Citigroup[①] off Top Spot
中国的银行取代花旗集团成为行业巨首

导读 中国股市连创新高，中国公司的股价与市值也顺势节节攀升。三家中国公司今天荣登全球十大公司排行榜。工商银行超越花旗银行一举成为世界第一银行，分析家预测中国石油赶超埃克森美孚也是指日可待。如今，中国股市的总值已首超GDP总量，如此高的股价，实在令人有高处不胜寒之感，处于排行榜的中国公司也应有高处不胜寒的同感。

Three Chinese companies are today ranked among the biggest in the world for the first time. The Asian giants have emerged within the top 10 because the Chinese stock market has hit record highs, pushing up the valuations[②] firms listed on the Shanghai exchange[③].

Higher share values mean that the Industrial and Commercial Bank of China[④] has overtaken Citigroup as the world's largest bank, although the US group recorded profits that were three times higher. Analysts say that PetroChina[⑤] could soon overtake Exxon Mobil as the largest company in the world, if it pursues plans to issue more shares to new investors.

But China's stock market is worth more than its GDP, sparking fears among some analysts that the steep rise in Chinese share prices may not be sustainable.[⑥]

China's advance up the corporate league table illustrates the Asian giant's massive

---

① 花旗集团(Citigroup)是当今世界资产规模最大、利润最多、全球连锁性最高、业务门类最齐全的金融服务集团。它是由花旗公司与旅行者集团于1998年合并而成，并于同期换牌上市的。花旗集团成为美国第一家集商业银行、投资银行、保险、共同基金、证券交易等诸多金融服务业务于一身的金融集团。花旗集团红伞商标下主要的品牌名称包括：花旗银行(Citibank)，CitiFinancial，Primerica，Smith Barney和Banamex。

② 估值，一个企业资产的可能现值。

③ 上海证券交易所成立于1990年11月26日，同年12月19日开业，为不以营利为目的的法人，归中国证监会直接管理。

④ 中国工商银行(Industrial and Commercial Bank of China，简称ICBC)，成立于1984年1月1日，总部设在北京，是中国内地规模最大的银行。该行是在中国人民银行专门行使中央银行职能的同时，从中国人民银行分离出的专业银行。

⑤ 中国石油天然气集团公司是根据国务院机构改革方案，于1998年7月在原中国石油天然气总公司的基础上组建的特大型石油石化企业集团，系国家授权投资的机构和国家控股公司。

⑥ 中国股票市场价值甚至高于中国国内生产总值，一些分析家认为中国股票价格的大幅上涨不会持续很长时间。

economic development over the past five years. Not everything is rosy, though. The country's drive to become a global force in science and technology faces obstacles, according to a recent report from the Organization for Economic Co-operation and Development①.

It blames state dominance of research and development, and the economy in general, combined with a shortage of talented scientists and managers. The report went on to say that "a high-technology myopia pervades current policy objectives and thinking on innovation".

Words and Expressions

steep [sti:p] *adj.*	大起大落的
rosy ['rəʊzɪ] *adj.*	充满希望的，乐观的
pervade [pə'veɪd] *v.*	弥漫，蔓延
share value	股票价值

Exercises

Exercise 1 Choose the best answer for each of the following questions.

1. For the time being, ________ Chinese companies are ranked as the biggest in the world.
   A. four B. one C. three D. two
2. ________ is now the largest petrol company in the world.
   A. PetroChina B. Exxon Mobil C. BP D. Shell Group

Exercise 2 Fill in each of the blanks with the appropriate words given. Change the form of the word when necessary.

overtake hit record high shortage of steep rise

1. *Yuan* ________ against US dollar for second straight day.
2. Singapore, June 18: Shanghai is set to ________ Singapore as the world's busiest port in 2008 as the Chinese economy continues with its stellar growth, an executive of the city-state's port operator said in remarks published Monday.
3. The festive season is ringing in cheer for the otherwise in red airlines. Finally, airlines see ________ in occupancy levels.
4. But "with no local budget allocated and ________ hands in the State Cultural Relics Bureau, the regulation could be a mere paper, with no force," said Dong.

---

① 经济合作与发展组织(经合组织)简写为OECD，是成立于1960年的一个国际联盟，以取代欧洲经济合作组织(OEEC)；总部设在巴黎。

Exercise 3 Translate the following sentences into English.

1. 部分分析家指出经合组织发布的年度报告并不令人满意，进而引起了人们的恐慌。(annual report, spark)
2. 沃尔玛的营业额超过其他同行，成为行业内的领军者。(turnover)
3. 不可否认，资源配置不合理将极大地影响经济发展的进程。(misallocation of resources)

Text 17 ALIBABA.COM IPO[①]: Magic-Carpet Ride
阿里巴巴 IPO:神话的延续

导读 在古阿拉伯神话中,阿里巴巴因一句"芝麻开门"开启了四十大盗的秘密宝藏而一夜之间富甲一方;而21世纪的阿里巴巴(Alibaba),全球著名的B2B电子商务服务公司,则是这一神话的延续:管理运营着全球领先的网上贸易市场和商人社区——阿里巴巴网站,为来自220多个国家和地区的1,200多万家企业和商人提供网上商务服务,是全球首家拥有百万商人的商务网站。在全球网站浏览量排名中,稳居国际商务及贸易类网站第一,遥遥领先于第二名,可谓是阿里巴巴神话在中国的延续。

In ancient Arabia, Alibaba became rich when he discovered the forty thieves' secret treasure trove; in modern times humble laborers find wealth by tapping Chinese initial public offerings. As such, a stampede for shares in Alibaba.com—a near-magical blend of China and the Internet—is pretty much assured. [②]

Like the eponymous fable, Alibaba.com is a good yarn. The holding company, Alibaba Group, was founded on a shoe-string and the upcoming IPO will make Chairman Jack Ma[③] one of China's richest men. Subsidiary Alibaba.com, an online business-to-business marketplace for mainly small and medium size suppliers and buyers, now boasts 24.6m users. As such, it taps into growth in both trade and the increasing participation of SMEs in the economy. Explosive growth in online advertising—JP Morgan[④] forecasts around 40 percent per annum this year and next, roughly double the rate of growth in the bigger US market—should benefit Alibaba.com, which charges for add-on marketing features like online storefronts. Goldman Sachs[⑤], an underwriter on the $1.3bn IPO, expects this year's net profit to increase 186 percent to $84m.

---

① IPO(Initial Public Offering)即股票对公众的初始发售,也就是我们一般所说的首次上市。当股票最初以一定价格在一级市场发行之后就在二级市场交易。一级市场由将股票分配给机构或个人投资者的承销商组成。一级市场本质上代表了公司股票在股票市场正式交易前发生的一切。

② 如此看来,几乎可以肯定,人们会对阿里巴巴(Alibaba.com)的股票趋之若鹜——这个网站可谓是中国与互联网近乎传奇的融合。

③ 马云,阿里巴巴创始人、首席执行官,被著名的"世界经济论坛"选为"未来领袖",被美国亚洲商业协会选为"商业领袖",是50年来第一位成为《福布斯》封面人物的中国企业家。

④ JP Morgan(JP Morgan Chase & Co)摩根大通。全球历史最长、规模最大的金融服务集团之一,由大通银行、JP摩根公司及富林明集团在2000年完成合并。摩根大通的总部位于纽约。

⑤ 高盛集团。国际领先的投资银行和证券公司,向全球提供广泛的投资、咨询和金融服务。拥有大量的多行业客户,包括私营公司、金融企业、政府机构以及个人。

Still, the relatively undemanding price tag and tight free float suggests Alibaba.com and its advisors are not counting on its China Internet credentials alone. The HK $ 10-12 share price equates to around 45 times forecast 2008 earnings on a pre-stock compensation basis[1], slightly above Alibaba.com's smaller B2B peers but a big discount to more high-profile Chinese Internet stocks like NASDAQ[2]-listed Baidu[3]. The company will have a free float of just 17 percent, and has already secured a clutch of cornerstone investors, including Yahoo Inc. of the US[4]. The Hong Kong listing, while logical, suggests Alibaba.com is playing it safe rather than seeking a higher NASDAQ-style multiple. That said, it would take a serious turn in market sentiment to stop Alibaba.com enjoying a fairy tale ending when it starts trading next month.[5]

Words and Expressions

trove [trəʊv] *n.* (有价值的)发现物,发掘到的财宝
tap [tæp] *v.* 开发,发掘(知识、资源等)
stampede [stæmˈpiːd] *n.* 风尚;热潮,风气
eponymous [ɪˈpɒnɪməs] *adj.* 与(标题)同名的
yarn [jɑːn] *n.* 故事,奇谈
shoestring [ˈʃuːstriŋ] *n.* 小额资本
add-on *adj.* 附加的,能被加上去的
storefront [ˈstɔːfrʌnt] *n.* 店面,铺面,铺面房
float [fləʊt] *n.* (公司或企业)发行股票上市/(可上市交易的)流通股
credential [krɪˈdenʃəl] *n.* 证明可信或可靠的事物
SME (small and medium size enterprises) 中小型企业

---

① 2008年预期市盈率

② 纳斯达克,是全美证券商协会自动报价系统(National Association of Securities Dealers Automated Quotations)英文缩写,但目前已成为纳斯达克股票市场的代名词。纳斯达克是全美也是世界最大的股票电子交易市场。

③ 百度,2000年1月创立于北京中关村,是全球最大的中文搜索引擎。

④ Yahoo 雅虎(Yahoo!,NASDAQ:YAHOO),是美国著名的互联网门户网站,20世纪末互联网奇迹的创造者之一。其服务包括搜索引擎、电邮、新闻等,业务遍及24个国家和地区,为全球超过5亿的独立用户提供多元化的网络服务,迄今为止,保持了全球第一门户搜索网站的地位。

⑤ 这意味着,当阿里巴巴下月开始交易时,只有市场人气的明显逆转,才会阻止阿里巴巴拥有一个神话般的结局。

Exercises

Exercise 1 Choose the best answer for each of the following questions.

1. In modern times humble labors find wealth by tapping Chinese ________.

   A. IPO B. SMEs C. FDI D. SOEs

2. What shows Alibaba.com and its advisor are not counting on its China Internet credentials alone?

   A. Undemanding price. B. Tight free float.

   C. Add-on marketing feature. D. Both A and B.

3. What could probably prevent Alibaba.com from enjoying a fairy tale ending when it starts trading next month?

   A. NASDAQ-listed Baidu. B. Goldman Sachs.

   C. JP Morgan. D. A serious turn in market sentiment.

Exercise 2 Fill in each of the blanks with the appropriate words given. Change the form of the word when necessary.

tap yarn storefront shoestring eponymous stampede secure add-on

1. The movie seems to ________ into a general sentimentality about animals.
2. In the early years, the business was run on a ________.
3. The team managed to ________ place in the finals.
4. Don Quixote, ________ hero of the great novel by Cervantes.
5. Besides computer hardware, the company also develops ________ software.
6. Falling interest rates has led to a ________ to buy property.
7. They run their business from a small ________.
8. He used to spin ________ about his time in the army.

Exercise 3 Translate the following sentences into English.

1. 这家公司于1995年在证券市场上市，至今运行状况良好。
2. 此项研究是整个研究计划的基础，因此我们必须投入大量的前期工作来确保它的顺利进行。
3. 我们需要利用我们现有的人员的专业知识和技能，只有这样我们才能在激烈的市场竞争中占有一席之地。

Text 18 Lenovo Says It Proves China's Products Are Among World's Best

联想证明中国产品是世界一流

导读 谁说中国不能制造伟大的产品？联想集团高级副总裁兼亚太区总裁麦大伟(David Miller)向全世界宣布：联想电脑的成功证明中国可以制作世界顶级品牌产品。联想电脑在一级方程式赛车、NBA球赛、奥运会等赛事中的运用足以证明联想电脑的安全性、移动性、可靠性达到世界一流水准。麦大伟把联想的成功归功于联想独特的全球资源配置(worldsourcing)战略。

The success of Lenovo①'s laptop computers proves China-made products can be among the world's best brands, the firm's Asia Pacific president said here Wednesday.

"People say great products don't come out of China," said David Miller② at a conference of the Management Association of the Philippines.

Yet Lenovo's "Thinkpad" computers were being used all over the world in Formula 1 racing, NBA basketball and in other high-profile events, he said.

Miller credited this success to innovation and to what he called "worldsourcing."

He said worldsourcing is defined as finding the most talented and innovative people with the right language proficiency from places with strong infrastructure and the finest IT facilities.

This is different from outsourcing③ which just looks abroad for lower labor costs.

Miller said his company had spread its resources all over the world with centers of innovation in Beijing, Yamato and Raleigh, North Carolina.

The benefits of worldsourcing will be felt by both developed and developing countries, Miller said, "The jobs are there. The hardest thing to find is the skills."

---

① 联想集团成立于1984年，由中科院计算所投资20万人民币及11名研究员创办。2003年，联想将其英文标识从"Legend"更换为"Lenovo"。Lenovo Group是全球PC的领导企业。联想在2005年5月完成对IBM个人电脑事业部的收购，这标志着新联想将成为全球个人电脑市场的领先者，一年收入约130亿美元，是一家极富创新性的国际化科技公司。联想的总部设在纽约的Purchase，同时在中国北京和美国北卡罗来纳州的罗利设立两个主要运营中心，通过联想自己的销售机构、联想业务合作伙伴以及与IBM的联盟，新联想的销售网络遍及全世界。

② 2006年8月17日，联想雇佣了42岁的前戴尔中国负责人David Miller担任联想亚太区总裁。

③ 外包，是指企业整合利用其外部最优秀的专业化资源，业务流程转移到另一家公司，从而达到降低成本、提高效率、充分发挥自身核心竞争力和增强企业对环境的应变能力的一种战略管理模式。

Speaking at the same forum, Arthur Tan, president of Integrated Microelectronics Inc.[①], said his Philippine company had acquired companies in China, Singapore and the United States to maintain its competitive advantage.

He said the company, which focuses on semiconductors and other electronic components, was looking to increase its facilities in China and to expand in Vietnam although he would not give any timetable.

Tan said that in 2000, potential partners would be impressed with his company's capabilities but balked when they discovered it was based in the Philippines.

"These must have been a misunderstanding. We thought you had a plant in China," Tan quoted them as saying. This prompted the company, one of the leaders in the Philippines' booming electronics industry[②], to look abroad.

Despite their acquisition and expansion abroad, Tan said his company had never laid anyone off or forced them to relocate.

Words and Expressions

laptop ['læptɒp] *n.*	便携式电脑
high-profile *adj.*	倍受关注的，高调的
worldsourcing ['wɜːld'sɔːsɪŋ] *n.*	全球资源配置
infrastructure ['ɪnfrəˌstrʌktʃə] *n.*	基础设施
outsourcing ['aʊtˌsɔːsɪŋ] *n.*	外包
semiconductor [semɪkən'dʌktə] *n.*	半导体
balk [bɔːk] *v.*	回避，退缩
acquisition [ˌækwɪ'zɪʃən] *n.*	收购
relocate [ˌriːləʊ'keɪt] *v.*	搬迁、迁移
credit ... to ...	把……归功于……
be impressed with	对……钦佩不已

Exercises

Exercise 1 Choose the best answer for each of the following questions.

1. The success of Lenovo's laptop can be attributed to ________.

   A. product innovation

---

① 菲律宾的综合微电子公司，简称 IMI。

② 亚太地区半导体产业的发展堪称一枝独秀。2002 年，亚洲集成电路销售占据全球 36%的市场份额，正式凌驾于欧、美之上，而 12.93%的年复合增长率更是令昔日老大们发出了“长江后浪推前浪”的惊叹。东南亚国家半导体产业中要属新加坡与马来西亚两国表现最佳，印尼、菲律宾和泰国等虽然产值规模仅在 12—48 亿美元之间，但增长也较为明显，竞争实力不可小觑。

B. world's excellent HR management

C. world's advanced technology application

D. all the above

2. In what way is outsourcing different from worldsourcing according to the passage?

   A. The former lays more emphasis on talents.

   B. The former attaches importance to language proficiency.

   C. The former focuses on strong infrastructure and the finest IT facilities.

   D. The former overstresses lower labor costs.

3. "The jobs are there. The hardest thing to find is the skills" means that ________.

   A. the most important and demanding task for business expansion is the technology and talents management

   B. worldsourcing benefits both developing and developed countries

   C. MNCs are lost to determine the suitable global strategy

   D. China has enough cheap labor resource

Exercise 2　Fill in each of the blanks with the appropriate words given. Change the form of the word when necessary.

impress　credit ... to ...　language proficiency　high-profile　lay off　boom

1. The ________ test requirement will be waived for applicants who have studied full-time for at least two years (or equivalent in part-time studies) at an accredited university.
2. Haier's success in the global market, ________ its innovative strategies and leaders like Parks, provides a model framework for IMBA students.
3. The reaction from China's Ministry of Commerce was swift and unyielding, suggesting that Beijing is not courting compromise in the ________ dispute.
4. Analysts seemed less ________ the deal, which they said would be unlikely to have a substantial impact on the nation's crowded banking sector.
5. If you want to invest in Chinese banks to tap the ________, you have plenty of choices.
6. GM Canada spokesman Stew Low said the ________ were part of the company's plan to keep its inventory in line with production and offset some of the value that was lost as a result of incentive plans.

Exercise 3　Translate the following sentences into English.

1. 全球资源配置主要是挖掘得到创新人才。
2. 联想已经在全球范围内扩张企业规模，在北京、日本、美国的北卡罗来纳均有研发中心。
3. 综合微电子中心公司正考虑增加在中国的投资设备，扩大在越南的市场份额，但暂时还没有具体的预定计划。

Text 19 How Corporate China Is Evolving

中国公司新面貌

导读 经历数十年的经济快速增长与参与全球竞争的历程，中国公司的面貌也呈现出耳目一新的新景观。往日中国公司可分成三大类：国有企业、合资企业与外国独资企业。如今，有些国有企业因受到政府的深厚关照仍然是一些行业的垄断企业；而有些企业却因国内市场国际化能全力以赴与数以百计的外资企业搏击，争夺市场；更有一些国内企业能勇敢走出国门，闯荡海外市场，开辟一片新大陆。这些中国公司虽然刚刚步入青春期，他们却能孜孜不倦、默默而执著地强身壮体，与世界级巨头过招。中国还出现了一股不可忽视的创新与创业型企业，他们通过开发新技术与探索企业经营的新路径，正在披荆斩棘地开辟一片前所未有的新天地，跨国公司巨头对这些乐此不疲的"年青人"和"创新家"万万不可小觑或忽视。

China's business landscape is changing rapidly. So must the way we comprehend it.

Years of rapid economic growth and exposure to global competition are redrawing the boundaries of China's business landscape. In the past, most companies there fell into one of three categories: state-owned enterprises, joint ventures between Chinese and foreign concerns, or wholly owned foreign operations. The new world of Chinese business calls for new ways to describe the playing field.

As in the past, some giant state-owned enterprises, protected from competition by a thicket of government regulations, continue to dominate their industries. But other companies in that category, now fully exposed to global competition, vie for business against hundreds of domestic and foreign companies targeting the same customers.

Other categories have emerged in recent years. Globalizing companies are stepping beyond China's borders to build substantial businesses overseas, organically or through acquisitions. The "restless adolescents" are operating beneath the radar of most global players but quietly and methodically building the capabilities needed to go global. And the innovators and entrepreneurs are blazing trails inside China by developing new technologies or pioneering new ways of doing business. Multinationals should awaken to the existence of—and the coming competition from—both the restless adolescents and the innovators.

To be sure, the lines demarcating these categories are constantly shifting, and some companies belong in more than one: Many of China's most dynamic, competitive companies, for example, retain vestiges of state ownership. Global executives will need a better understanding of Chinese customers, competitors, suppliers, or even business partners, regardless of where they fall along the ownership spectrum—from wholly private sector to wholly government owned.

How Chinese CEOs Do Business

The outlook and career experiences of the CEOs who head many of today's rapidly growing and increasingly confident Chinese companies are markedly different from those of Western executives. Understanding these differences can help to explain behavior that otherwise might seem curious to the executives of many multinationals—and could also suggest competitive opportunities.

Nowhere is the contrast with Western corporate leaders starker than it is for the chief executives of state-owned Chinese enterprises. Most of these CEOs have spent their careers shuffling between the private and public sectors. A capable leader might start out as a senior provincial-level executive in a state-owned enterprise, then hold a provincial-level Communist Party post, follow it up with a stint as the CEO of the state-owned enterprise, and move back to the party infrastructure to serve as the mayor of a major city or as a provincial governor. A final career step might be attaining a senior position in the central government or the party—for instance, a seat on the State Council or the Politburo.

Because the career of a typical CEO of a state-owned enterprise usually straddles the corporate and political spheres, these chief executives pay careful attention to politics—in particular, to developments in the Communist Party. In fact, it's not unusual for such CEOs to link the timing of long-term strategic decisions to plans outlined in the annual National People's Congress (China's legislature) or to other significant political events, such as trips to China by foreign leaders or the creation of new government agencies. What's more, the symbiotic relationship between the enterprise and the state makes such CEOs sympathetic to corporate social and economic goals beyond maximizing shareholder value.

China Mobile's rural-expansion strategy shows how one major state-owned enterprise has grown while supporting national-development goals. Since 2004, the company has extended mobile service to millions of people in the vast countryside to support the government's rural-infrastructure program, which includes initiatives linking rural areas through a mobile-telecommunications network. Government objectives such as maintaining social stability by keeping China's huge workforce employed and by redressing economic and social inequities are partly responsible for the importance that many CEOs of state-owned companies attach to top-line revenues. In fact, we find that chief executives in both the public and the private sector talk more about revenue growth, market leadership, and competitive advantage than about shorter-term financial objectives, such as higher earnings. The emphasis on driving top-line growth to keep factories humming and employees on payrolls often means that Chinese companies are generalists playing in several different business areas and markets.

Foreign players therefore have an opportunity to carve out niches in rapidly growing but underserved segments. Some pharma multinationals, for example, avoid head-on competition with Chinese companies in large product categories, such as antibiotics, which today account for as much as 30 percent of the total pharma market but are declining in importance. These multinationals are instead targeting smaller, faster-growing therapeutic areas—for instance, oncology and hypertension.

Perhaps not surprisingly in a rapidly expanding market, Chinese CEOs rely less on rigorous analysis, market research, or a detailed understanding of customer preferences than their counterparts in developed markets do. Instead, some of them make decisions instinctively, feel comfortable with rapid and flexible responses to new industry trends and shifts, and have a keen interest in holding down costs in order to boost competitiveness and to keep companies growing.

These tendencies also create opportunities for multinationals. The dealer strategies of Chinese automakers, for example, emphasize low-cost facilities in favorable locations that pull in customers. Few of these companies have focused on providing a high-quality showroom experience. GM, by contrast, applies to each of its dealerships strict customer service standards—all the way down to details such as how many seconds should elapse before a dealer greets a customer who enters a showroom and how many times a telephone should ring before a dealer answers it.

To be sure, such strategies aren't a silver bullet for multinationals: Local pharma companies continue to hold a 70 percent market share in China, and GM is locked in tough competition with other foreign carmakers and with Chinese ones as well. But unless multinationals use such approaches, success will be even more elusive. A better understanding of Chinese companies and of the executives who lead them is an important starting point when multinationals decide how to compete.

Words and Expressions

thicket ['θɪkɪt] *n.*	丛林，草丛，密集的东西
vie [vaɪ] *v.*	竞争
blaze [bleɪz] *v.*	开拓
trail [treɪl] *n.*	路径
demarcate [dɪ'mɑːkeɪt] *v.*	划定界线，区别，分开
vestige ['vestɪdʒ] *n.*	痕迹，遗迹
spectrum ['spektrəm] *n.*	光谱，范围，领域，系列
stark [stɑːk] *adj.*	僵硬的，顽固不化的，严厉的
shuffle ['ʃʌfl] *v.*	滑来滑去；把……移来移去
stint [stɪnt] *n.*	连续不断的一段时间从事某件事
Politburo [pə'lɪtbjuərəʊ] *n.*	政治局
straddle ['strædl] *v.*	不表明态度，骑墙观望
symbiotic [ˌsɪmbaɪ'ɒtɪk] *adj.*	共栖的，共生的
payroll ['peɪrəʊl] *n.*	工资单（计算报告表）

generalist ['dʒenərəlɪst] *n.* （有多方面知识和经验的）通才，多面手
niche [nɪtʃ] *n.* 适当的位置，恰当的处所
pharma ['fɑːmə] *n.* 药品
therapeutic [ˌθerə'pjuːtɪk] *adj.* 治疗的
oncology [ɒŋ'kɒlədʒɪ] *n.* 肿瘤学
hypertension ['haɪpə'tenʃən] *n.* 高血压，过度紧张
elusive [ɪ'luːsɪv] *adj.* 难以达到的，难找的
State Council 国务院

Exercises

Exercise 1 Choose the best answer for each of the following questions.

1. Which of the following categories is a new emergence according to the passage?
   A. State-owned enterprises.
   B. Joint ventures between Chinese and foreign concerns.
   C. Wholly owned foreign operations.
   D. Wholly private sectors.
2. Which of the following statements is not true, according to the opinion of the author?
   A. Corporate leaders of China have quite different career experiences from their Western counterparts.
   B. The CEOs in state-owned enterprises enjoy the biggest contrast with Western corporate leaders.
   C. More often than not, CEOs of SOEs shift their roles between political and corporate spheres.
   D. Because of the symbiotic relationship, such CEOs often show mercy for national economic goals.
3. As far as various approaches multinationals use are concerned, which of the following is not suggested?
   A. To target smaller, faster-growing therapeutic areas.
   B. To improve service standards.
   C. Such approaches are sure to bring success.
   D. To understand more about Chinese companies and the CEOs is vital for multinationals.

Exercise 2 Fill in each of the blanks with the appropriate words given. Change the form of the word when necessary.

vestige spectrum shuffle straddle stark

1. Oh, come on. Don't ________ the fence.
2. They will carry on the struggle till their land is rid of the last ________ of imperialism.
3. There's a wide ________ of opinions on this problem.

4. The arithmetic searching for oil is ________.

5. Don't ________. Give me a clear answer.

Exercise 3 Translate the following sentences into English.

1. 各商行互相竞争以招揽顾客。

2. 公司工资单上一部分是原工资，一部分是实发工资。

3. 我太太花钱如流水。

Chapter Three Made in China

中国制造

Text 20 A Year Without "Made in China"

没有"中国制造":生活一年,度日如年

导读 中国制造的产品正以它的合理价格和精美品质风靡海外市场,深受外国消费者的喜爱。中国制造的玩具陪伴着异国孩童金色童年的成长,中国制造的彩灯点亮了他国千家万户的圣诞树,中国制造的家电为外国消费者带去了日复一日、年复一年的家庭温馨与生活愉快。当一个美国家庭发现家里的一切都是"中国制造"时,悄然进行了一场抵制"中国制造"的尝试。可长达一年的试验结果告诉他们:没有了"中国制造",生活度日如年。一年之后,这个家庭又别无选择地回归到了"中国制造"的温馨生活。

Last year, two days after Christmas, we kicked China out of the house. Not the country obviously, but bits of plastic, metal, and wood stamped with the words "Made in China." We kept what we already had, but stopped bringing any more in.

The banishment was no fault of China's. It had coated our lives with a cheerful veneer of toys, gadgets, and $10 children's shoes. Sometimes I worried about jobs sent overseas or nasty reports about human rights abuses, but price trumped virtue at our house. We couldn't resist what China was selling.

But on that dark Monday last year, a creeping unease washed over me as I sat on the sofa and surveyed the gloomy wreckage of the holiday. It wasn't until then that I noticed an irrefutable fact: China was taking over the place.

It stared back at me from the empty screen of the television. I spied it in the pile of tennis shoes by the door. It glowed in the lights on the Christmas tree and watched me in the eyes of a doll splayed on the floor. I slipped off the couch and did a quick inventory, sorting gifts into two stacks: China and non-China. The count came to China, 25, the world, 14. Christmas, I realized, had become a holiday made by the Chinese. Suddenly I'd had enough. I wanted China out.

Through tricks and persuasion I got my husband on board, and on Jan. 1 we launched a yearlong household embargo on Chinese imports. The idea wasn't to punish China, which would never feel the pinprick of our protest. And we didn't fool ourselves into thinking we'd bring back a single job to unplugged company towns in Ohio and Georgia[①]. We pushed China out of our lives because we wanted to measure how far it had pushed in. We wanted to know what it would take in time, money, and aggravation to kick our China habit.

We hit the first rut in the road when I discovered our son's toes pressing against the ends of his tennis shoes.[②] I wore myself out hunting for new ones. After two weeks I broke down and spent $60 on sneakers from Italy. I felt sick over the money; it seemed decadent for a pair of children's shoes. I got used to the feeling. Weeks later I shelled out $60 for Texas-made shoes for our toddler daughter.

We got hung up on lots of little things. I drove to half a dozen grocery stores in search of candles for my husband's birthday cake, eventually settling on a box of dusty leftovers I found in the kitchen. The junk drawer has been stuck shut since January. My husband found the part to fix it at Home Depot but left it on the shelf when he spotted the telltale "Made in China."

Mini crises erupted when our blender and television broke down. The television sputtered back to life without intervention, but it was a long, hot summer without smoothies. We killed four mice with old-fashioned snapping traps because the catch-and-release ones we prefer are made in China. Last summer at the beach my husband wore a pair of mismatched flip-flops my mother found in her garage. He'd run out of options at the drug store.

Navigating the toy aisle has been a wilting affair. In the spring, our four-year-old son launched a counter-campaign in support of "China things." He's been a good sport, but he's weary of Danish-made Legos, the only sure bet for birthday gifts for his friends. One morning in October he fell apart during a trip to Target[③] when he developed a sudden lust for an electric purple pumpkin.

"It's too long without China," he wailed. He kept at me all day.

The next morning I drove him back so he could use his birthday money to buy the pumpkin for himself. I kept my fingers off the bills as he passed them to the checker.

My husband bemoans the Christmas gifts he can't buy because they were made in China. He plans to sew sleeping bags for the children himself. He can build wooden boats and guitars, but I fear he will meet his match with thread and needle.

"How hard can it be?" he scoffed.

---

① 美国的俄亥俄州和佐治亚州。

② 我们碰到的第一个问题就是儿子的网球鞋已经小得无法再穿了，脚趾都顶鞋帮了。

③ Target，美国第二大连锁超市，仅次于沃尔玛（Wal-Mart）。公司位于明尼苏达州明尼阿波利斯美市，为客户提供当今时尚前沿的零售服务。

The funny thing about China's ascent is that we, as a nation, could shut the whole thing down in a week. Jump-start a "Just Say No to Chinese Products Week," and it will collapse amid the chaos of overloaded cargo ships in Long Beach Harbor[①]. I doubt we could pull it off. Americans may be famously patriotic, but look closely, and you'll see who makes the flag magnets on their car bumpers. These days China delivers every major holiday, Fourth of July included.

I don't know what we will do after Dec. 31 when our family's embargo comes to its official end. China-free living has been a hassle.

I have discovered for myself that China doesn't control every aspect of our daily lives, but if you take a close look at the underside of boxes in the toy department, I promise it will give you pause.

Our son knows where he stands on the matter. In the bathtub one evening he told me how happy he was that "the China season" was coming soon.

"When we can buy China things again, let's never stop," he said.

After a year without China I can tell you this: You can still live without it, but it's getting trickier and costlier by the day. And a decade from now I may not be brave enough to try it again.

Words and Expressions

coat [kəʊt] *v.* 涂上一层,外加一层

trump [trʌmp] *v.* 战胜

creeping [ˈkriːpɪŋ] *adj.* 逐渐蔓延的,悄悄的

wreckage [ˈrekɪdʒ] *n.* 破片;残骸

stack [stæk] *n.* 堆,垛

aggravation [ˌægrəˈveɪʃən] *n.* 加重;增剧;恶化

decadent [ˈdekədənt] *adj.* 堕落的,腐朽的

toddler [ˈtɒdlə] *n.* 初学走路的孩子

telltale [ˈtelˌteɪl] *n.* 标识,指示器

erupt [ɪˈrʌpt] *v.* 突然发生,爆发

sputter [ˈspʌtə] *v.* 发劈啪声,噼噼啪啪地作响

flip-flop *n.* 凉鞋

navigate [ˈnævɪgeɪt] *v.* 使通过;横渡,跨越

wilting [ˈwɪltɪŋ] *adj.* 萎缩的

Legos *n.* 垒高拼装玩具(商标名称)

lust [lʌst] *n.* 渴望,热烈追求

---

① 洛杉矶长滩海港

bemoan [bɪ'məʊn] *v.* 惋惜;感叹
scoff [skɒf] *v.* 嘲笑
hassle ['hæsəl] *n.* [口]激烈争论;困难,麻烦
jump-start *v.* 起动，发动
cargo ship *n.* 货船
pull off 努力实现，赢得
car bumper 车档
be weary of 厌烦，不耐烦
fall apart 崩溃
shell out 交付，支付

Exercises

Exercise 1 Choose the best answer for each of the following questions.

1. Why did the author want "China" out?
   A. She wanted to measure how far China had penetrated into their life.
   B. She thought she would bring back some job opportunities to unplugged company towns in Ohio and Georgia.
   C. She wanted to punish China.
   D. She was tired of "Made in China."
2. During the embargo, the author got hung up on lots of little things except ________.
   A. she drove to half a dozen grocery stores in search of candles for her husbands birthday cake
   B. they killed four mice with old-fashioned snapping traps
   C. she drove to buy an electric purple pumpkin for her son
   D. her husband bemoans the christmas gifts he can't buy
3. After a year without China, the author came to the conclusion that ________.
   A. without China things, they can still live very well
   B. they can still live without China things, but its getting trickier and costlier by the day
   C. they cannot live without China things
   D. they can resist what China is selling

Exercise 2 Fill in each of the blanks with the appropriate words given. Change the form of the word when necessary.

trump eruption meet one's match chaos coat

1. Sometimes I worried about jobs sent overseas or nasty reports about human rights abuses, but price ________ virtue at our house.
2. Our crises ________ when our blender and television broke down.

3. He can build wooden boats and guitars, but I fear he will ________ with thread and needle.
4. The house was in ________ after the party.
5. It had ________ our lives with a cheerful veneer of toys, gadgets, and $10 children's shoes.

Exercise 3 Translate the following sentences into English.

1. 在这件事上他知道他的立场在哪。
2. 我们碰到的第一个问题就是发现所有的火柴都已经湿了。
3. 我们也不会欺骗自己,认为我们把一个就业机会还给了俄亥俄州和佐治亚州的某家公司。

Text 21 Made-in-China Christmas for Americans
美国圣诞节“中国造”

导读 当圣诞老人与红鼻鲁道夫享受北极冰雪风光之时，他的小精灵们早已飞到了中国南方的乡镇忙碌圣诞节采购。世界另一头的北美大地漫天雪花飞舞，又一个银装素裹的圣诞节即将来临，家家户户忙碌购买圣诞用品：圣诞树，圣诞礼物，圣诞袜，彩灯，彩条……一看标签，这些东西竟然都是小精灵们在中国辛勤采购的成果！目前，全球70%的圣诞玩具及装饰品包括人造圣诞树都产于中国，连装饰白宫的圣诞树也是来自中国。中国小商品出口基地浙江义乌，机声隆隆，车水马龙，倾城为美国制造一个个“中国造”圣诞节。

While Santa Claus lives it up with Rudolph at the North Pole, his elves have relocated to southern China's towns and villages. Some 70 percent of the world's Christmas ornaments and other paraphernalia now originate in officially atheist China's Mainland. Tinsel, Santas, mistletoe, and artificial trees of every shape and hue are churned out at a relentless pace by thousands of factory workers in Guangdong, Zhejiang and Jiangsu provinces.

According to the China General Administration of Customs[①], Guangdong exported more than $620 million worth of Christmas products in 2004. For the country as a whole the figure was over $1 billion.

Even the White House now celebrates a Made-in-China Christmas. In 2003, seven of the trees adorning the US president's residence were manufactured in China.

In fact more than two thirds of the worlds artificial Christmas trees are made in the single city of Shenzhen.

And while the world celebrates Christmas, Santa's Chinese elves are enjoying a bit of a quiet period after having toiled for the majority of the year. "Our busy period is really February to October," says He Li, assistant sales manager of Yiwu Festival Gifts Company[②]. The company has annual sales of over $12 million and employs between 800-1,000 workers. It exports 90 percent of its products to the US, Russia and Chile and specializes in manufacturing hanging toys, trees and Christmas gifts.

Yiwu[③], where the company is located, is today one of the Christmas industry's global

---

① 中国海关

② 义乌市福斯特工艺品公司

③ 义乌，位于浙江中部，是中国最大的小商品出口基地。

centres. Last year, Yiwu posted sales of $2.5 billion, $1.5 billion of that in exports. Like many places in China, it has abundant cheap labor. Two-thirds of the 316,000 farmers in the surrounding countryside have left the land to become part of Yiwu's mega-export machine. An additional 400,000 migrant workers have come from other provinces.

Similarly, another town Xiaoguanzhuang now has 45 large businesses and more than 400 processing workshops, producing angels, trees and reindeers. According to Xinhua, China's official news agency, more than 7,000 farmers living in Xiaoguanzhuang collectively manufactured some 100 million Christmas decorations for exports in 2004, earning close to $48.3 million.

Many of the Pearl River and Yangtze River delta Christmas product manufacturers now have their own websites in English and Spanish.

Words and Expressions

elf [elf] *n.*	小精灵
paraphernalia [ˌpærəfəˈneɪlɪə] *n.*	配件
atheist [ˈeɪθɪɪst] *n.*	无神论者
tinsel [ˈtɪnsl] *n.*	装饰的、薄的闪光金属片、条、线
mistletoe [ˈmɪsltəu] *n.*	槲寄生,常青植物,通常用作圣诞节装饰物
hue [hjuː] *n.*	色彩;样子
relentless [rɪˈlentlɪs] *adj.*	稳定持续的
adorn [əˈdɔːn] *v.*	装饰
toil [tɒɪl] *v.*	辛苦地工作
mega-export machine	百万出口生产大军
processing workshop	加工车间

Exercises

Exercise 1 Choose the best answer for each of the following questions.

1. In which part of China are the most of Christmas products manufactured?

   A. Eastern part. B. Southern part.

   C. Western part. D. Northern part.

2. Which of the following statements is not an example showing China's predominance in Christmas ornament production?

   A. The atheist Chinese government has shifted its interest to Christianity.

   B. The exportation of Christmas products from China exceeded $1 billion in 2004.

   C. Shenzhen occupies over 2/3 of international artificial Christmas tree production.

   D. The Made-in-China Christmas trees have won popularity in the White House.

3. Where is Festival Gift Company located?

A. Pearl delta.   B. Chongqing.

C. Xiaoguanzhuang.   D. Yiwu.

Exercise 2 Fill in each of the blanks with the appropriate words given. Change the form of the word when necessary.

churn out adorn collectively toil live it up

1. Some locals who used to be in rags ________ at posh hotels in Bluefields and Managua, others stock up on wide-screen TVs and expensive beer.
2. Why should he ________ and moil, and be at so much trouble to pick himself up out the mud, when, in a little while hence, the strong arm of his Uncle will raise and support him?
3. The sugar plantations ________ with windmills.
4. Tennessee's coal-burning power plants ________ CO_2.
5. In probability theory, a set of events is ________ exhaustive if at least one of the events must occur.

Exercise 3 Translate the following sentences into English.

1. 如今,连白宫里用的圣诞装饰品也都是中国产的。
2. 周边农村三分之二的农民们都放下了农活加入到义乌圣诞产品生产的百万大军中来。
3. 2004年一年中,该村七千多名农民总共生产了约一亿件圣诞装饰品以供出口,赚了近4,830万美元。

Text 22　Made by America in China

在中国的"美国制造"

导读　超过1600亿多美元的中美贸易顺差确实令人惊讶不已，究其根源其中相当一部分的顺差来自在华的西方公司所为，很多产品与其说是"中国制造"，还不如说是"在中国的美国制造"。西方公司在华投资以各种形式赢得钵满盆盈：在美国销售1双100美元的运动鞋仅有15美元留在中国，中国为此得支付工资、运费等开支，而剩下的85%则由美国公司分享；通用汽车、摩托罗拉、飞利浦等跨国公司在华建起了一座又一座工厂的同时，也培育了当地的消费水平，顺势把产品卖给了当地生活日益富足的消费者；在中国制造的产品因低的成本返销到美国后，给美国消费者带去大量的实惠，给这些公司创造了丰厚的利润，给美国投资者也赚取了良好的投资回报。

Before our eyes, two giant nations—India and China—are simultaneously embracing both commercialism and globalization. The world economy is being transformed as a result, as Forbes[①] Senior Editor Robyn Meredith explains in her new book, *The Elephant and the Dragon: The Rise of India and China and What It Means to All of Us*. Each weekday through July 27, Forbes.com will post a new excerpt from the book.

In past centuries, China was a technological leader, and it prospered as a result. By the 14th century, China had became a pillar of international trade by moving goods along the Silk Road—overland trading routes[②] across China, through the Arab world and onto Europe. China's inventions include paper, gunpowder, the magnetic compass and even wallpaper, and one of its biggest exports was porcelain, which Europeans couldn't duplicate for more than a century.

What a sharp contrast to the manner in which China successfully trades today. Instead of doing the inventing as the West watches with envy, China excels at building Western inventions cheaper than Westerners can build them at home. China has shifted from a hub of invention to one of rote production.

As the outside world watches China's numbers rise and rise—economic growth is sizzling, exports are skyrocketing—a panic has ensued. But the real boom in China is the global economy itself. Much of the global economy has simply moved to China, and it is owned and run by the same multinationals that controlled it before.

---

① 美国《财富(福布斯)》杂志，每期刊登60多篇对公司和公司经营者的评论性文章，语言简练，内容均为原创。

② 陆上丝绸之路，是历史上横贯欧亚大陆的贸易交通线。

A large portion of the frighteningly lopsided US-China trade deficit can be traced to goods made by Western companies in China, then shipped home for sale. In practice, "Made in China" often really means "Made by America in China".

For multinational companies like Philips[①], General Motors and Motorola, China's development has been a virtuous circle—as companies have built more factories, the nation has gotten richer, enabling Chinese people to buy more of their products.

Meanwhile, most foreign companies are making money in China now and are passing on some of the gains to their American customers in the form of lower prices, and keeping some for themselves and their investors as higher profits.

In many other ways, China seems strong but it is weak. Chinese manufacturing might require more brawn than brains,[②] and as a result, most of the commercial gains that come from China land in the pockets of foreigners. For instance, when China exports a shoe that sells for $100 in the US, just $15 of the price stays in China in the form of workers wages, transportation costs or other value. American companies keep the remaining $85.

China must transform itself further if it is to reap the full rewards of its own economic rise. Even though Chinese workers have been the big winners overall because their incomes have risen, they have few rights and little recourse to fair courts, so it is easy for unscrupulous, newly capitalist bosses to take advantage of them. China's army of migrant workers, the tens of millions who pour from the countryside into the cities hoping to find work, are particularly powerless.

The other big losers from the shift of the global economy to China are American workers whose jobs have been moved to China, and they are hard to count because the rise of China is creating some jobs in America at the same time it eliminates others. Just as the effect of China's strong economic growth on America is more complex than it appears at first glance, so is the effect on American jobs.

The bulk of China's job gains have come from factory work, and most Americans no longer work in factories but in the service industries. Yet white-collar workers also have reason to worry: Increasingly, American companies and other multinationals are hiring Chinese workers to do white-collar work.

Just as an American parent might work overtime on the assembly line to pay for a child's college tuition, China is trying to encourage its next generation to work with their minds rather than their hands. As factories move to China, products that are built in China are increasingly designed and engineered there as well.

The Chinese government has asked foreign companies to create research and development facilities, not just factories. Over 700 foreign investors—including Microsoft,

---

① 总部位于荷兰的飞利浦公司在全球 60 多个国家拥有大约 123,800 名员工。

② 中国的制造业要求更多的是体力劳动,而不是脑力劳动。

Philips and Intel[①]—have set up R&D centers in China in recent years.

By bringing the global economy to India and China—both by hiring Indians and Chinese and by selling products to them—Western companies are changing the face of the world economy and thus the way we live, for those in the East as well as those in the West.

Words and Expressions

simultaneously [ˌsɪml'teɪnɪəslɪ] *adv.*	同时地
embrace [ɪm'breɪs] *v.*	拥抱;欢迎
excerpt ['eksɜːpt] *n.*	摘录,引用
porcelain ['pɔːsəlɪn] *n.*	瓷器,瓷
duplicate ['djuːplɪkeɪt] *v.*	复制,复写
sizzling ['sɪzlɪŋ] *adj.*	令人振奋的,表现良好的
skyrocket ['skaiˌrɒkɪt] *v.*	涨,猛涨
ensue [ɪn'sjuː] *v.*	跟着发生,继起
lopsided [ˌlɒp'saɪdɪd] *adj.*	倾向一方的,不平衡的
recourse [rɪ'kɔːs] *n.*	求助的对象
unscrupulous [ʌn'skruːpjuləs] *adj.*	肆无忌惮的,无道德的
excel at	擅长于(某项活动)
rote production	机械的、生搬硬套的制造
virtuous circle	良性循环
the bulk of	大半,大多数

Exercises

Exercise 1　Choose the best answer for each of the following questions.

1. By the 14th century, China had became a pillar of international trade, because ________.
   A. China's numbers rise and rise—economic growth was sizzling, exports were skyrocketing
   B. China was a technological leader at that time
   C. many foreigners did business in China
   D. Chinese product prices were very low
2. Most of the commercial gains that come from China land in the pockets of foreigners, because ________.

---

① 英特尔,成立于1968年,为迅猛发展的计算机工业提供关键元件,包括性能卓越的微处理器、芯片组、板卡、系统及软件等。

A. most products are invented and designed by them

B. foreign companies and other multinationals are hiring Chinese workers to do white-collar work

C. China excels at building Western inventions cheaper than Westerners can build them at home

D. most foreign companies are big and strong

Exercise 2 Fill in each of the blanks with the appropriate words given. Change the form of the word when necessary.

the bulk of   sizzling   excel at   transform   lopsided

1. Michael Cullen, who was a historian before he was a politician, cautioned that economic ________ are not one-off.
2. One good way to keep the forum ________ is to realize that it is always necessary to reply to articles.
3. Sun Microsystems announced Tuesday it has finished the process of making ________ its core Java technology available as open-source software under the GNU general public license version 2 (GPLv2).
4. Russian President Vladimir Putin has demanded that the Cabinet should ________ work throughout the presidential election campaign.
5. I think a ________ development is an unbalanced development, with some economic sectors more in advance than others for example.

Exercise 3 Translate the following sentences into English.

1. 中美经贸关系正变得如同两个国家的安全关系一样复杂。
2. 中国必须增加进口以满足其活跃的国内经济。
3. 美国必须认识到美国的贸易逆差是因为它超过自身能力消费而造成的。

Text 23 China's New Model Army

中国造"中华尊驰"闪亮登陆汽车王国

导读 "中国造"小商品誉满全球，备受各国消费者的青睐。而如今，"中国造"的大宗商品——轿车，也登上了国际市场的舞台，驶入素有世界汽车王国的德国与邻近的其他欧洲国家。由中国华晨汽车推出的"中华尊驰"BS6 型轿车，其设计出自意大利大师手笔，并经受了各种恶劣条件测试，如西藏－45℃超低温与海南岛 38℃高温的考验。BS6 型轿车锁定的客户为欧洲中等收入消费者，定价为 20,000 欧元，与韩国现代、通用雪佛兰并驾齐驱，逐鹿欧洲车市。2007 年华晨出口汽车达 15,500 辆，2008 年有望出口 3 万辆，2009 年 6 万辆，2010 年 10 万辆。

Europe's crowded mid-size car segment will get an exotic new entrant this month with the launch of Brilliance Jinbei Automobiles BS6 sedan①.

The car, branded Zhonghua in China②, will debut in Germany and its neighboring countries, marking the first major foray by a Chinese carmaker into one of the world's most competitive and sophisticated car markets.

Brilliance boasts of the car's Italian design and road tests at "extreme operating conditions" ranging from minus 45 Celsius in Tibet to 38 degrees on the tropical island of Hainan.

The BS6 will target middle-income buyers, cost about 20,000 ($26,800) and compete head-on with well-established models produced by Koreas Hyundai and Kia and General Motors Chevrolet brand. ③

---

① 华晨金杯汽车有限公司，前身是沈阳金杯客车制造有限公司，于 2003 年更名，为华晨中国汽车控股有限公司的重点生产企业。

② 在中国国内名为"中华尊驰"，也就是在德国展出的 BS6 轿车，该款汽车是一款迎合中等收入者的中低档轿车。

③ 韩国现代(Hyundai)；起亚(Kia)；通用汽车(General Motors)旗下的雪佛兰(Chevrolet)

HSO Motors Europe[1], which has a five-year contract with Brilliance to sell the cars in Europe, is projecting sales of 15,000 this year, and 75,000 by 2010. Hans-Ulrich Sachs, who runs HSO, proved his credentials for selling Asian cars to skeptical Europeans when he introduced Hyundai cars to Germany in the early 1990s.

The launch marks a significant moment for China's burgeoning car industry as it seeks to follow Japanese and Korean producers into the rich but saturated markets of the developed world.

HSO will initially sell in Germany, Belgium and the Netherlands, moving to Poland by as soon as late May, followed by other European countries.

HSO is deliberately setting the bar high by launching in Europe's largest car market, and the homeland of some of the world's most renowned luxury brands and exacting car-buyers.

"Germany is one of the most quality-demanding markets in Europe, and if you do your job here, you do it in the neighborhood as well," says Mr Sachs.

HSO will add Brilliance's BS4 compact sedan and BC3 coupe[2] to its European offering by 2008.

When Brilliance first began selling its own brand of cars in 2003, the vehicles were widely criticized for the poor quality of their finishing. When the company reported a large financial loss in 2005, many analysts thought it would withdraw from the business and stick to making buses and to the joint venture it has with BMW to manufacture cars for the Chinese market.

However, Brilliance has since brought out new models that are seen as an improvement in terms of quality. Its sales grew sharply last year, with the Junjie[3] sedan alone selling nearly 36,000 units in its first year.

Even with the improved vehicles, however, some analysts think Brilliance will find it tough going trying to sell mid-size, mid-level cars in Europe, where the segment is already well-served.

"Going into Europe with a mid-level sedan will be very difficult to pull off," says Michael Dunne, president of Automotive Resources Asia, a consultancy recently acquired by JD Power.

"There will be some initial sales from curious buyers, but unless they are very good on quality and cost, there will not be much follow-through." Initial reviews of the BS6 have been mixed. While a writer for the *Detroit News* in Geneva said that Brilliance's three models on show "looked sharp", *Auto Express* magazine last year described the BS6's styling as "bland" and its drive quality as "spongy, with lots of body roll".[4]

---

① 欧洲 HSO 汽车贸易公司，总部设在卢森堡。

② BS4 紧凑型轿车和 BC3 型双门跑车

③ “骏捷”为中华轿车旗下一品牌。

④ 尽管《底特律新闻报》一名驻日内瓦记者表示，华晨在日内瓦车展亮相的 3 款汽车“外观惹眼”，但《汽车快讯》杂志去年称 BS6 汽车的设计“平淡无奇”，其驾驶时性能“不够稳定，车身晃动很厉害”。

Mr Sachs demurs that the car will not sell well, saying that he learned from the Hyundai launch to offer "first-class service right from the beginning."

The Brilliance cars will come with a 36-month warranty and mobility guarantee. The 15,000 target is realistic, he claims, noting that Hyundai sold 33,000 units in Germany in its first year, 1992.

Unlike Brilliance, some other Chinese car companies, including Chery Automobile and Shanghai Auto, have chosen to improve their products in their home market before venturing abroad.

Brilliance, like its smaller competitor Great Wall, has decided it will learn more quickly about what US and European customers want by launching its vehicles there, even if it means some short-term problems.

The strategy could prove risky for the early entrants if they falter on service or quality, analysts say. "The risk, of course, is that they get shut out for a number of years if there are lots of complaints," says Mr Dunne.

Even with stronger domestic sales in 2006, there are still doubts about the sustainability of Brilliance's own-brand cars. "The key challenge is to run a profitable business," says Yu Bing, automotive analyst with Central China Securities. "Large numbers of sales do not mean very much if the business is not profitable."

Losses in the first half of last year were ￥176m ($22.7m), although this was a third of the losses in the same period the year before.

Chen Qiaoning of TX Investment Consulting in Beijing, says that while the feedback on Brilliance's new models has been good, the company needs to sharpen its marketing edge and reduce costs. "Otherwise, no matter how large the sales are, the rate of return on investment will not be very satisfying," he says.

Words and Expressions

segment [ˈsegmənt] *n.* 部分,细分市场
exotic [ɪgˈzɒtɪk] *adj.* 异国情调的,异国风味的,非本国的
entrant [ˈentrənt] *n.* 新成员
sedan [sɪˈdæn] *n.* 轿车,小汽车
head-on *adj.* 迎头相撞的;正面相撞的
burgeoning [ˈbɜːdʒnɪŋ] *adj.* 迅速增长的
saturated [ˈsætʃəreɪtɪd] *adj.* 饱和的
demur [dɪˈmɜː] *v.* 表示反对;提出异议
warranty [ˈwɒrəntɪ] *n.* (商品)质保单
falter [ˈfɔːltə] *v.* 摇晃,蹒跚
boast of 自夸,自吹自擂
set the bar high 抬高门槛

Exercises

Exercise 1 Choose the best answer for each of the following questions.

1. Which brand is not the direct competitor of BS6 among the middle-income buyers?

   A. Hyundai. B. Chevrolet. C. Buick. D. Kia.

2. Which of the following is not the evaluation that the foreign media's have given to BS6?

   A. The models of the Brilliance are attractive.

   B. The styling of BS6 is nothing exciting.

   C. It is very safe to drive BS6 for its high quality.

   D. The stability of BS6 is disappointing.

3. What means the most to Brilliance's own-brand cars now in accordance with some analysts?

   A. Large sales. B. Profit.

   C. Large market share. D. More investment.

Exercise 2 Fill in each of the blanks with the appropriate words given. Change the form of the word when necessary.

debut boast of head-on burgeon set the bar high

1. We confide in our strength, without ________ it; we respect that of others, without fearing it.
2. Despite the resulting disfigurement she's facing life's challenges ________—and even enjoys being one of the UK's unlikeliest pin-ups.
3. The recent ________ of Apple's iPhone provides a great example of how employees enamored by fancy applications and interfaces might opt to spend more out of their own pockets for a device that better meets their work and personal needs.
4. His efforts brought together the ________ hip-hop community and inspired gangs to battle creatively through rapping and breaking rather than through violence.
5. Prison Break ________ for Fall dramas— Fox's jailhouse tale delivers one of the seasons most captivating and intense storylines.

Exercise 3 Translate the following sentences into English.

1. 竞争激烈的欧洲中型汽车市场将迎来一个外来的新进入者。
2. 中国发展迅速的汽车业计划效仿日本和韩国汽车制造商的做法,进军富裕但较为饱和的发达国家市场。
3. HSO 汽车贸易公司选择在德国这一欧洲最大的汽车市场推出该款汽车,是有意抬高门槛。

Text 24 Made in China Labels Don't Tell the Whole Story
"中国制造"——盛名背后的故事

导读 位于中国南部的城市深圳,硕大的工厂内数以百计的工人正在忙碌地包装计算机磁盘,工厂为日本日立公司拥有,产品发往地是美国。每天数以万计发往美国或世界其他各国的产品看似"中国制造",其实是由在华的跨国公司制造。来自日本、韩国、美国的跨国公司仅把中国当成他们全球生产链的最后一站——组装车间。正是这种全球供应链模式把中国推到"中国制造"威胁论的风口浪尖,而真正受益的却是处于产业链上游的跨国公司、外国的零售商和外国消费者。这些跨国公司与零售商是推行廉价"中国制造"的无形之手,他们获取了产业链所产生利润的大块,是大赢者。而输者是上述在日立工厂的低薪中国工人与跨国公司原所在地的失业工人。

Hundreds of workers here at a huge factory owned by the Japanese company Hitachi[①] are fashioning plates of glass and aluminum into shiny computer disks, wrapping them in foil. The products are destined for the United States, where they will arrive like billions of other items, labeled "Made in China."

But often these days, "Made in China" is actually "Made by Someone Else"—by multinational companies from Japan, South Korea and the United States that are using China as the final assembly station in their vast global production networks.

Analysts say this evolving global supply chain—which often tags goods at their final assembly stop—is increasingly out of step with global trade figures, which serve to inflate China into a bigger trade threat than it may actually be.

That kind of distortion is likely to appear once again on Friday, when the US Commerce Department is expected to announce that America's trade deficit with China swelled to a record of $200 billion last year.

It may look as though China is getting the big payoff, but over all, the biggest winners are consumers in the United States and other rich countries, who have benefited enormously from China's production of cheaper toys, clothing, electronics and other goods.

At the same time, US multinationals and other foreign companies, including retailers, are big winners, because they are the largely invisible hands behind the factories pumping out inexpensive goods from China. And they are reaping the bulk of the profit from the trade.

---

① 日本日立公司于1910年创建,至今已发展为大型的国际化公司,产品包括信息系统、电子设备、动力和产业系统、家用电器及其他产品。

"Basically, in the 1990s, foreign firms based in America, Europe, Japan and the rest of Asia moved their manufacturing operations to China," said Yasheng Huang, a professor at the Sloan School of Management at Massachusetts Institute of Technology[①]. "But the controls and therefore profits of these operations firmly rest with foreign firms. While China gets the wage benefits of globalization, it does not get to keep the profits of globalization."

To the extent that there are any real losers, they are mostly lower-wage workers elsewhere, like the ones at Hitachi, who lost their jobs in Japan, along with workers in other parts of Asia and in the United States who suffered as employers began relocating factories to China. Indeed, despite the big shift to China, US imports from Asia as a whole have hardly changed in the last 15 years.

In fact, about 60 percent of China's exports are controlled by foreign-financed companies, according to the latest Chinese customs data. In categories like computer parts and consumer electronics, foreign companies command an even greater share of control over the exports, analysts say.

Foreign expertise has been critical as manufacturing supply chains become increasingly complex, involving multiple countries that separately produce individual components that are then shipped to China for final assembly[②]. Since such a system can render global trade statistics misleading; some experts say that a more apt label would be "Assembled in China."

Because so many different people in different places touch a particular product, other experts say you might as well just throw away the trade figures.

"In a globalized world, bilateral trade figures are irrelevant," said Dong Tao, an economist at UBS[③]. "The trade balance between the US and China is as irrelevant as the trade balance between New York and Minnesota."

China's supply of cheap labor helped bring about $465 billion in foreign direct investment into China from 1995 to 2004, making the country one of the hottest destinations in the world for foreign capital.

Japanese and South Korean companies are coming to China in force. Panasonic of Japan now has 70,000 employees working in China; Toshiba's largest information technology production site in the world is in the Chinese coastal city of Hangzhou. And Samsung, the South Korean company, has 23 factories, 50,000 employees and all of its notebook PC production in China. Its last computer notebook factory in South Korea closed last year.

---

① 麻省理工学院

② 随着生产供应链越来越复杂，外国的专门技术一直都是至关重要的。在这种供应链中，各个零部件由不同的国家生产，最后都运到中国进行组装。

③ 瑞银集团是1997年瑞士联合银行(UBS)与其竞争对手瑞士银行公司(Swiss Bank Corp.)合并后的产物。瑞银集团不同于花旗和汇丰这样的综合金融超市，管理私人财富才是它的核心业务。

The migration has left footprints in trade statistics. In 1990, Japan was America's dominant trading partner in the Pacific, and Asia accounted for 38 percent of all US imports.

Last year, however, China was Asia's dominant trading power. The country's trade with the United States has soared about 1,200 percent since 1990. And yet Asia's share of imports into the United States has held remarkably steady, at 38 percent. In other words, if production labels simply read "Made in Asia," almost nothing changed from 1990 to 2005, except that many goods got a lot cheaper as China took on a greater role as the world's factory floor.

Even as that shift was taking place, most Asian countries retained and even expanded their powerful influence in the global supply chain, designing increasingly sophisticated models, making the preassembly components, and carrying out the marketing and brand management. So, while China now has an estimated $200 billion trade surplus with the United States, it also has a $137 billion trade deficit with the rest of Asia.

To be sure, American and European companies are moving more of their manufacturing to China. Dell and IBM computers used to be primarily made in the United States. Now, most of their PCs are assembled in China.

Bigger multinationals could be on the way. Airbus① is now considering building passenger jets in China. And General Motors② is considering exporting some of the cars it makes in China.

Thousands of Chinese factories have created millions of jobs for the country's low-wage migrant laborers, who earn about 75 cents an hour. But so far, Chinese companies in these industries have not been able to climb from basic manufacturing into design work and beyond. China's rise is in striking contrast to that of Japan in the 1980s, when Japan was producing brands like Toyota, Honda, Mitsubishi and Sony. China, by contrast, has few if any global brands beyond Lenovo and Haier, which are still struggling to build name recognition. ③

"The biggest beneficiary of all this is the United States," said Tao, the UBS economist. "Look, a Barbie doll④ costs $20 but China only gets about 35 cents of that."

Chinese officials rarely miss an opportunity to argue that the trade statistics showing huge surpluses for China are misleading indicators of the country's prosperity.

"What China got in the past few years is only some pretty figures," said Mei Xinyu of

---

① 空中客车公司(Airbus)是业界领先的民用客机制造商。

② 通用汽车公司(GM)是全球最大的汽车公司。

③ 尽管如此,中国崛起成为世界贸易的动力与上世纪80年代的日本在发挥这样作用时形成了鲜明的对比。当时的日本人创建了自己的品牌,如丰田、本田、三菱和索尼。除了联想和海尔以外,中国几乎没有什么叫得响的全球品牌。

④ 芭比娃娃,世界上最受欢迎的洋娃娃。

the Ministry of Commerce Research Institute. "American and foreign companies have gotten the real profit."

Still, China's economy is booming, and an aggressive class of entrepreneurs is emerging at home that resembles the overseas Chinese who built business empires in exile during the 20th century. These are people like Yin Mingshan①, a 68-year-old multimillionaire in the central city of Chongqing, who is fashioning himself as a Chinese Henry Ford②.

"We are the biggest exporter of motorcycles in China," Yin said.

Yin started out selling books in the 1980s, then engines and motorcycles in the 1990s. Today, his company, Lifan Group, has just opened a huge factory. Yin says his next goal is to export cars to the United States.

Don Brasher, who operates Global Trade Information Services, said this about the Chinese transformation, "That's how the Japanese got started. Remember, in the 1950s, the Japanese started exporting motorcycles. And 20 years later, it was cars."

Words and Expressions

fashion ['fæʃən] *v.*	制造，将某物做成某形状
aluminum [ælju'mɪnjəm] *n.*	[化]铝
striking contrast	鲜明的对比
wrap... in foil	把……用箔纸包裹
global supply chain	全球供应链
out of step	步调不一致
trade statistics	商业统计
trade surplus	贸易顺差
pump out	抽空
the bulk of	大多数，大半
bilateral trade	双边贸易

Exercises

Exercise 1　Choose the best answer for each of the following questions.

1. According to the passage, which Japanese company fashions plates of glass and aluminum into shiny computer disks?

   A. Sony.　　B. Haier.　　C. Hitachi.　　D. Toshiba.

2. The US Commerce Department is expected to announce on Friday that America's trade

---

① 尹明善，全国政协委员、重庆市工商联会长，还是第一批当选当地工商联会长的民营企业家。于1992年起担任重庆力帆集团董事长。

② 美国汽车制造家，管理学家，福特汽车公司创始人。

deficit with China swelled to a record of ________.

A. ¥200 billion last year B. $200 million last year
C. $200 billion next year D. $200 billion last year

3. According to some experts, a more apt label for commodities exported from China would be "Assembled in China" because ________.
   A. labor is very cheap in China
   B. all the companies from South Korea and Japan are shifting their manufacturing plants to China
   C. China is Asia's dominating trade power and has overtaken Japan
   D. parts of products are manufactured in different countries, but the final product is shipped from China

Exercise 2 Fill in each of the blanks with the appropriate words given. Change the form of the word when necessary.

assembled distortion render out of step

1. The application note explains the possible effects such as increased gain error and ________ when using high impedance to drive an ADC (analog-to-digital converter 模数转换器) without a buffer.
2. China's banking industry is still ________ with economic and social development in China in two aspects.
3. Not only is risk prediction unreliable but, when applied to individuals rather than groups, the margins of error are so high as to ________ any result meaningless.
4. American car manufacturer, Henry Ford installed the first conveyor belt-based ________ line in his car factory in Fords Highland Park, Michigan plant, around 1913-14.

Exercise 3 Translate the following sentences into English.

1. 实际上,中国是全球最大的最终组装工厂,当地的附加值极少。
2. 美国制造业失业率逐年上涨,这主要是由于劳动生产率的大幅提高。

Text 25 Nations Dust off Their Antidumping Duties in Response to Chinese Pricing

中国成为世界反倾销头号目标

导读 世界各国对进口商品的官方壁垒日趋下降,而中国企业成为反倾销目标的案例却有增无减。目前中国已成为世界各国反倾销的头号目标,WTO公布报告的数据显示,2006年下半年一共有82件新的反倾销调查,其中有33件是针对中国的。WTO反倾销协议规定,进口产品以低于正常价值的价格进入另一国,则该产品被视为倾销。有三种方式参照、判断价格是否低于正常价值:① 该产品在本国的销售价格;② 向其他国出口价格;③ 成本核算。一般优先以第一、第二种方法作为判断依据。由于中国至今被美国、欧盟等主要贸易伙伴视作为"非市场经济",在反倾销调查中,中国产品的正常价值经常要通过参照所谓第三国的国内同类产品市场销售价格来确定该出口产品的正常价值。

Countries official blocks on imports have fallen to record lows, although that trend seems to be reversing as complaints against unfair competition from China increase.

New data show that "trade defense instruments" (TDIs)—principally "antidumping" duties levied against imports sold more cheaply abroad than at home and "countervailing" duties charged against government-subsidised goods—dropped to the lowest in the first half of this year since the World Trade Organisation was created in 1994. ①

But Cliff Stevenson, a trade consultant who collects the figures, said there had been a rapid uptick in the past three months. If the trend continued, he said, "antidumping will still be relatively low post-WTO creation, but not a record low, and certainly significantly above the 1980s average."

Recent high global commodity prices have prevented many companies successfully from filing antidumping cases, as it is harder to show they have been damaged by artificially low import prices.

The EU brought no antidumping cases at all in the first six months of the year, though it has brought several since recently extended antidumping duties against Chinese

---

① 最新数据表明,2007年上半年各国采取的"贸易防卫手段"减少至1994年世贸组织(WTO)成立以来的最低水平。"贸易防卫手段"主要是对国外售价低于国内售价的进口产品征收反倾销税,以及对政府补贴产品征收反补贴税。[trade defense instruments (TDIs)贸易防卫手段; antidumping duties 反倾销税; countervailing duties 反补贴税;government-subsidized goods 政府补贴产品]

energy-saving light bulbs for a year.

China has been by far the most common target of antidumping cases this year, and India, the biggest user of antidumping duties.

With rising complaints from its companies against China, the US has opened a new front that the EU may follow. Washington recently reversed a two-decade precedent and imposed countervailing duties against Chinese glossy paper—used in books and packaging—despite designating China as a "non-market economy"① in which prices are not set by open competition, making government subsidies hard to determine.

Since then, several more US countervailing duty cases have been opened against China as add-ons. One Washington lawyer said, "Since many subsidies are not specific to individual industries, if you prove it once you can go after the whole Chinese economy."②

Last week the US Commerce Department③ confirmed the duties and in the case of one Chinese company raised them to 44 percent, more than four times higher than its preliminary levy.

Beijing has hit back by seeking to have the US duties declared illegal in the World Trade Organization,④ a case that could set a vital precedent but one that may take years to resolve.

So far the EU, although it is watching the US case closely and reviewing its own use of trade defense instruments, has not followed suit with a countervailing duty case.

Words and Expressions

levy ['levɪ] *v.*	征收,课税
uptick ['ʌptɪk] *n.*	[商](股票)报升(成交价格比上一个交易高的成交或价格)
file [faɪl] *v.*	提起诉讼
designate ['dezɪgneɪt] *v.*	指定,认定
add-on *n.*	附加,追加
antidumping duty	反倾销税
dust off	重新起用
official block	官方限制
record low	创记录低点
trade consultant	贸易顾问
a new front	新战线
glossy paper	铜版纸
go after	追究

---

① 非市场经济体

② 由于许多补贴不是针对特定行业,只要证明了一次,你就能追究整个中国经济。

③ 美国商务部

④ 中国政府进行了反击,将案件上诉到世贸组织,希望世贸组织宣布美国反补贴税为非法。

Exercises

Exercise 1 Choose the best answer for each of the following questions.

1. The trend that countries' official blocks on imports seems to be ________.
   A. unchanged B. reversing
   C. upwards D. continuing
2. The EU brought no antidumping cases at all in ________.
   A. the first six months of the year B. the second six months of the year
   C. the whole D. the last year
3. ________ has been the biggest user of antidumping duties.
   A. China B. The US
   C. EU D. India
4. The US recently reversed a two-decade precedent and imposed countervailing duties against ________.
   A. Chinese energy-saving light bulbs B. Chinese cars
   C. Chinese glossy paper D. Chinese textile

Exercise 2 Fill in each of the blanks with the appropriate words given. Change the form of the word when necessary.

reverse levy designate energy-saving antidumping duties

1. Wed like to ________ Shanghai as the loading port because it is near the production area.
2. China has formally imposed ________ on imports of polyester chips and polyester fiber from South Korea, in its final decisions in two long-running trade investigations.
3. Earlier this year, America took aim at banks that were helping Mr Kim's regime to launder money, a pinch that may have caused North Korea to ________ with the nuclear test.
4. The commissioner would assess registration processes, and could ________ fines if a regulator fails to root out unfair practices.
5. The application of ________, low pollution and environmentally-friendly products and materials should be popularized.

Exercise 3 Translate the following sentences into English.

1. 世界各国对产品进口的官方限制已降至创纪录低点。不过,随着对中国不公平竞争的指控增多,这种势头似乎正在逆转。
2. 随着美国公司对中国的投诉越来越多,美国开辟了一个欧盟可能会效仿的新战线。
3. 尽管欧盟一直在密切关注美国的案件,审议自己对贸易防卫手段的使用,但它并没有效仿美国的做法,提起反补贴税案。

Text 26 Mattel Apologizes to the Chinese People
美泰公司向中国人民的道歉

导读 近来"中国制造"的质量在西方国家遭受一些质疑，美国玩具制造商巨头美泰声称涂层含铅量超标，前后3次宣布召回中国制造的2,100万玩具。瞬间西方媒体对"中国制造"的质量质疑四起，中国企业成了"质量门"的"替罪羊"。然后姗姗来迟的美泰公司的道歉道出了"质量门"真相：是美泰公司的设计问题，而不是代加工的中国公司问题。美泰公司表示承担所有责任，并向中国人民和购买问题玩具的美国消费者表示道歉。

Mattel was forced to deliver a humiliating public apology to the Chinese people on Friday over the damaging succession of product recalls of China-made toys that the US toymaker has announced in recent months.

In a carefully stage-managed meeting in Beijing with a senior Chinese official, which, unusually, was open to the media, Thomas Debrowski, Mattel's executive vice-president for worldwide operations, read out a prepared text that played down the role of Chinese factories in the recalls.

"Mattel[①] takes full responsibility for these recalls and apologizes personally to you, the Chinese people, and all of our customers who received the toys," Mr Debrowski said.

The apology was in stark contrast to recent comments from Robert Eckert, Mattel's chief executive. In testimony to the US Senate last week, he suggested that the fault for the groups recent product recalls lay with outside contractors. "We were let down, and so we let you down," he said.

The apology came as Simplicity, a US-based company that makes baby products, recalled 1m Chinese-made cots over a design flaw that has been blamed for the deaths of two infants.

In recent months, California-based Mattel has announced three recalls of 21m toys made in China, where the group conducts two-thirds of its manufacturing.

But while some of the toys were recalled because they used excessive amounts of lead paint, the majority—about 18m—were deemed unsafe because of Mattel design flaws

---

① 美泰玩具为全球《财富》500强企业之一，在儿童产品之设计、生产、销售方面处于领导地位。总部位于美国加州，并在36个国家设有销售机构，产品销往150多个国家和地区。主要品牌包括 Barbie Doll, Harry Potter, Hot Wheel, MatchBox, Fisher Price 等。

rather than shoddy manufacturing. Doggie Day Care, Batman and Polly Pocket[①] toys were recalled because they contained small magnets that could be dangerous if swallowed.

Mr Debrowski said Mattel understood and appreciated "the issues that this has caused for the reputation of Chinese manufacturers."

In a later statement, Mattel said that some reports had "mischaracterized" its comments and said it had "apologized to the Chinese today just as it has wherever its toys are sold." But the statement made clear that it was also apologizing to the country and its reputation over the magnet-related recalls.

The apology comes weeks after the owner of one of the Chinese factories used by Mattel committed suicide in the wake of the first recall announcement.

Joe Lampel, a professor of strategy with the Cass Business School[②] in London, said Mattel's volte-face had been driven by a need to build bridges with Beijing. The groups reputation with consumers had been affected, he said. "They have to salvage some of their business relationship with China. They need the goodwill of the government."

The Chinese government has argued that the toy recalls unfairly damaged the credibility of its manufacturers at a time when widespread questions have been raised about the quality of China-made goods.

Li Changjiang, head of the government's product quality watchdog, who led the Chinese delegation at yesterday's meeting, said Mattel should take steps to "improve their quality control measures."

He said that much of the US groups profits were generated by factories in China. "This shows that our co-operation is in the interests of Mattel, and both parties should value our co-operation. I really hope that Mattel can learn lessons and gain experience from these incidents."

Mattel, which has been making toys in Asia for several decades, has been considered a model for how to outsource manufacturing.

Words and Expressions

humiliating [hjʊˈmɪlɪeɪtɪŋ] *adj.*	耻辱的
recall [rɪˈkɔːl] *n.*	召回(残损产品等)
stage-managed *adj.*	精心安排的
stark [stɑːk] *adj.*	(指区别)明显的
cot [kɔt] *n.*	(有围栏的)幼儿床
shoddy [ˈʃɒdɪ] *adj.*	做工粗糙的,劣质的
volte-face *n.*	(意见或计划的)完全转变,大转变

① 均为原产于中国的儿童用品品牌,分别为汪汪日托磁性玩具、蝙蝠侠、波利口袋。

② 伦敦卡斯商学院,位于伦敦的中心地区,它是欧洲领先的商业管理和教育的学院。

salvage ['sælvɪdʒ] *v.* 挽救，挽回

outsource [aut'sɔːs] *v.* 外包

play down 减低……的重要性

let sb. down 让某人失望

Exercises

Exercise 1 Choose the best answer for each of the following questions.

1. How many toys made in China have been recalled by Mattel in recent months?

   A. 15 million. B. 18 million. C. 20 million. D. 21 million.

2. The majority of the toys were deemed unsafe because of ________.

   A. shoddy manufacturing B. high price

   C. design flaws D. lead paints

3. All of the following are the toys that were recalled because they contained small magnets that could be dangerous if swallowed except ________.

   A. Doggie Day Care B. Batman

   C. Polly Pocket D. Harry Potter

4. China conducts ________ Mattel's manufacturing.

   A. two-thirds B. one-third C. one-fourth D. two-fifths

Exercise 2 Fill in each of the blanks with the appropriate words given. Change the form of the word when necessary.

testimony flaw shoddy volte-face humiliating

1. The report reveals fatal ________ in security at the airport.
2. I always complain about bad service or ________ goods.
3. Her claim was supported by the ________ of several witnesses.
4. This represents a ________ in government thinking.
5. It was the most ________ night of his life.

Exercise 3 Translate the following sentences into English.

1. 美国玩具商美泰上周五被迫向中国人民发表了一份谦卑的公开致歉。
2. 与北京打造关系的需要，促成了美泰政策的大转变。
3. 数十年来，美泰一直在亚洲生产玩具，并被视为制造业外包的典范。

Text 27 From "Made in China" to "Invented by China"
从"中国制造"到"中国创造"

导读 能让世界各国政府、各家公司董事会屡感敬畏的是现代中国能够制造出无与伦比的数据的魅力：一是变小数据，如"中国价格"，无论是生活日常用品如袜子还是具有高科技含量的半导体，中国公司总是能让其成本一降再降；二是变大数据，如中国的手机用户一度超越4亿4千万，水泥消费占全球的40%。现在使他们更担忧的是中国人的创新能力。经过20年不屈不挠的努力，中国进入了一个又一个的制造行业，并取得了骄人的业绩，再过20年，中国又将从"中国制造"跨入"中国创造"。眼下一些数据已经足以使他们开始诚恐诚惶：中国的年科研经费已超越日本，仅次于排位第一的美国；中国的专利申请量世界排位已赶上了德国，排世界第五；中国每年培养的具有本科学位的工程师是35万之多，几乎是美国的三倍。

One of the specialties of modern China is an ability to generate statistics that strike fear into governments and boardrooms around the world.

Companies talk endlessly about the "China price"—how Chinese manufacturers have driven down the cost of goods, from socks to semiconductors. At other times it has been the number of mobile phone users in China (440m) or the proportion of world cement it consumes (40 percent).

Now the theme is turning to science. Having spent two decades muscling in on one manufacturing sector after another, China wants to spend the next two decades moving from "Made in China" to "Invented in China." Here, too, it has some numbers to show it is serious.

According to the Organisation for Economic Co-operation and Development, China overtook Japan last year in terms of spending on research and development and ranks in second place behind only the US. In the last decade, R&D has more than doubled as a share of the country's gross domestic product China has also just overtaken Germany in terms of patent filings to stand fifth in international rankings.

Japan and South Korea invested heavily in universities to modernise their economies in the past and China is doing the same. The number of university students has more than quadrupled since 1998 to 16m. While the US produces 137,000 engineers a year with at least a bachelor's degree, China churns out 352,000.

Not only are one-quarter of foreign PhD candidates in the US Chinese but a growing number of them are heading back home: Beijing says 170,000 Chinese who studied abroad have returned, 30,000 of them last year.

Multinationals are lining up to open research centers in China, inspired in part by the abundance of local scientists who are paid only about 20 percent of that which western counterparts receive. Academics estimate that 250 – 300 foreign companies have R&D centres in China.

Having watched first Japan, then South Korea develop knowledge-based economies, China's leaders are in a hurry to do the same, especially given the rapid rise in the country's own labor costs. President Hu Jintao in speeches regularly extols the cause of "independent innovation."

It all looks like another episode in the relentless advance of the Chinese economic juggernaut.[①] Yet beneath the surface, China's science drive faces a host of problems, ranging from academic fraud[②] to weak financial markets. At the corporate level, Chinese innovation remains weak. Having a top-down government plan for fostering innovation is one thing; turning it into reality is a much harder task.

Indeed, the problems are so entrenched that a recent report by CLSA,[③] the regional brokerage, maintains that China lacks the legal and economic environment to foster innovation. It concludes, "China is not an innovative economy and has no innovative companies."

The sheer weight of numbers and scale of the Chinese economy[④] will ensure that some research-based companies come through. But whether it is a trickle or a flood will depend on how well China overcomes these obstacles.

The problems begin with academic research. China may be spending a lot more money in the laboratory but there are big questions about the results. Many potential worries were brought to the fore by a recent scandal at Jiaotong University in Shanghai where Chen Jin, a dean, claimed to have invented a sophisticated form of microchip that could process 200m instructions per second. Instead, an inquiry revealed he had scraped the name off a Motorola product and claimed the work as his own.

The scandal was not as damaging as the one in South Korea involving Hwang Woo-suk, a scientist whose claims to have produced the world's first stem cells cloned from human embryos were revealed to be a fraud. But it did expose the same problem of a government desperate to show off research triumphs. Like Mr Hwang, Mr Chen had been given generous public grants, while the announcement of his chip design was trumpeted at a press conference attended by leading government officials and which made front-page news.

Even before the Jiaotong revelations, Chinese academia was witnessing a slew of allegations about endemic plagiarism and fraudulent research. A Chinese magazine article

---

① 上述种种,似乎是中国经济战车一往无前的又一表现。

② 学术造假

③ 里昂证券(CLSA Asia-Pacific Markets,全名里昂证券有限公司)于1986年创办,总部设于香港,是一家欧资金融机构,主要在亚太区从事证券经纪、投资银行及私人投资业务。

④ 中国经济的数字与规模

exposed academics and students who had created counterfeit versions of respected journals so that it would seem their work had been published.

"People used to think that only officials could be corrupt," says Tang Anguo, director of the higher education institute at East China Normal University in Shanghai. "But I can tell you that in Chinese academia, there are many similar cases [to the Chen one]."

The statistics show quality might be suffering. In 2004, China was in ninth place in the ranking of published scientific papers and a handful of Chinese scientists have made the cover of international journals such as *Nature and Science*. However, China ranked only 124th in the average number of citations per paper—a measure of the modest influence of much of its scientific output.

It is not just the academic research apparatus that needs an overhaul if China is to be more innovative, according to many observers, but also the education system. University teachers say there is too much emphasis on theory and rote learning and insufficient attention given to problem-solving and working in a team. Classes are also overloaded: Some doctoral advisers have more than 50 candidates to supervise.

A report by McKinsey estimates that only 10 percent of the engineering graduates of Chinese universities have the practical and language skills needed to work for a multinational company. The consultancy warns of a looming talent shortage. The Chinese even have a phrase for this type of student—"stuffed ducks" who are good at memorizing facts and passing exams but have little initiative.

With its Confucian heritage①, China places great emphasis on education, but there is also a heavy deference towards authority. Employers regularly complain that although they hire graduates who seem brilliant on paper, it can be very hard to get them to voice opinions. Japan and South Korea all had to overcome this sort of reticence in their young graduates and the Chinese government is trying to address some of these problems. It has introduced changes in the curriculum that emphasize communication and teamwork and a core of elite universities has been established, which will be given additional resources. Yet even top universities operate under very tight budgets.

One of the biggest obstacles to innovation might not be in the lab or the classroom, however, but the fate of stock market. Over the last couple of decades, small private companies have been one of the main engines of innovation, yet China's financial system does not provide enough support to private entrepreneurs. State-controlled groups garner around 75 percent of bank credit in China and dominate the ranks of the 1,300 companies on the stock market.

Although research companies sometimes need years and millions of dollars to get a product to market, China's entrepreneurs often have to raise start-up capital from family members or informal networks of lenders. "Informal networks work really well to set up a

---

① 儒家学说的传统遗产

backyard factory," says Andrew Grant, head of the China practice at McKinsey. "But they do not work if you want to shift to an operation of 1,000 people."

In Japan and South Korea, research has been concentrated in big companies with the resources to take chances, such as Sony or Samsung. But in China the large companies are mostly state-owned and run by executives allergic to taking big risks. "One of the keys will be the financial system," says Andy Rothman, an economist at CLSA who prepared its report on China's science drive. "The question is, can it become a genuine system that allocates funds to private sector companies to fund their own research?"

On top of these obstacles, Chinese innovation faces the further threat of intellectual property theft. The immediate threat to research from patent violations can be exaggerated: Companies are usually more concerned about someone making fakes of a finished product than having secrets stolen from a lab. But both Chinese and foreign groups regularly warn that such legal uncertainties will inhibit investment in knowledge industries.

Against these deep-seated problems, there are two wild cards that could work in China's favour. The first is the role of the multinationals. The extent of multinational research is hard to gauge because some of the R&D centres in China are more about public relations than science. Sylvia Schwaag Serger, science counselor at the Swedish embassy in Beijing, who has written several papers on Chinese research, estimates that only 30 overseas companies are doing innovative research.

In the long run, however, multinationals could provide a strong platform for China's innovation push. A young generation of scientists is being trained at Microsoft, Intel and other leading companies in how to manage complex research projects that span different disciplines, how to establish links with university researchers and how to collaborate with other companies that have niches of expertise①.

Armed with such skills, some of these young scientists are bound to strike out on their own. "There will inevitably be a spill-over from the multinationals into the Chinese economy," says Ms Schwaag Serger.

The other swing factor is the returnees. Of the 30,000 overseas graduates who returned last year, some will have been enticed by government grants and others by the booming economy. Many talk about a patriotic urge to make a contribution to their country. The returnees bring not just the skills they learnt abroad but also a greater willingness to throw ideas around.

"The success of Chinese scientists in the west shows that they can be innovative," says Wang Baoping, research director in China at Novo Nordisk, the Danish diabetes specialist. "What they need is the right environment."

For two decades, the huge Chinese Diaspora has helped accelerate the country's entry into manufacturing, with both capital and management know-how. Now it could provide

① 专有技术所持有的特定市场

the same crucial boost to China's innovation drive.

Words and Expressions

extol [ɪk'stɒl] *v.*	赞扬
entrenched [in'trentʃt] *adj.*	根深蒂固，不容易改的（风俗习惯）
scandal ['skændl] *n.*	丑行，丑闻，诽谤，耻辱，流言蜚语
fraud [frɔːd] *n.*	欺骗，欺诈行为，诡计，骗子，假货
revelation [ˌrevə'leɪʃən] *n.*	显示，揭露，被揭露的事，新发现，启示
academia [ˌækə'diːmjə] *n.*	学术界，学术环境
plagiarism ['pleɪdʒərɪzəm] *n.*	剽窃，剽窃物
overhaul ['əʊvəhɔːl] *n.*	检查
concentrated ['kɒnsntreɪtɪd] *adj.*	集中的，浓缩的
inhibit [ɪn'hɪbɪt] *v.*	抑制，约束
gauge [geɪdʒ] *v.*	测量
returnee [rɪtɜː'niː] *n.*	回国人员，返回者
patent filing	专利申请量
churn out	大量炮制
line up	接二连三
a core of	一批
Chinese diaspora	华侨

Exercises

Exercise 1　Choose the best answer for each of the following questions.

1. According to the Organisation for Economic Co-operation and Development, China overtook ________ last year in terms of spending on research and development and ranks in second place behind only the US.

   A. England　　B. Germany　　C. Japan　　D. Korea

2. Yet beneath the surface, what problems does China's science drive face?

   A. Academic fraud.　　B. Short of money.

   C. Weak financial markets.　　D. A and C.

3. Over the last couple of decades, ________ have been one of the main engines of innovation.

   A. state-controlled groups　　B. small private companies

   C. collective companies　　D. joint venture companies

Exercise 2 Fill in each of the blanks with the appropriate words given. Change the form of the word when necessary.

strike out drive down deep-seated inhibit

1. The corporate giants try to ________ wages in order to make superprofits.
2. There is a deep in-built suspicion of financial institutions based on confusion and a ________ mistrust.
3. Industrial countries tend to support domestic production and thereby ________ imports and encourage exports.
4. The company was ________ in new directions in the field of drama.

Exercise 3 Translate the following sentences into English.

1. 在大学圈子里面，人们普遍认为，政府的不当干预是阻碍学术发展的最大障碍。
2. 在儒家传统的熏陶下，中国对教育非常重视，但也极度尊重权威。
3. 除了上述障碍，中国创新还面临着知识产权剽窃的进一步威胁。

Text 28 The Future of Chinese Global Brands
中国品牌全球化的未来

导读 你身上的运动装与脚下的跑步鞋也许是中国制造，但大多应该是西方公司的著名品牌。可是再过一二十年，中国企业的品牌也将走向世界。中国自有品牌的电子、家电、媒体乃至汽车公司已经在国际市场上崭头露脚，培育世界品牌，开发全球产品。尽管他们国际化的途程将布满艰难险要，但他们的出现将改变美国公司一统天下的市场竞争状况，也将会给全球消费者带来新的品牌、新的产品。中国品牌走向全球有5大途径……

While your workout clothes and running shoes are probably made in China, chances are that they carry a Western brand name. All that's going to change in the coming decade as Chinese companies take their brands global.

Athletic shoes and apparel are just one area where US consumers will start to see Chinese brands popping up, according to the cover story in the *Premier Issue of Change Waves*[①], a new monthly newsletter produced by the DC-based research and consulting futurist firm Social Technologies.

"Chinese electronics, appliances, media, and even automotive companies are developing their international brand presence and globalizing their products," explains futurist John Cashman, author of the article, who runs Social Technologies Shanghai office. "While challenges lie ahead for Chinese companies with global ambitions, over time these rising stars will alter the competitive landscape for US companies and give consumers access to new brands and products."

In the article, Cashman offers five forecasts for the future of Chinese global brands, including the following.

Mergers and acquisitions will yield the most prominent Chinese global brands in the near term—with guidance and funding from the central government, Chinese companies are pursuing a global strategy of acquiring foreign businesses. This allows them to gain both instant expertise and already-known brands, and may be the quickest path for them to own recognized global brands. Example: Lenovo, which bought IBM's personal computer division in 2005.

Many successful Chinese global brands will grow first in the developing world—many

① Social Technologies旗下的一份时事分析月刊。每期都有报告、采访、书评等，涉及人们的日常生活，商业和技术。Social Technologies是一家国际性研究和咨询公司。

Chinese companies are testing the waters in countries where they can capitalize on the appeal of low-cost products. Example: High-tech companies Huawei and ZTE have operations in Africa, India, Brazil, and several Asian countries; appliance maker Haier also has a growing business in several regions including Africa; and Li Ning has opened sporting goods stores in Bulgaria and Russia.

Social Technologies View

Cashman forecasts that while Chinese brands won't overwhelm the global market in the next five years, a few will successfully shed their low-value reputation and become more closely associated with quality, distinctive design, and emotional meaning. In short, they will be branded①.

The 2008 Olympics will be a turning point for Chinese brands. The event will propel some of China's most aggressive brands to the global stage through partnerships and sponsorships. Watch for future leaders and competitors.

US companies can stay ahead of aspiring Chinese firms by focusing on customer service and quality, since these are areas the Chinese have yet to fully master.

Words and Expressions

apparel [ə'pærəl] *n.*	衣服,服饰
newsletter ['njuːzˌletə] *n.*	时事通讯,时事分析
futurist ['fjuːtʃərist] *n.*	未来主义者
merger ['məːdʒə] *n.*	(两个或以上公司的)合并,并吞
overwhelm [ˌəuvə'welm] *v.*	压倒,制服(某人[某事物])(尤指以数量胜);击败
propel [prə'pel] *v.*	推进,推动
pop up	出现,发生(尤指出乎意料)
rising star	新星
test the water	摸清底细
turning point	转折点,转机
watch for	(为某人/某事)注视或监视

Exercises

Exercise 1 Choose the best answer for each of the following questions.

1. According to the passage, which may be the quickest path for Chinese companies to own recognized global brands?

   A. Sponsorship.

---

① 小部分企业将脱掉低声誉的帽子从而成为拥有高质量,独具特色的产品设计以及颇有情感意义的公司。总之,他们会拥有自己的品牌。

B. Paying more attention to customer service and quality of products.

C. Mergers and acquisition.

D. Founding the R & D center abroad.

2. Which of the following is not coincident with the forecasts of John Cashman?

A. US companies are the powerful opponent of Chinese companies.

B. Chinese brand will overwhelm the global market in the next five years.

C. There are great challenges for Chinese brands to be global.

D. Many successful Chinese global brands will grow first in the developing countries.

3. By the example of Huawei, ZTE and Li Ning, the author means that ________.

A. the 2008 Olympics will bring many chances for Chinese companies

B. the future of Chinese global brands is definitely bright

C. many successful Chinese global brands will grow first in the developing world

D. the government of China helps these companies a lot

4. What is the turning point for Chinese brands according to the article?

A. The 2008 Olympics.

B. China entered into WTO.

C. Opening and reform of China in 1987.

D. The meeting of APEC in Shanghai.

5. US companies are better than Chinese companies on ________.

A. employees　　B. business plans

C. promotion　　D. customer service and quality of products

Exercise 2　Fill in each of the blanks with the appropriate words given. Change the form of the word when necessary.

merger　overwhelm　propel　sponsorship

1. The British Air Force succeeded despite ________ odds against them.

2. The company offers integrated business applications in various ways. Now, it is our National Badminton Team's major ________.

3. Company directors were ________ into action.

4. Enterprises that don't have the heft or profits for a splashy initial public offering are finding they can get a coveted overseas listing through a reverse ________.

Exercise 3　Translate the following sentences into English.

1. 研究显示,中国仍是全球第二大经济体,但其人均国内生产总值只有美国的 9.8%。(GDP)

2. 购买力平价被视为衡量相对生活成本的更好尺度,因为它的衡量基础是各个家庭用本国货币所能购买的商品和服务。(PPP,the relative cost of living)

3. 美国消费者的购物兴趣正在减弱。(shy away from)

Chapter Four China's Buying

中国采购

Text 29 China Digs for Raw Materials to Sustain Fast Growth

中国觅求全球资源以维持快速发展

导读 长期以来中国在制造方面具有无与伦比的竞争力。眼下中国公司正在采用同样的竞争方法来提高矿产采掘与原材料精炼产量，以满足国内日益膨胀的需求并利用大宗商品价格高涨之机进行牟利。对自然资源的狂热追求不仅蔓延到国有企业马鞍山钢铁厂附近的荒山区域与位于安徽其他地区的私人矿区，也触及到千里之外的澳洲铁矿区与非洲苏丹油田。

China has long excelled at manufacturing. Now its companies are applying the same ruthless business methods to increasing production of mined and refined raw materials, in an effort to meet swelling domestic demand and cash in on high commodities prices.

This resources mini-boom has produced scores of mines like the one under construction in the rough hills near the Ma'anshan Steelworks in central China, where gangs of workers are racing to dig up enough iron ore to meet the company's target of doubling steel output within three years.

Even amid this frenzy of growth, executives at the state-owned Ma'anshan cast a jealous eye at the breakneck expansion of privately-owned mines elsewhere in Anhui province.

"We are making a stable transition from old to new mines, to make sure that our dependence on imports will not increase," says Cui Xian, in charge of mining at Ma'anshan, China's ninth largest steelmaker. "But the private mines can go even faster. They only have to choose an area where it is easy to mine."

China's hunger for natural resources is being felt around the world, from the iron ore mines of outback Australia① to the oil fields of Sudan, and has been a big factor in forcing up global prices to generational highs. But along with this has come the rush to lift output

① 澳大利亚内地的铁矿。澳大利亚的铁矿总储量为350亿吨，是世界上最大的铁矿资源国之一。

at home. State enterprises like Ma'anshan have raced to tie up resource deposits but the greatest impetus has come from private companies.

China's much publicized forays offshore in search of raw materials, and oil in particular, to feed the double-digit annual growth of its economy have overshadowed the fact that it remains a continent rich in many resources itself. About 90 percent of China's primary energy needs are supplied locally.

Although that figure will decline over time as oil imports rise, it still sets China apart from neighbors such as Japan and South Korea, which have relied almost entirely on imports and nuclear power. Local producers have heftily lifted domestic output of alumina, copper, zinc, coking coal, lead and iron ore[①] over the past 12 months.

The same advantages enjoyed by Chinese manufacturing are at work in the resources sector. Producers have access to cheap capital and labor and pliant local governments desperate to attract business to their regions.

The expansion has also produced the same problems that bedevil China's economic development in general. Coal mining accidents kill around 5,000 workers a year, although reliable figures are elusive. Mines have wreaked havoc on the environment. In addition, the jump in domestic output has for some minerals brought global prices down, just as Chinese overcapacity in manufacturing has for consumer goods.

The central government has also boosted the resources sector, by giving freer rein to entrepreneurs and, to a limited extent, foreign investors, in order to kick-start production and help meet demand. Until recently, the resources sector was largely closed to both local private and foreign investment.

Alumina, the powder refined from bauxite that is used to make aluminum, has seen the most explosive growth. High global prices and a decision by the government to allow private entrants into a market long dominated by a state monopoly is projected to ruthlessly push Chinese production up from about 4.3m tonnes a year in 2000 to more than 27m tonnes by the end of the decade. The government protected the alumina monopoly enjoyed by the state-controlled Chalco[②] before and after its overseas initial public offering in late 2001, to ensure the listing was successful.

But when local smelters complained about how shortages of alumina were driving up prices and leaving them short of the raw material, the government opened up the industry.

With potentially huge profits to be gained from getting alumina to the market quickly, private companies, with the support of local governments, poured money into new plants. So rapidly did production rise that China will go from being an importer of 7m tonnes of alumina in 2005 to a position of balance in 2008.

---

① 氧化铝、铜、锌、焦炭煤、铅和铁

② 中国铝业贵州分公司，它在2002年从被誉为中国铝业排头兵的贵州铝厂分立出来，有资产总额71.24亿元。

"It had been in the making for about two years, but once it was unleashed, it came through in a torrent," says Jim Lennon, of Macquarie Research, in London.

With little need for the kind of feasibility studies required by multinationals to test their business and environmental cases, the plants were built cheaply and quickly. "Before I visited the sites, I could not believe how quickly they went up. I had to see it with my own eyes," says a local metals consultant.

The explosion in production of alumina has reverberated around the world and blown back into China itself. Global prices have slid from a high of $650 (£329) a tonne earlier this year to about $250 now. As a result, many of the plants built in the past two years, which are uneconomic at below $300 a tonne, will have to close.

The rapid construction of iron ore mines, prompted by a 70 percent increase in global contract prices in 2005, also comes with a self-destruct button. The new mines, which have pushed Chinese production up by about 40 percent this year, are mainly in drought-stricken northern China and use scarce water.

On top of this, the focus on quick profits and the poor quality of Chinese ore—about 10 tonnes of dirt need to be dug up to find a tonne of ore—is devastating the environment around the mines. In the short term, however, the mines have delivered fat profits.

"Based on current market prices, the rule of thumb is a one-year return period on equipment investment and a three-year return period on total investment," says a Macquarie Research report. Unlike in developed countries, the Chinese private mines do not need to factor in the cost of cleaning up the site after it has been mined out.

Ma'anshan says it will double its production of iron ore by the end of the decade, with each new mine taking three to five years from feasibility to production. But Ma'anshan is in the slow lane compared with the privately-owned Dachang Mine Corp. nearby, which can commission and open a mine in half the time.

Dachang is on track to boost output from the 1.4m tonnes of iron ore mined last year to 5m tonnes in 2010. Chai Yansong, a senior mine manager, proclaims, "Our aim is to be one of the top 10 iron ore producers in China by the end of the decade."

Words and Expressions

amid [ə'mɪd] *prep.* 在……中
rush [rʌʃ] *n.* 大量急需,争购
impetus ['ɪmpɪtəs] *n.* 动力,刺激
overshadow [ˌəʊvə'ʃædəʊ] *v.* 使……显得逊色,遮盖
pliant ['plaɪənt] *adj.* 温顺的,容易摆布的
bedevil [bɪ'devl] *v.* 长期搅扰
elusive [ɪ'luːsɪv] *adj.* 难以捕捉的,难以掌握的,逃避的,躲避的
havoc ['hævək] *n.* 大破坏,浩劫

overcapacity [ˌəʊvəkəˈpæsətɪ] *n.* 生产能力过剩
rein [reɪn] *n.* 控制，主宰
entrepreneur [ˌɒntrəprəˈnɜː] *n.* 创业者，企业家
kick-start *v.* 使……尽快启动
monopoly [məˈnɒpəlɪ] *n.* 垄断，专利
unleash [ʌnˈliːʃ] *v.* 放开，发动
torrent [ˈtɒrənt] *n.* 激流，洪流
reverberate [rɪˈvɜːbəreɪt] *v.* 产生广泛的影响
scarce [skeəs] *adj.* 缺乏的，稀少的
devastate [ˈdevəsteɪt] *v.* 彻底破坏
commission [kəˈmɪʃn] *v.* 正式委托
cash in on 从中牟利

Exercises

Exercise 1 Choose the best answer for each of the following questions.

1. The greatest impetus of resource deposits has come from ________.
   A. state enterprises B. private companies
   C. central government D. resource imports
2. Which of the following advantage is inaccessible to the producers ?
   A. Low taxation. B. Cheap capital.
   C. Pliant local governments. D. Cheap labor.
3. According to the article, the domestic output of ________ have not been heftily lifted over the past year.
   A. alumina and coking coal B. bronze and tin
   C. zinc and iron ore D. lead and copper
4. The expansion has produced the following problems except ________.
   A. devastating the environment B. coal mining accidents
   C. overcapacity in manufacturing D. increases of imports

Exercise 2 Fill in each of the blanks with the appropriate words given. Change the form of the word when necessary.

havoc unleash kick-start elusive foray reverberate commission

1. The company's first ________ into the computer market is a success.
2. The government's proposals ________ a storm of protest in the press.
3. Continuing strikes are beginning to play ________ with the national economy.
4. The government's attempt to ________ the economy has failed.
5. A solution to the problem of toxic waste is proving ________ in the extreme.

Exercise 3 Translate the following sentences into English.

1. 去年因生产成本降低，利润有所增加。
2. 电、煤气和水垄断经营过去被认为是自然而然的。
3. 这件事持续影响着整个金融界。

Text 30 Ramping up Investment All Round
中国投入巨资 寻求海外能源

导读 伴随着神华集团融资规模达662亿人民币并在首日上市交易时大涨87%，以及中石油创造全球IPO纪录，融资规模达668亿人民币，成为全球市值最大的公司，中国已奠定其全球第二大石油及能源消费国的地位。中国持续强劲的经济增长，意味着能源消耗将不断上升，然而国内的能源储备远不能满足日益上升的需求，因此中国正在对任何潜在的能源来源加大投资并将触角伸向海外。在未来10年内，中国将有40%以上石油和煤炭以及50%以上天然气需从国外进口。中国能源巨头如中石化、中石油、中海油均清一色国字头，全进入全球500强行列，他们资本实力雄厚，业务布满全球，具有寻求海外能源的超强实力。

If Chinese domestic investor sentiment is anything to go by, the local energy sector is in for boom times. In October, a unit of the Shenhua Group, China's largest coal company, raised $8.9bn in an initial public offering in Shanghai. Until this week, it was the largest IPO in the world this year, but it was 30 times oversubscribed[①], locking up about $350bn in funds during the lottery for shares, and then jumped an astounding 87 percent on the first day of trading.

Later, PetroChina[②], a unit of China National Petroleum Corp[③], surpassed Shenhua's landmark when it became the first company in the world to be valued at more than $1,000bn after a dramatic stock market debut in Shanghai. The stock market was already buffeted in the run-up to the IPO, with share prices falling as investors sell stock to enter the PetroChina lottery.

China is already the world's second-largest oil and energy consumer. As a result of a surge in investment in capital-intensive and energy-hungry industries[④] since 2000, energy consumption has grown disproportionately to gross domestic product this decade. The use of coal, for example, China's primary fuel, has doubled in the past five years, mainly to fuel a surge in construction of power plants. The power plants, in turn, have been required less for the household consumer than to drive the huge numbers of new steel, cement and aluminum plants.

---

① 超额认购

② 中石油

③ 中国石油天然气集团公司

④ capital-intensive industry 资金密集型产业；energy-hungry industry 高耗能产业

The government has set tough energy efficiency benchmarks[1] for industry, which have—so far—not been met, and is trying to impose European-style fuel standards[2] for vehicles. But for all its efforts to moderate consumption, China's continued powerful economic growth means that energy use will keep rising.

China recognized as long ago as 1993, when it became a net oil importer, that it would have to globalize both its search for energy and the lumbering state-owned industry. Companies such as PetroChina, Sinopec, CNOOC[3] and Shenhua, now featuring in the Fortune 500, were all formed in the late 1990s as part of efforts to build globally-competitive enterprises. All of them, aside perhaps from Shenhua, which is blessed with huge coal reserves at home, have proceeded to build large overseas portfolios. And all of them, including Shenhua, have listed overseas, submitting themselves to the disciplines of global capital markets.

On top of coal, gas and oil, China is ramping up investment in just about any potential source of energy available to it. Nuclear power; coal-to-liquids; coal-bed methane gas; liquefied natural gas[4] and wind power—all are expanding rapidly.

In some respects, the most powerful operators in the sector are the energy companies themselves. All state-owned, their bosses enjoy ministerial-level status and trappings[5]. When they were formed, much of their expertise came out of the existing government bureaucracy.

The regulator, the energy bureau in the planning ministry, the National Development and Reform Commission[6], is small and understaffed by comparison, something the government may finally rectify in the next 12 months. A draft energy law to allow the creation of an energy ministry could be submitted to the cabinet this year, laying the ground for legislation to complete the process.

The companies have been given a degree of licence to go offshore in search of energy assets, but at home they are constrained by numerous regulations, most importantly the government's power to set prices.

The price controls, which have turned into a price freeze in the last six months of this year, as part of a raft of measures to control inflation, have prompted an almost annual stand-off between the government and Sinopec, the main refiner, in recent years. The last time China raised prices at the pump[7] 17 months ago.

With the government declining to allow local prices to rise in line with global levels,

---

① 能耗指标

② 欧洲燃油标准

③ CNNOOC (China National Offshore Oil Corporation)中海油

④ coal-to-liquids 煤变油;coal-bed methane gas 煤层气;liquefied natural gas(LNG)液化天然气

⑤ 部长级地位和待遇

⑥ 国家发改委

⑦ 成品油价格

refiners have been losing tens of millions of dollars on imported oil. At the year's end, they have usually been compensated out of public funds.

In the meantime, however, the companies play cat-and-mouse with the government, cutting production, to register their displeasure with government policy, resulting in embarrassing shortages.

Another area of tension has been over liquefied natural gas, which also flowed from price controls. Despite huge demand from richer coastal cities for LNG, as a clean-burning fuel, the controls made signing long-term contracts uneconomic when global prices began to rise rapidly in about 2002. The NDRC also ordered state companies to enter into long-term contracts only if they were able to secure equity in the resource itself.

But in a series of deals signed this year in Australia, PetroChina bucked the NDRC's guidelines, signing contracts at global prices, and without purchasing equity. Such market-driven behaviour is likely to become increasingly the norm.

Words and Expressions

debut ['deɪbjuː] *n.*	初次登场（文中指首日交易）
buffet ['bʌfɪt] *n.*	冲击
disproportionate [ˌdɪsprə'pɔːʃənɪt] *adj.*	不成比例的，不均衡的
lumbering ['lʌmbərɪŋ] *adj.*	动作迟缓的
list [lɪst] *v.*	（股票）上市
understaffed [ˌʌndə'stɑːft] *adj.*	人员不足的
rectify ['rektɪfaɪ] *v.*	调整
stand-off *n.*	对立
equity ['ekwətɪ] *n.*	股权
market-driven *adj.*	市场主导的
market sentiment	市场行情
power plant	发电厂
net import	净进口
overseas portfolios	海外投资组合
submit to	服从；提交

Exercises

Exercise 1　Choose the best answer for each of the following questions.

1. Which company was the first one in the world to be valued at more than ＄1,000bn?

   A. Shenhua Group.　　B. PetroChina.　　C. Sinopec.　　D. CNOOC.

2. Why is there a surge in construction of power plants?

   A. For the household consumer.

B. For more steel, cement and aluminum plants.

C. For the government buildings.

D. For more schools.

3. All of the following are the potential source of energy mentioned in the passage except ________.

   A. nuclear power   B. coal-to-liquids   C. LNG   D. solar energy

4. Which of the following statements is true according to the passage?

   A. As a result of a surge in investment in labor-intensive and energy-hungry industries, energy consumption has grown proportionately to gross domestic product this decade.

   B. Companies such as PetroChina, Sinopec, CNOOC and Shenhua have all proceeded to build large overseas portfolios.

   C. The price controls have prompted an almost annual stand-off between the government and Sinopec.

   D. The NDRC also ordered state companies to enter into short-term contracts only if they were able to secure equity in the resource itself.

Exercise 2 Fill in each of the blanks with the appropriate words given. Change the form of the word when necessary.

in turn   lay the ground   give a degree of   be blessed with   on top of

1. He gets commission ________ his salary.
2. Increased production will, ________, lead to increased profits.
3. She ________ excellent health.
4. Years of hard work have ________ for his success.
5. The companies have ________ license to go offshore in search of energy assets.

Exercise 3 Translate the following sentences into English.

1. 新债券的认购已超额了。
2. 每年加薪幅度将与通货膨胀挂钩。
3. 在某些方面，能源行业最强大的运营商就是能源企业自身。

Text 31 Airbus in $17.4b Deal with China

来自中国的巨额订单飞向空中客车

导读 一笔高达174亿美元购买欧洲空客商用飞机的巨额订单在法国总统萨科齐访问中国之时正式签订。萨科齐总统抵达北京的第二天中法两国又趁热打铁签订了一项建造两座价值118亿美元核反应堆的合同。如此“大手笔”的巨额合同着实让浪漫的法国人深感“不虚此行”。

China has signed an €11.7 billion ($17.4 billion) deal for 160 commercial planes from Airbus[①], a spokeswoman for the European aerospace giant has told CNN.

The announcement of the deal coincides with a state visit by French President Nicolas Sarkozy to China.

The second day of Sarkozy's trip provided a further boost for French business as the French firm Areva[②] secured a contract to build two nuclear reactors.

According to the French daily newspaper *Le Monde*, the deal with the China Guangdong Nuclear Power Corporation (CGNPC) in southern China is worth €8 billion ($11.8 billion).

Amelia Xu, a senior communications officer with Airbus, which is based in the French southern city of Toulouse[③], said the company had negotiated two deals.

The first deal is to provide 150 aircraft to the China Aviation Supplies Export and Import Group[④]. The second will mean the delivery of 10 planes to China Southern Airlines, Xu said.

The Airbus deal is for the manufacturer's medium-sized aircraft, including 110 of its A320s[⑤] and 50 A330s[⑥].

The deal will not, however, be for any of the new A380[⑦] super jumbo jets that went into service earlier this year.

The agreements were signed after the French President met with Chinese Chairman

---

① 欧洲空中客车公司创建于1970年，是一家集法国、德国、西班牙与英国公司为一体的欧洲集团，总部设在法国图卢兹。空客公司是世界领先的大型民用客机制造商。

② AREVA(阿海珐)集团是一家法国核工业公司，全球500强企业之一，是世界排名第一的核能企业。

③ 图卢兹，法国南部城市，空客公司总部所在地。

④ 中国航空器材进出口集团公司(CASGC)

⑤⑥⑦ A320、A330、A380均为欧洲空客公司研制的客机系列。

Hu Jintao in the Great Hall of the People, inside the Chinese parliament building in Beijing. Sarkozy arrived in China Sunday seeking to boost trade and bilateral ties.

His three-day visit was also expected to address key international issues including the environment and Iran.

The French leader told the Chinese news agency Xinhua ahead of the visit that he was counting on China's support in preventing Iran from acquiring nuclear weapons.

Words and Expressions

boost [buːst] *v.*	推进，提高
coincide with	符合（一致，与……重合），同时发生
secure a contract	订立合同
negotiate a deal	达成交易
jumbo jets	大型喷气式客机
go into service	投入使用
bilateral ties	双边关系
news agency	通讯社
count on	依靠，指望

Exercises

Exercise 1 Choose the best answer for each of the following questions.

1. China has signed an €11.7 billion ($17.4 billion) deal for 160 commercial planes from Airbus, whose HQ is located in ________.
   A. Paris　　B. Marseilles　　C. Toulouse　　D. Lyons
2. The deal is to provide 10 aircrafts to ________.
   A. China Aviation Supplies Export and Import Group
   B. China Southern Airlines
   C. China Southeast Airlines
   D. China Airlines

Exercise 2 Fill in each of the blanks with the appropriate words given. Change the form of the word when necessary.

boost　secure　negotiation　forge　deteriorate　separate

1. The company has ________ a new contract with its staff.
2. All the people who know this secret represent a ________ risk.
3. Our integrity as a nation is threatened by these ________ forces.
4. The ship ________ ahead under a favorable wind.
5. The physical ________ of the manufacturing class in England was still noticeable in the

1930s, more than a century after the height of the Industrial Revolution.

6. The publication of this book ________ my confidence.

Exercise 3 Translate the following sentences into English.

1. 会上,这个候选人向听众发表了雄辩的演说。
2. 经过双方协商,他们最终成功订立了合同。
3. 经过长达一年的研发阶段,新机器已于去年 10 月投入使用。

Text 32 Ultra-luxury Cars Enjoy Fast Sales Growth in China

超豪华汽车"井喷"中国市场

导读 拥有一辆高级轿车，乃至一辆超豪华汽车已成为中国有钱人的时尚。BMW 旗下的英国豪华车制造商劳斯莱斯宣称今年将向包括香港市场在内的中国提供 70 辆幻影超豪华轿车，使中国市场一举超越日本成为继美国、英国之后的劳斯莱斯第三大市场。另一制造高档汽车公司奔驰集团也宣称其旗下的迈巴赫(Maybach)高档车在中国销量也将翻番，一辆限量版超豪华 Maybach's 62 在北京的零售价竟达 100 万美元之多。

How are rich people in China showing off their success?

Owning one or more luxury and even ultra-expensive cars appears to be one of the most popular ways.

Boosted by the ever-increasing numbers of people getting rich as a result of the nation's booming economy, demand for these cars is in the fast lane, offering rich pickings for the world's top luxury carmakers.

British brand Rolls Royce[①], owned by German carmaker BMW[②], said it expects to sell 70 Phantom vehicles this year in China including Hong Kong which will enable the world's most populous country to unseat Japan as the firm's No 3 single market after the United States and the United Kingdom.

On Thursday in Hong Kong, Rolls Royce delivered its largest order yet—14 Phantoms to Sir Michael Kadoorie's Peninsula Hotel[③].

To further boost China sales, the brand plans to add three dealerships in Hangzhou, Shenzhen and Chengdu. It now has one each in Shanghai, Beijing and Guangzhou.

In a telephone interview on Friday, Jenny Zheng, general manager of Rolls Royce Motor Cars Greater China, said, "China's thriving economy is creating very successful people in all business areas at a staggering pace. This is a big opportunity for us and other luxury car manufacturers."

"The more important thing is that our customers here are much younger than those in other markets," Zheng said.

Rolls Royce owners in China are on average more than 10 years younger than elsewhere,

---

① 劳斯莱斯汽车公司，它是著名的英国豪华汽车制造商。

② 德国宝马汽车公司，它是驰名世界的汽车企业，也被认为是高档汽车生产业的先导。

③ 米高嘉道理爵士旗下的半岛酒店，它位于香港，一直以来都被誉为世界最佳酒店之一。

she added.

Maybach①, another ultra-luxury car brand, which is controlled by Mercedes Car Group②, is also enjoying fast sales growth in China.

Anthea Wang, a spokeswoman of Mercedes China, said, "Maybach's sales here will more than double this year from 2005," but she declined to reveal a specific figure. "China is very close to one of Maybach's top five markets in the world," she said.

To lure Chinese buyers, Maybach's 62 Special Edition made its global debut at last month's Beijing international auto show. The model retails in China for a cool $1 million.

Maybach now has two exhibition and sales centres in Beijing and Shanghai. Wang said it is considering building a third centre in Guangzhou "in the near future."

Many of the ultra-luxury cars displayed at the 10-day Beijing auto show were sold, raising more than 100 million *yuan* ($12.8 million), a fact that demonstrates the immense purchasing power of rich Chinese people.

However, Yale Zhang, the Shanghai-based director of emerging markets vehicle forecasts for auto consultancy CSM③ Asia in Shanghai, said ultra-luxury cars will account for a tiny ratio of China's entire vehicle market as only those super rich people will buy them.

Words and Expressions

thrive [θraɪv] *v.*	繁荣,兴旺,蓬勃发展
staggering [ˈstæɡərɪŋ] *adj.*	惊人的,难以置信的
cool [kuːl] *adj.*	(俚语)整整的,满满的
immense [ɪˈmens] *adj.*	极大的,巨大的
the fast lane	快车道
Special Edition	特款,特别版;号外,专刊
account for	占

Exercises

Exercise 1 Choose the best answer for each of the following questions.

1. The top three markets of Rolls Royce are US, UK and ________.

   A. Japan B. China C. France D. Switzerland

2. The features of China's ultra-luxury car market are including following except ________.

   A. the customers are much younger than those in other markets

---

① 迈巴赫,在1921年到1940年间它曾是活跃于欧洲地区的德国超豪华汽车品牌与制造厂,从属于梅赛德斯汽车集团。迈巴赫可以说是当代豪华礼车品牌的巨擘之一。

② 梅赛德斯汽车集团,它属于戴姆勒·克莱斯勒集团。

③ 汽车行业咨询机构,CSM是Customer Service Management(客户服务管理)的缩写。

B. ultra-luxury cars will account for a large ratio of China's entire vehicle market as China is very prosperous now

C. ultra-luxury cars enjoy fast sales growth in China

D. the competition between the ultra-luxury car manufactures will become fiercer than before

3. What don't the ultra-luxury car manufactures do to expand their business?

A. Opening auto shows.

B. Adding dealerships in metropolitan cities.

C. Building more centers.

D. Cutting the price down.

Exercise 2　Fill in each of the blanks with the appropriate words given. Change the form of the word when necessary.

immense　stagger　debut　boost　lure

1. An advertising program to ________ local products abroad is necessary for this company.
2. Industry often seeks to ________ scientists from universities by offering them huge salaries.
3. What they have achieved within my lifetime is ________.
4. The government will be building new hotels, an ________ stadium, and a fine new swimming pool.
5. The ________ of a new foreign policy will improve the relationship of the two countries.

Exercise 3　Translate the following sentences into English.

1. 作为克莱斯勒汽车和菲亚特的合作伙伴，奇瑞汽车被普遍认为具有最强的研发能力，有着中国汽车生产行业的最强阵容。
2. 随着中国经济的繁荣，以及世界上很多大国对汽车需求的迅速增加，绝大多数中国的汽车品牌近几年都取得了比较大的发展。
3. 针对这种华而不实的浮夸，汽车行业咨询机构 CSM 的分析师认为，"他们只是在试图吸引公众的关注。"

Text 33 China's Hunger for Luxury Goods Grows
面对奢侈品,中国的胃口越来越大

导读 随着中国经济的发展,购买力的提升,越来越多的消费者开始注重生活品质的提高,对奢侈品的需求呈现出不断膨胀的趋势。各大国际奢侈品品牌为此纷纷涌入中国市场,从名车到名表,从珠宝到首饰,再从高档烟酒到名牌服装,纷至沓来。一辆宾利雅致728超豪华车在北京的售价为120万美元,为世界第一价;卡地亚(Jeweler Cartier)的一款钻石项链在中国售出了300万美元的天价。目前中国已是世界第三大奢侈品市场,预计到2015年,中国将超过日本跃居成为世界第二大奢侈品消费国。

China is on a spending spree[①] for luxury goods, and it has only just begun.

The country is now the third-biggest consumer of luxury goods, accounting for 12 percent of sales worldwide, up from 1 percent just five years ago, according to a recent report from Goldman Sachs. If the high living continues as expected, China will surpass Japan to become the world's second-largest purchaser of luxury goods by 2015, when it could account for 29 percent of the world's luxury sales, the report said.

"There's a lot of prestige buying in China now," said Edward Bell, director of planning in Beijing for the Ogilvy advertising firm. "People who buy luxury brands see the products as extensions of themselves everywhere, but in China this is taken very seriously."

Consider: British carmaker Bentley[②] has sold more Mulliner 728 limousines, at $1.2 million the world's most expensive car, in Beijing than in any other city in the world. Also, Chinese yuppies, known as chippies, bought 23,600 BMWs last year, 50 percent more than in 2004. With about 5.2 million potential luxury car buyers, China, industry analysts say, could soon become the world's largest buyer of luxury automobiles.

Some of the spending is driven by China's growing number of millionaires. The country now has 300,000 people with a net worth of more than a $1 million each, according to Merrill Lynch & Co.[③] But young urban salaried workers are also lapping up luxury goods. Yang Qingshan, secretary-general of the China Brand Association[④], recently said

---

① 无节制的疯狂开销

② 本特利(Bentley)于1920年创建了他的汽车公司,开始设计制造他多年来梦寐以求的运动车。

③ 美林公司,世界最著名的证券零售商和投资银行之一,总部位于美国纽约,是世界最大的金融管理咨询公司之一。

④ 中国国际品牌协会,成立于2003年。中国国际品牌协会的主要任务是大力培育中国国际品牌,使之走向世界,积极参与国际品牌竞争。

about 13 percent of China's population, or 170 million people, now buy top-tier brands.

Luxury goods companies have launched sumptuous marketing campaigns, and chic advertisements for pricey foreign goods cram most magazines. Jeweler Cartier, whose China revenues almost doubled last year, a period in which it sold a single diamond necklace for $3 million, recently created a massive ice replica of its flagship Paris store[①] at the famous winter festival in northern Harbin city, and company executives said they soon expect to have 30 stores in China, second only to the number in the United States.

In fact, nearly every company active in China's $1.2 billion-a-year luxury goods market has said it plans to expand, and glass-and-granite boutiques hawking fashionably rumpled Italian suits are springing up even in less prestigious cities such as Shenyang in northeastern Liaoning province.

Parts of Chinese culture have always been fond of money and the things it can buy. Ritualistic and traditional symbols for prosperity, such as fish, adorn almost every palace, temple, school, office building, and home. No Chinese festival is complete without paying due homage to *qian*, or money.

"Money is the new god in China today," said Dr. Ding Ningning, director of social studies at the Development Research Center of the State Council. "People are in a selfish mood. They want to show off and be extravagant."

The Hurun Report, a socialite magazine in Shanghai, recently interviewed 600 Chinese millionaires to identify their preferred brands. Christie's was voted the best auctioneer, Vacheron Constantin the best watch, Davidoff the best cigar, Giorgio Armani the best designer, Hennessy, Chivas Regal, and Dom Perignon the best liquors, Princess the best yacht, and Ferrari the best sports car.

With China's economy continuing to boom, luxury marketers are counting on escalating profits, except for one big problem—the plethora of anonymous factories that spin out imitation $5,000 suits for $50 a piece.

At a recent luxury goods industry conference in Hong Kong, companies said China's lack of a system of intellectual property rights is the biggest problem they face in the country. Rip-offs aside, Chinese companies have also taken several international brand names for themselves. For example, there are 200 different "Valentino" brands in China, said Valeria Azario, an executive with V. S. Ltd., which manages the original Italian Valentino brand.

Recently, a group of luxury brand owners—Burberry, Chanel, Gucci, Louis Vuitton, and Prada[②]—tried a novel approach to cracking down on fakes. Since the factories producing these goods are difficult to locate, they tried to get China's new justice system to

---

① 巴黎的旗舰店,即规模最大的店。

② Burberry, Chanel, Gucci, Louis Vuitton, and Prada 均为奢侈品牌,分别是巴宝丽、香奈儿、古奇、路易威登和普拉达。

clamp down on markets where the fakes are sold. The luxury goods makers had some success but few expect them to thwart the imitators any time soon.

But there is still expected to be a growing market for the real thing. Paul McGowan, chief executive of Added Value, a division of the advertising firm WPP[①], recently said his organization's research showed that Chinese tend to buy luxury products without a lot of study or research.

"China is still in its infancy and it's still status and show that are the main market drivers" of luxury sales, McGowan said.

Some rich Chinese consumers readily confess they like to walk out of a shop knowing they've overpaid. Said Isabella Ma, 32, wife of a wealthy electronics manufacturer in Beijing, "Why be shy to confess it."

Words and Expressions

spree [spriː] *n.*	无节制的狂热行为
surpass [sɜːˈpɑːs] *v.*	超过,胜过
prestige [presˈtiːʒ] *n.*	影响力,魅力,威望
yuppie [ˈjʌpɪ] *n.*	城市少壮职业人士,雅皮士
top-tier *adj.*	顶级的
sumptuous [ˈsʌmptʃʊəs] *adj.*	奢侈的,豪华的
chic [ʃiːk] *adj.*	漂亮的,雅致的
flagship [ˈflæɡʃɪp] *n.*	旗舰;最佳者,王牌
hawk [hɔːk] *v.*	兜售,叫卖
rumple [ˈrʌmpl] *v.*	弄皱,压皱
ritualistic [ˌrɪtʃʊəˈlɪstɪk] *adj.*	惯常的,仪式主义的
extravagant [ɪkˈstrævəɡənt] *adj.*	奢侈的,铺张的,浪费的
auctioneer [ˌɔːkʃəˈnɪə] *n.*	拍卖商
yacht [jɒt] *n.*	快艇
escalate [ˈeskəleɪt] *adj.*	迅猛上升的
plethora [ˈpleθərə] *n.*	过多,过剩
rip-off *n.*	伪劣便宜货;乱开价的高价物
locate [ləʊˈkeɪt] *v.*	探明,找到
thwart [θwɔːt] *v.*	阻挠,反对,挫败
lap up	贪婪地追求;热爱
ice replica	钻石仿品
spring up	涌现,迅速萌发
crack down on	制裁,对……严打

① 英国最大的广告与传播集团,全球广告业收入排名第3位。

clamp down on　　　　　　　　取缔，严格限制

Exercises

Exercise 1　Choose the best answer for each of the following questions.

1. China is now the ________ biggest buyer of luxury goods.

   A. second　　B. third　　C. fourth　　D. fifth

2. According to Edward Bell's words, which of the following sentence is true?

   A. In China, people who buy luxury brands see the products as extensions of themselves everywhere.

   B. In China, people buy luxury brands just because they want to use their money.

   C. In China, people are in a selfish mood, and they want to show off and be extravagant.

   D. In China, people often lap up luxury goods for fun.

3. Which is not the reason that makes Chinese rush to buy luxury goods?

   A. China's growing number of millionaires.

   B. Luxury goods companies have launched sumptuous marketing campaigns.

   C. Parts of Chinese culture have always been fond of money and the things it can buy.

   D. People in China want to turn the country into an agrarian utopia.

4. There are ________ different "Valentino" brands in China.

   A. 100　　B. 200　　C. 300　　D. 400

Exercise 2　Fill in each of the blanks with the appropriate words given. Change the form of the word when necessary.

prestige　extravagant　rumple　escalate　spring up

1. What started as a small difficulty has ________ into a major crisis.
2. The ________ conferred in many cultures has a professional job, such as a doctor or lawyer.
3. Towns had ________ in what had been a dry desert.
4. In many places of China, people often complain about the government's ________.
5. We could see from the ________ sheets that the bed had been slept in.

Exercise 3　Translate the following sentences into English.

1. 中国消费者越来越愿意购买大件，如住房、汽车分期付款。
2. 导致中国对奢侈品牌缺乏认识的另一个结果是该品牌在其国内没有影响，但在中国却被认为是奢侈品牌。

Text 34 China Border Town: Gateway to Cheap Vietnam Resources
昔日宁静边镇,如今喧闹商埠

导读 历程30年的中国改革开放触及到神州大江南北,连昔日边疆小镇也沐浴在经济蓬勃发展的金色阳光之中。浦寨位于广西凭祥市西南端,与越南国境相连,遥远望去它仅是一个普通铁路的交叉口,看不出是通往世界著名边民易货通商之地。一辆辆满载大米、橡胶、木薯淀粉、咖啡、煤炭、铝钒矿等无所不有的卡车源源不断过境驶入世界第四大经济大国,隆隆驶向相反方向邻国的是满车的摩托车与机电部件。一个昔日宁静的小镇如今已成为连接中越乃至中国与东南亚贸易互市的大商埠。

At a dusty border crossing on a remote section of the China-Vietnam border, Puzhai[①] looks more like a railway crossing than an entry point into the world's most resource-ravenous economy.

Trucks ferrying every commodity imaginable—rice, rubber, tapioca, coffee, coal and bauxite—stream across the border into the world's fourth-largest economy. Motorcycles and machine parts rumble across in the other direction.

Puzhai is just a small border crossing but it heralds the future of trade in this region of China, which is bent on boosting a free flow of goods with its neighbors in Southeast Asia to keep raw materials flowing and its economy on track.

China needs all the raw materials it can get hold of to power an economy roaring ahead at more than 10 percent a year. And it's at the threadbare—and unofficial—Puzhai border that resource buyers save on import duties—one way or the other.[②]

"Things are getting busier and busier," said a man who gave his name only as Wei and has run a shop hawking Vietnamese wares at the border for the past decade.

Pointing to the trucks queuing amid the swirling dust of the deceptively low-key crossing, the vendor said, "Those are for minerals. Trucks for farm products look different."

Guangxi, the poor southern autonomous region left behind by the country's economic growth, hopes to cash in on a free trade agreement between China and the Association of

① 浦寨,位于凭祥市西南端,与越南国境相连。有"中国国际商业城"之称。

② 中国给予边民互市贸易免征进口关税和进口环节增值税,以及边境小额贸易减半征收进口关税和进口环节增值税政策。

Southeast Asia Nations[1].

The innocuous plot of dry, dusty land is fast becoming an import-export hub, heralding what the regional government of Guangxi wants on a larger scale, particularly when it completes a major free trade zone in the Beihai Bay.

"The autonomous region enjoys every advantage for closer economic cooperation and trade ties with Southeast Asian countries," Li Wenjie, deputy director-general of Guagxi's commerce department, told the *China Daily* newspaper.

The region—which is roughly the size of Britain and has depended on its sugar cane production—plans to import more energy and mineral resources from ASEAN members, while raising exports of finished products.

Official data showed Guangxi's trade with ASEAN members rose 50 percent in 2006 to about \$1.82 billion from 2005. ASEAN members were also the second most important foreign investor in Guangxi.

An official with the Puzhai trade administration, who declined to be identified, told Reuters the border trade totaled 3 billion *yuan* (\$400 million) last year, with farm products and minerals accounting for most of the business.

Not bad for a tiny border town about 200km west of Guangxi's capital Nanning.

There are no armed guards, just two ramshackle huts on either side of a long metallic bar. No-one inspected cargo rumbling across on trucks, carts or even human backs.

Chinese and Vietnamese people cross the line freely with identity cards issued by local authorities.

Ironically, Puzhai is just a few kilometers away from the official Pingxiang border — known as the Friendship Pass[2].

During the Vietnam War, Pingxiang was known as a portal for arms as the Nanning-Hanoi railway runs through the city.

Local officials said Chinese firms export most of their motorbikes through the border. About half of Chinese-made machinery and automobile parts destined for Vietnam also go through the crossing.

In the other direction, imports of iron ore and magnesium to China had risen sharply over past years.

Puzhai parking lot was chock-a-block with lorries ready to carry resources across into China. A road link is under construction that would connect the border town with a newly built highway to Nanning.

"I come here very often," said one taxi driver from Nanning. "Many want to start business here."

---

① 东南亚国家联盟(Association of Southeast Asian Nations，简称东盟)和中国拟于2010年前建立世界最大的自由贸易区。

② 友谊关是中国九大名关中唯一一个国际关隘，原名镇南关。离凭祥市18公里，距越南凉山16公里。

Words and Expressions

ravenous ['rævənəs] *adj.* 贪婪的，渴望的，狼吞虎咽的
tapioca [ˌtæpɪ'əʊkə] *n.* (食用)木薯粉，[植]木薯
herald ['herəld] *v.* 预报，宣布，传达，欢呼
threadbare ['θredbɛə] *adj.* 穿破旧衣服的；俗套的
hub [hʌb] *n.* 毂，中心
swirl [swɜːl] *v.* 打漩，盘绕；头晕
low-key *adj.* 抑制的，低调的
vendor ['vendə] *n.* 卖主，小贩，摊贩
autonomous [ɔː'tɒnəməs] *adj.* 自治的
metallic [mɪ'tælɪk] *adj.* 金属(性)的
rumble ['rʌmbl] *v.* 辘辘行驶；低沉地说
ore [ɔː] *n.* 矿石，含有金属的岩石
magnesium [mæg'niːzjəm] *n.* 镁
portal ['pɔːtəl] *n.* 入口
chock-a-block *adj.* 挤满的，塞满的，充满的
cash in on 靠……赚钱，乘机利用

Exercises

Exercise 1 Choose the best answer for each of the following questions.

1. In accordance with the information in the article, the following statements are true except ________.
   A. Guangxi enjoys every advantage for closer economic cooperation and trade ties with Southeast Asian countries
   B. Guangxi plans to import more energy and mineral resources from ASEAN members
   C. cargo rumbling across on trucks, carts or even human backs must be inspected
   D. imports of iron ore and magnesium to China had risen sharply over past years
2. What is not the thing that the Chinese firms export to Vietnam?
   A. Motorbikes. B. Machinery and automobile parts.
   C. Coal. D. Machine parts.

Exercise 2 Fill in each of the blanks with the appropriate words given. Change the form of the word when necessary.

boost herald autonomous rumble tiny

1. Although Puzhai is a ________ border town, it takes an important role in China-Vietnam trade.

2. Official data showed Guangxi's trade with ASEAN members rose 50 percent in 2006 to about $1.82 billion from 2005, which ________ that the further development in the future.
3. In ________ regions legally founded, ethnic minorities have the right to develop their economy and culture.
4. Many trucks ________ across the exit of the trade center, taking finished products to Vietnam.
5. Foreign trade ________ the development of China economy.

Exercise 3　Translate the following sentences into English.

1. 中国在深入发展与东盟国家的经济合作和贸易方面具有各种优势条件。
2. 随着中国经济的以平均每年超10%的速度迅猛，其对各种原材料的需求日益增长。
3. 满载着机器及汽车零部件的卡车轰鸣而过，边境小镇浦寨呈现出一派繁忙的景象。

Text 35 Coffee Sales Booming in China
咖啡——中国新生代消费者的宠儿

导读 中国人数千年来以茶为饮，而源自上世纪80年代一曲“味道好极了”的广告叩开了中国大众咖啡消费市场的大门。如今中国的咖啡消费以每年10%的速度增长，5年之内的消费量翻了一番。中国咖啡消费者偏爱速溶咖啡，喜爱喝卡布奇诺或拿铁，而不是偏苦的意浓咖啡。

It's no secret that emulating the west has become a big sport in China. And one western tradition that's rapidly gaining momentum in China is drinking coffee. While better known for its tea consumption, the demand for coffee more than doubled between 2001 and 2006 and is currently estimated to be growing by 10 percent a year, according to the International Coffee Organization①(ICO).

The ICO credits Nestlé's aggressive marketing of its instant Nescafé② brand in the mid-80s with helping spur the Chinese coffee culture. Today, instant coffee still accounts for approximately 90 percent of retail sales, according to the ICO.

Its first-mover advantage③ helped Nestlé maintain its grip on the coffee market with a 45 percent share of retail sales. Together with competitors Kraft's Maxwell House④ and Sara Lee⑤, these three brands account for 70 percent of the market, reports the ICO.

In 1998, Starbucks⑥ opened its first coffee outlet in China. Today, the company has 450 stores in China, with more than 200 stores in 21 mainland cities, the region experiencing the fastest growth.

But there are some contrasts between Chinese coffee consumption and that of the west. According to the ICO, Chinese often eat when drinking coffee, leading to a smaller take-away business than in western countries. The ICO also says that most Chinese coffee drinkers prefer cappuccinos or lattes to espresso, which is considered to be too bitter.

---

① 国际咖啡组织是一个政府间组织，1963年成立于伦敦，由咖啡进口国和出口国组成。

② 雀巢咖啡

③ 先行者优势

④ 麦斯威尔咖啡。“滴滴香浓，意犹未尽”是麦斯威尔一贯遵循的准则。

⑤ 美国沙莉集团，总部设在芝加哥，是一家消费产品巨头。生产多元产品，包括食品、咖啡等饮料，个人消费品，如服装等，以及家庭和个人护理用品。

⑥ 星巴克是当今世界上最大的咖啡专卖连锁店。

Words and Expressions

momentum [məʊ'mentəm] *n.* 动力,发展势头

instant ['ɪnstənt] *adj.* (食品)速溶的

grip [grɪp] *n.* 掌握,控制

espresso [e'spresəʊ] *n.* (蒸汽加压煮出的)浓咖啡

cappuccino 卡布奇诺咖啡

latte 拿铁咖啡

Exercises

Exercise 1 Choose the best answer for each of the following questions.

1. The consumption of coffee turns out ________ every year reported by the ICO.

A. to decrease about 10 percent B. to increase about 10 percent

C. to decrease exactly 10 percent D. to increase exactly 10 percent

2. Which kind of coffee do our Chinese people like least by comparison?

A. Cappuccinos. B. Lattes. C. Nescafé. D. Espresso.

3. Kraft's Maxwell House and Sara Lee, take 70 percent of the market, together with their competitor ________.

A. Starbucks B. Nestlé C. ICO D. Lattes

Exercise 2 Fill in each of the blanks with the appropriate words given. Change the form of the word when necessary.

first-mover advantage instant coffee consumption

1. With ________, caffeine measurements are based on the amount of its powder used to make the drink.

2. Everybody must cut back on ________ in time of war.

3. ________ was initially touted as crucial in the Internet economy, although now there is a growing backlash against it.

Exercise 3 Translate the following sentences into English.

1. 岩石滚下山坡时,冲力愈来愈大。

2. 这些措施可以促进消费的提高和当地经济的发展。

Text 36 Formidable China Effect Keeps the Commodity Bulls Running

强盛中国令大宗货物市场“牛气十足”

导读 日益强盛的中国公司对大众商品的持续采购，在全球范围内又掀起一阵风波。西方媒体长篇累牍报道：世界大宗货物价格之所以如“火箭升空”般的持续上扬是源自中国难以满足的需求。而事实上中国对大众商品的消费并不是其价格直线上升的直接原因，真正原因是来自华尔街以及西方各国投机机构的推波助澜。历史告诫：一轮经济增长的周期有涨有跌，大众商品价格也是如此。IMF 预测：尽管全球需求持续增长，但在 2010 年前铝与铜的真实价格将分别下跌 35% 与 57%。

The commodity indices may be drooping, but the investment community seems unmoved.

New commodity funds are still popping up all over the place. Pension funds such as Calpers and Hermes[①] have recently said they are beefing up their commodity exposure.

There are respectable long-run arguments for commodities as an investment class. But is it just coincidence that funds are seeing the light after a record-breaking four-year bull market?

Commodities, we are told, have a better long-run return than stocks or bonds, and a fairly low correlation with them. They are therefore likely to provide a return when funds need it most.

Underlying both those propositions is evidence that commodities are a hedge against inflation.[②]

A recent study showed that in the inflationary period 1970 - 81, commodities did more than twice as well as US stocks. Over the low-inflation period 1982 - 2004, they did rather worse—10 percent a year versus 13.3 percent.

So if you expect today's low inflation to persist, the return from commodities may prove a little disappointing. So might the benefits from diversification.

Let us look further at how those returns are made up.

---

① Calpers 美国最大的公共养老基金公司。Hermes 爱马仕，法国奢华消费品的代表，共有十四个系列产品，如皮具、箱包、男女服装，香水等，多为手工精心制作。

② 从这些投资方案的隐含优势中，我们显然可以看出大宗货物的投资可以免除通货膨胀的负面影响。

Over the past half-century, the real spot price of non-fuel commodities has fallen by 1.6 percent a year on average. But the return on forward contracts[①]—which is what we are talking about—has two other parts: The yield on the collateral put up against the contract, and the so-called roll return.

This latter is, in turn, made up of two parts. First is the risk premium, whereby far-out contracts are priced at a discount to what either the buyer or the seller of protection thinks the actual price will be.[②] That is, the investor demands a reward for providing the hedge.

Then comes the so-called convenience yield[③], whereby end-users of a commodity tend to bid up a futures contract as it nears expiry, so as to guarantee physical supply.

The snag is that, in principle, the size of the roll return—which is a vital factor in the whole argument—should depend on the balance of supply and demand. The more investors there are offering hedges, the less the return ought to be.[④]

As it happens, for the past couple of years oil futures contracts have been expiring at a discount, or contango.[⑤]

The International Monetary Fund notes, in its latest *World Economic Outlook*, that many oil traders blame this directly on the presence of more investors in the market.

For the real commodities bulls, all this is mere detail. What about China and the super-cycle? What about the fact that metals prices have gone up 180 percent in real terms in the past four years?

Against this, the bears[⑥] can point to the historical correlation between metals prices and the US housing market. That market is turning down.

For all that, the China effect remains formidable.

The IMF argues that in developing countries, consumption of commodities rises steeply until output per head reaches $15,000-$20,000. Thereafter, it levels off as the economy tilts towards services. China's output per head is around $6,400.

So whatever the immediate outlook for the Chinese economy, the essential demand story remains intact.

The supply story is another matter. It may take several years for new sources of metals to come on stream. But reserves are practically limitless. There is no OPEC-type cartel to hold prices up, nor much prospect of one.

The same applies to agricultural commodities. Bulls here point to global warming,

---

① 远期合同

② 后者又由两部分构成,首先是如果获得收益低于买方或是卖方的投保价格,那么便可以获得保险费。

③ 拥有实物而不是合同,或是衍生(derivative)产品所获得的利益及保险费。

④ 越多的投资者套牢,则越少的利润回报。

⑤ 正像过去的几年一样,石油期货合同的最终价往往会出现折价或溢价现象。

⑥ 卖空的人,在股市以赢取低额买进的利润。

water shortages and the like. Maybe so. But it may be that crops will simply shift around the world, and that supply will keep coming.

As for the balance of supply and demand in metals, the IMF has done an elaborate exercise involving its own fairly bullish projections on world growth, and data from the Australian government on green field and brown field sites planned around the world[①].

Its bald conclusion is that in spite of continued growth in demand, the real price of aluminum will fall 35 percent by 2010, and of copper by 57 percent.

It may prove that investors are running to catch a bus that is grinding to a halt. If the IMF is right, the long-term case for commodities will be far more compelling in a few years' time.

I wonder whether investors will see it that way.

Words and Expressions

correlation [ˌkɒrɪˈleɪʃən] *n.*	相关性
hedge [hedʒ] *n.*	套期保值，套牢；防御、保护方法
diversification [daɪˌvɜːsɪfɪˈkeɪʃən] *n.*	多样性（这里指多样化投资）
collateral [kɒˈlætərəl] *n.*	抵押物，担保品
expiry [ɪkˈspaɪərɪ] *n.*	到期
contango [kənˈtæŋgəʊ] *n.*	期货溢价，期货升水
tilt [tɪlt] *v.*	倾斜
compelling [kəmˈpelɪŋ] *adj.*	使人非注意不可的，引人入胜的
pop up	弹出
beef up	加强，补充；使更大，更好
spot price	现价
risk premium	保险费
physical supply	实物供应
come on stream	成为主流
green field	待开发区
brown field	待重新开发的城市用地

Exercises

Exercise 1 Choose the best answer for each of the following questions.

1. By which, far-out contracts are priced at a discount to what either the buyers or the seller of protection thinks the actual price will be?

   A. Spot price. B. Roll return. C. Risk premium. D. Convenience yield.

---

① 来自澳大利亚对于全球范围内的待开发地区以及待重新开发的城市用地的官方统计数据。

2. According to IMF, China is on all these phases but ________ right now.

A. initial B. steeply developed

C. on the way D. budding

Exercise 2 Fill in each of the blanks with the appropriate words given. Change the form of the word when necessary.

come on stream pop up correlation compelling expire

1. The menu ________ when you click twice on the mouse.
2. The record exposes the ________ of social power with wealth.
3. There is no ________ reason to believe him.
4. His terms of office ________ at the end of June.
5. Headquarters has assign the new task to each branch, the ones in Asian is to make this line of product ________ the next spring.

Exercise 3 Translate the following sentences into English.

1. 越来越多的投资者倾向于套牢来避免通过膨胀所带来的损失。
2. 当经济发展快速并且逐渐趋于平稳时,经济的增长则倾斜于服务行业。
3. 中国的强势影响将成为世界经济中引人注目的有利力量。

Text 37 China's Surging Coal Demand Leaves Costly Queues at Australian Port

饥渴中国煤船 挤破澳洲港口

导读 2007年中国煤耗量超26亿多吨，占全球的三分之一，其中累计进口煤炭达5,300多吨，澳大利亚是中国煤业实体的进口大国之一。纽卡斯尔港是澳大利亚最大的港口之一，也是全球最大的煤炭出口港。近日由于世界煤炭需求猛增，来自中国等国家70艘煤船在纽卡斯尔港沿海岸排起了40英里的长队，等待进港装载煤炭。这种挤破澳洲港口的情景着实使澳洲煤炭供应商与港口管理部门万分难堪，束手无策。

After 38 years as a skipper, little fazes Dave Rolston, master of one of the six tugboats operating in Newcastle①, among Australia's biggest ports and a world leader for coal exports.

But on an outing earlier this month Mr Rolston appeared flummoxed by news that the queue of ships waiting to enter the port and load coal had stretched that morning to a record 70 vessels.

"This is by far the worst it's ever been," he says. "We're working as fast as we can but these ships just keep arriving."

As his tugboat reached a Manila-registered ship a few miles out of the port's heads, the boat's radar screen showed a queue that stretched 40 miles down the coast—two-fifths of the way to Sydney.

Newcastle is suffering from one of the most striking examples of the infrastructure bottlenecks that have arisen across Australia because of surging Chinese-led demand for coal and other commodities.

The average wait for a ship to load up at Newcastle is now three weeks and delays are costing the coal industry about A$1m ($786,000, £407,000) a day according to industry estimates, as producers pay so-called demurrage charges to anchor until a berth becomes available.

Gloucester Coal, one of the producers affected by the queuing, recently described the situation as "a disgrace" that is "costing Australia money."

---

① 纽卡斯尔港是澳大利亚最大煤炭出口港，占据了澳大利亚煤炭三分之一的出口量。它地处盛产煤炭的新南威尔士州，年装船能力共计94Mt。

To ease the problem, coal producers recently voted to reintroduce quotas[①], a decision that still needs approval from the Australian competition regulator. But the use of quotas is controversial and has regularly split the big coal companies, leading to a series of policy back-flips.

The delays at Newcastle also illustrate the difficulties of timing costly infrastructure developments to coincide with peaks in demand in a cyclical sector such as coal. Meanwhile, Chinese and other coal purchasers have no incentive to stop their ships from waiting in the queue since producers pick up the bill for delays.

Unlike many state-controlled ports in emerging markets such as India, which are also facing capacity constraints, Newcastle runs as a private operation with investment decisions in the hands of the coal companies. However, another part of the transport chain, the railway network that links Newcastle to the coal-producing Hunter Valley, remains state-owned, which has led to some mutual recrimination.

Brian Nicholls, an industry veteran who has managed several Australian coal mines, says, "The rail system and the coal loading capacity have got to work in harmony, which hasn't been the case for the Hunter Valley."

Meanwhile Garry Webb, chief executive of Newcastle Port Corporation, is adamant Newcastle can expand considerably. Standing in front of a giant aerial photograph of the port, he points to several projects that will ensure annual capacity will soon rise from 90m tonnes to 102m tonnes, and eventually reach 120m tonnes.

"We all know that the coal industry is well cashed up," Mr Webb says. "The government is not going to get back into the funding of coal loading when it got out of it in 1989. Our policy is now very much hands-off. Any kind of interventionism would be a recipe for disaster because it would take away the efficiencies of the commercial world."

Newcastle's love affair with coal is almost as old as British settlement of Australia.[②] The colony's first commercial export cargo was a shipment of 50 tonnes of coal to Bengal in 1799. But Mr Webb argues the port needs to look beyond its longstanding coal customers.

While coal accounts for 90 percent of the volume handled in Newcastle, it represents 66 percent of the total value of goods.

The rest is made up of products ranging from Australian wheat to oranges arriving from Brazil.

Quotas have helped reduce queues in the past, but the system continues to divide producers. Xstrata, the UK-listed mining group, has consistently backed quotas, a position

---

① 配额制度是对有限资源的一种管理和分配，是对供需不等或者各方不同利益的平衡。

② 纽卡斯尔与煤业的亲密关系，几乎与英国殖民澳大利亚的历史一样悠久。

at odds with that of Rio Tinto and BHP Billiton, the world's largest mining company. ①

Chris Lynch, who oversees BHP②'s coal activities, recently told analysts that "quota systems are never a good system. They basically subsidise inefficient production".

Certainly no one is expecting quotas to act as a magic wand. A spokeswoman for Coal & Allied, a subsidiary of Rio Tinto③ says, "There is no quick-fix solution to this issue. Any system must effectively manage coal logistics for at least a two- or three-year time-frame until investment in rail and port capacity matches demand."

Words and Expressions

tugboat ['tʌgˌbəʊt] *n.*	拖船
flummox ['flʌməks] *v.*	使混乱,使失措
demurrage [dɪ'mʌrɪdʒ] *n.*	滞期费,滞期
anchor ['æŋkə] *n.*	锚
berth [bɜːθ] *n.*	泊位
recrimination [rɪˌkrɪmɪ'neɪʃən] *n.*	反责,反控
adamant ['ædəmənt] *adj.*	强硬的(东西),坚定不移的,固执的
hands-off *adj.*	不插手的,不干涉的
quick-fix *adj.*	快速的
timeframe ['taɪm'freɪm] *n.*	时间表
aerial photograph	航空摄影学

Exercises

Exercise 1 Choose the best answer for each of the following questions.

1. It can be inferred from the passage that that Australia suffers from infrastructure bottlenecks because ________.

   A. surging Chinese-led demand for coal and other commodities

   B. purchasers have no incentive to stop their ships from waiting in the queue since the producers pick up the bill from delays

   C. the infrastructure system and commodity loading capacity do have not got to work in harmony

---

① 过去,配额制的确曾有助于减少排队情况,不过,这项制度仍然在分化生产商。英国上市矿业集团斯特拉塔(Xstrata)始终支持配额,这一立场与力拓(Rio Tinto)和全球最大矿业公司必和必拓(BHP Billiton)相左。

② BHP公司成立于1885年,总部设在墨尔本,是澳大利亚历史最悠久、规模最大的公司之一。

③ 力拓矿业公司1873年成立于西班牙。2000年成功收购澳大利亚北方矿业公司,成为在勘探、开采和加工矿产资源方面的佼佼者,是全球第二大采矿业集团,仅次于必和必拓公司。

D. all of the above

2. Who will pick up the bill for the delay?

   A. Producers. B. Buyers.

   C. Government. D. Customers.

3. The reason of the Newcastle capacity has not expanded is that ________.

   A. it is a timing costly project

   B. it lacks funding

   C. the transport chain partly belongs to privacy and partly state

   D. all of the above

Exercise 2 Fill in each of the blanks with the appropriate words given. Change the form of the word when necessary.

flummox constraint veteran recrimination

1. It's natural to ________ against someone who has tried to put the blame on you.
2. Furthermore, the increasing use of outward processing facilities in the Mainland has enabled Hong Kong's productive capacity to expand by multiples even amidst the local capacity ________, and hence helped maintain the price competitiveness of Hong Kong's products.
3. It will do us much good to chat with these ________ workers.
4. She can ________ anybody by the lip.

Exercise 3 Translate the following sentences into English.

1. 铁路系统和港口的煤炭装船能力不能协调一致是瓶颈问题产生的原因之一。
2. 配额制度的确有助于减少排队的情况，但有人认为它的主要作用是鼓励资助效率低下的企业。
3. 很多新兴市场的港口，如印度，是国家控制的，而纽卡尔港是以私营方式运营的。

Chapter Five China's M & A

中国并购

Text 38 China Goes Shopping

中国海外"大采购"

导读 中国股价飙升着实使中国公司赚得盆满钵溢，手握大把真金白银在全球四处寻觅收购机会。中国公司海外收购的目的有三：收购相对廉价的资产或战略资源性企业，寻求海外扩张，学习海外先进技术与管理经验。如收购海外银行股权后，可学习如何追踪客户和资金流。除收购海外实业公司外，中国公司还购买了一些金融或投资机构的股权。但自购买后，其股价一直跌跌不休，损失不少。也许中国公司要学会的是不要仓促收购，应耐心等待底部到来，择机抄底。

They are over-sized, over-valued and over here. Chinese buyers, their share prices soaring, are prowling the globe for acquisitions. Targets kicked into play, such as Australian miner Rio Tinto, inevitably attract their eye—as do those whose owners never imagined hanging out for the sale signs. What motivates the newest breed of buyers?

Chinese companies have raised over ＄200bn in debt and equity[①] in the past two years and are itching to pick up relatively cheap assets. Another attraction is the prospect of global reach and technology transfer. Big Chinese banks, for example, earn less than 3 percent of their pre-tax income overseas and have much to learn about, say, investment banking services. Like the Japanese banks before them, Chinese lenders also want to follow their clients and money flows; hence the spate of deals in Africa. The recent brace of US stakes comes after bilateral banking assets tripled in the past decade to ＄31bn, according to Moody's[②].

These goals inform China's more subtle approach. In a reversal of the abortive 2005 bid for US oil major Unocal, Chinese buyers are willing to settle for minority stakes. They

---

① 债券股票市场

② 美国穆迪公司是全球最著名的信用评级、风险评估公司。

are also prepared to forego voting rights, as with the Sovereign Wealth Fund's[①]10 percent stake in Blackstone, the US private equity firm. And, since technical expertise and human capital is part of the attraction, management jobs are seldom on the line[②].

A more commercial attitude also prevails, although that will not necessarily extend to pricing discipline—or to rival bids from Chinese entities. However, some dud performance has put the focus on price, at least among Chinese bloggers. Blackstone shares are down almost 20 percent since Beijing's June investment; Barclays[③], in which China Development Bank took a stake in July, has fallen 36 percent, precluding further hasty acquisitions. Subsequent structuring shows lessons have been learnt, by, for example, using convertible bonds[④] for protection from price fluctuations. With deep-pocketed Chinese crowding the auction rooms, sellers have less to fear from retreating private equity firms.

Words and Expressions

soaring [ˈsɔːrɪŋ] *adj.*	猛增的，剧增的
prowl [praʊl] *v.*	四处觅食，徘徊，潜行
itch [ɪtʃ] *v.*	渴望；发痒，痒
spate [speɪt] *n.*	大量，一大批
brace [breɪs] *n.*	支架，支撑
reversal [rɪˈvɜːsəl] *n.*	翻转，倒转，反转
abortive [əˈbɔːtɪv] *adj.*	流产的，堕胎的
forego [fɔːˈgəʊ] *v.*	放弃，在之前，居先
dud [dʌd] *adj.*	无用的
blogger *n.*	写博客的人
preclude [prɪˈkruːd] *v.*	妨碍，阻止
convertible [kənˈvɜːtəbl] *adj.*	可改变的，可交换，可兑换的
deep-pocketed *adj.*	腰缠万贯的
auction [ˈɔːkʃn] *n.*	拍卖
bid for	投标
money flow	资金流
human capital	人力资本
on the line	模棱两可，处于危险中

---

① 主权财富基金，它既不同于传统的政府养老基金，也不同于那些简单持有储备资产以维护本币稳定的政府机构，而是一种全新的专业化、市场化的积极投资机构。

② 由于技术专长和人力资源也是吸引力的一部分，管理职位很少会受到威胁。

③ 巴克莱银行，它是英国最大商业银行之一，1862 年成立，总行设在伦敦。

④ 可转化债券，它指含股票认购权的公司债，可按约定的换股价将债券转换成发行公司的股票，可以理解为一支纯债券再加上一支股票期权的混合金融工具。

Exercises

Exercise 1 Choose the best answer for each of the following questions.

1. What has prompted Chinese buyers to search the globe for acquisitions?
   A. The fact that they have raised enough capital in debt and equity in the past two years.
   B. Their desire for global reach.
   C. The prospect of technology transfer.
   D. All of the above.
2. It can be inferred from the text that the bid for Unocal aborted because ________.
   A. the buyer was unwilling to settle for minority stakes
   B. the bid quotation was too low
   C. the buyer was reluctant to give up voting rights
   D. the buyer wanted to follow their clients and money flows
3. Which of the following is not a characteristic of this breed of Chinese buyers?
   A. They hold more commercial attitude.
   B. They are willing to settle for minority stakes.
   C. They are prepared to give up voting rights.
   D. They quote reasonable prices.

Exercise 2 Fill in each of the blanks with the appropriate words given. Change the form of the word when necessary.

forego be itching to asset equity bid for

1. One of the quickest ways to judge whether a company is creating ________ or gobbling up investor's cash is to look at their Return On Equity (ROE 股本回报率).
2. Accordingly, it had undertaken not only to ________ the use of nuclear weapons but also to conclude a safeguards agreement with IAEA (International Atomic Energy Agency).
3. After you made your views crystal clear to Jim, he ________ show everyone in the club what he's made of. He identifies with the club, and is proud of it.
4. Several firms have ________ the contract to build the new concert hall.
5. ________ is a risk interest or ownership right in property.

Exercise 3 Translate the following sentences into English.

1. 随着腰缠万贯的中国人涌进拍卖大厅，卖家已经减少了对私人股份公司日益退缩的恐惧。(deep-pocketed)
2. 海尔集团把投标价格从之前的12.8亿美元提升到22.5亿美元想竞购美国美泰公司。(bid for)
3. 你肯定很高兴，你想出差都想好几个月了。(be itching to)

Text 39 Hey, Big Spender
嗨，来自中国的大买家

导读 来自中国的一股并购浪潮正在冲刷着整个世界，中国公司海外“大采购”再次成为西方媒体焦点。2002年是中国加入WTO之后的第一年，海外并购额仅为2亿美元；2004年中国企业海外并购额达到70亿美元，包括联想集团收购IBM个人电脑业务的17.5亿美元；2007年超300亿美元，2007岁尾，中国投资公司向美国摩根士丹利公司投资50亿美元使2007年成为中国并购交易史上具有划时代意义的一年：中国公司和政府在海外的收购额首次超过了海外买家在中国的收购额。难怪老外直呼：中国大买家来啦！

China's investments in the rest of Asia are booming.

China's outward investment drive has become the subject of growing media and political attention, as increasingly internationally minded Chinese companies have begun scouring the globe for takeover targets. Yet despite the hype, this shopping spree is not quite what it appears, being in some ways more modest in ambition (for now, at least) than many suppose.

Back in 2005 when Lenovo, China's leading maker of personal computers (PCs), bought IBM's PC division for $1.25bn, some pundits hailed the deal as the beginning of a wave of big acquisitions abroad by Chinese companies. Certainly, China's overseas mergers and acquisitions (M&As) have soared recently. In 2006 Chinese companies did 103 crossborder deals worth $20.7bn, according to Dealogic. That is a dramatic rise from 2004 levels, when Chinese firms made 53 overseas purchases valued at $3.8bn.

But Lenovo's splashy takeover of the iconic US high-tech brand has so far proven to be an exception. That is because the bulk of Chinese acquisitions abroad are taking place with far less fanfare in emerging markets—often in China's own backyard, Asia. Of the top ten Chinese crossborder M&A deals by dollar value this year, all but two of the acquired companies were in Asia. As the volume of outbound M&A continues to increase, many expect Chinese investment in Asia to accelerate even more. "A lot of Chinese companies want to buy a company in Singapore, Pakistan, Malaysia, and we're going to see an increasing number of transactions between India and China," says Hong Chen, chairman and CEO of the Hina Group①, a boutique investment bank② in Beijing that initially

① 汉能投资集团，致力于中国与世界各地的跨境投资银行与投资基金管理业务。
② 新型投行或专业小投行，一般它们规模不大，业务专注于某个领域。

focused on Silicon Valley but opened a Singapore office and stationed a staffer in Hong Kong, China in 2006. Other observers point out that the big population of overseas Chinese scattered throughout Southeast Asia is especially well suited to act as liaisons for mainland Chinese businessmen.

For the most part, takeover targets in Asia have little to offer Chinese companies in the way of fancy technology or global brands. But they have another attraction: They are often less difficult for Chinese firms inexperienced in M&As to digest. For example, business leaders in China may be better able to apply experience gleaned at home to other Asian countries with similar income levels and customer needs. Take China Mobile's $460m acquisition of Paktel[①], a Pakistan-based mobile-phone operator, earlier this year. It marked the Chinese telecoms giant's first successful overseas acquisition. As M&As go, it was not exactly ambitious: China Mobile's subscriber base is over 230 times that of Paktel. Still, analysts say China Mobile could share with Paktel useful insights into working around underdeveloped payment systems and selling more expensive services as customers' incomes grow.

Salary Gap

As a further spur to investment in Asia, in much of the region salaries are likely to be roughly on a par with those in China. This is no small matter, say many who have worked on deals in China. Not only does moderate pay hold down business costs, but Chinese executives are also unsettled by the prospect of managing Western counterparts with salaries higher than their own. Mr Chen of the Hina Group offers the theoretical example of an Italian clothing company that boasts an upscale brand but lacks its own manufacturing capability or sales force in China. It would make perfect sense for a Chinese manufacturer eager to boost thin margins to snap up the Italian firm and market its clothes in China. Yet Mr Chen says so far deals like this have been few and far between in large part because of managers' income disparities. A typical salary for a Chinese vice-president might be $20,000 or $30,000 a year. "So they think, 'how can we have someone reporting to us who makes $100,000 a year?'," he says. Such cultural conflicts have in fact bedevilled TCL, a Chinese television-maker that purchased France's Thomson in 2004 in what was perhaps the highest-profile Chinese M&A in Europe to date. In May TCL declared its European unit insolvent.

But the biggest incentive for Chinese firms to stay close to home may be the fact that developing Asian countries eager to promote growth are relatively more likely to welcome Chinese investment than Western countries—which are more inclined to view China with some trepidation as a powerful new economic competitor. Many companies acquired by the Chinese know that they can also secure a better platform for selling into China. That is a huge carrot, especially for Asian businessmen who want to take advantage of the booming

---

① 巴科泰尔,它成立于1990年,是巴基斯坦第一个开展业务的移动运营商。

regional trade that China is anchoring. A case in point: Bank of China's $965m purchase in 2006 of Singapore Aircraft Leasing, the largest such firm in Asia. The bank framed the acquisition as a way to boost its non-interest income and potentially develop new business with airline companies. But the deal could also give Singapore Aircraft Leasing a stronger foothold in China's aviation market, one of the fastest-growing in the world. When Bank of China announced the deal, it pledged to tap its own contacts in the Chinese airline industry to drum up business for the Singaporean firm. "The rest of the Asian region really needs to do business with China," says one Hong Kong-based banker.

Indeed, the watershed event for China's outbound M&A strategy was the unsuccessful $18.5bn bid by China National Offshore Oil Corp (CNOOC) to buy US-based Unocal in 2005. That deal went down in flames as US Congressmen warned the Bush administration that approving it would amount to handing over America's energy security to the Chinese government (CNOOC is a state-owned enterprise). Some observers say China's resolve to avoid any similar public loss of face in the future has made it tougher since then to win central government approval for offshore purchases. A transaction is unlikely to get Beijing's green light unless it looks likely to sail through free of political hassle in the M&A target's home country.

The US seems a particularly unwelcome place for Chinese M&As. Even before the CNOOC-Unocal debacle, Lenovo had to get clearance for its IBM deal from the Committee on Foreign Investment in the US, an inter-agency government body charged with review-ing sensitive foreign investments.

This sort of prying will hardly encourage more Sino-American corporate marriages. But rumours do still make the rounds about the potential for Chinese companies to make high-profile US buys. Earlier this year the Chinese press ran stories suggesting mainland carmakers might bid for Chrysler[①], which its German parent, Daimler, was trying to unload. Although Cerberus[②], a US private-equity firm, emerged as the eventual buyer, sceptics had never taken a Chinese bid for Chrysler seriously. "Can you imagine a Chinese company going in and trying to close down a plant in Dearborn, Michigan?", asks one American lawyer based in China.

Daring and Defiant

To be sure, no one doubts that as Chinese firms gain more crossborder M&A experience, they will venture into Western countries in higher numbers and with greater success. The revelation in mid-May that the Chinese government will invest $3bn in the Blackstone Group[③], a leading American investment firm, shows that the Chinese will be both daring and defiantly freewheeling about spending their money. No doubt, many will

---

① 克莱斯勒品牌,典型的美国汽车品牌。

② Cerberus 成立于 1992 年,管理资金和账户高达 165 亿美元,是全球最大的私人投资公司之一。

③ 黑石集团,它是一家全球领先的另类资产管理公司及金融咨询服务提供商。

be keeping a close eye on the progress of the Blackstone deal and the continued evolution at Lenovo to see if China can play the M&A game in the West. (Lenovo has struggled to gain market share in the US and in April announced the lay-off of 5 percent of its global workforce.) That said, Asia already looks like a hotbed of Chinese dealmaking.

Words and Expressions

scour [skauə(r)] *v.*	走遍(某地)以搜寻某人(某物)
hype [haɪp] *n.*	夸大其词,夸张,装饰,渲染
spree [spriː] *n.*	戏耍,宴会,喧闹
pundit ['pʌndɪt] *n.*	某一学科的权威,专家
hail [heɪl] *v.*	热情地承认
splashy ['splæʃɪ] *adj.*	颇受好评的;容易溅开的;遍布斑点的
iconic [aɪ'kɒnɪk] *adj.*	图标的,醒目的
fanfare ['fænfɛə] *n.*	吹牛;喇叭或号角嘹亮的吹奏声
outbound ['aʊtbaʊnd] *adj.*	向外去的;驶向外国的
boutique [buː'tiːk] *n.*	流行女装商店;精品店
liaison [lɪ'eɪzn] *n.*	联络,组织、单位间的交流、合作
glean [gliːn] *v.*	点滴搜集;拾
spur [spɜː] *n.*	鼓舞,刺激物;马刺
upscale ['ʌpskeɪl] *adj.*	高标度端的
disparity [dɪ'spærətɪ] *n.*	不一致,不等
bedevil [bɪ'devl] *v.*	使痛苦,使苦恼
insolvent [ɪn'sɒlvənt] *adj.*	资不抵债的,无力偿还的,破产的
trepidation [trepɪ'deɪʃən] *n.*	惊慌
anchor ['æŋkə] *v.*	赖以支撑;抛锚使停泊
foothold ['fʊthəʊld] *n.*	立足处,根据地,据点
aviation [ˌeɪvɪ'eɪʃn] *n.*	航空,飞行,飞机制造业
watershed ['wɔːtəʃed] *n.*	流域(分水岭)
hassle ['hæsl] *n.*	激战;争论,与……争辩
debacle [deɪ'bɑːkl] *n.*	解冻;崩溃
pry [praɪ] *v.*	窥探,刺探,打听
defiantly [dɪ'faɪəntlɪ] *adv.*	挑战地,对抗地
freewheeling [friː'wiːl] *v.*	轻松快活地行动,凭惯性前进
hotbed ['hɒtbed] *n.*	温床,滋长地
sceptic ['skeptɪk] *n.*	持怀疑态度的人
on a par with	同等,同位,同价
snap up	抢购;加快脚步,加速,增长
drum up	大力争取(支持,顾客等)

Exercises

Exercise 1 Choose the best answer for each of the following questions.

1. Which is mentioned in the text as something that Chinese companies lack in overseas M&As?

   A. Experience. B. Money.

   C. People. D. Technology.

2. Which of the following is not a reason why Asia has become a hotbed for Chinese M&As?

   A. Income levels and customer needs in other Asian countries are similar to those in China.

   B. A large number of overseas Chinese work as liasons.

   C. Asian M&A targets can share Chinese buyers with their technological expertises and global brands.

   D. Other Asian developing countries are eager to promote business relationship with China.

3. What impact has CNOOC's abortive bid for Unocal exerted on Chinese M&As?

   A. It has spurred Chinese buyers to search for more takeover targets.

   B. Chinese buyers and government have become more cautious of potential political hassles.

   C. Chinese buyers become more conscious of salary disparities.

   D. It has become easier for other Chinese buyers to pull through Congressional scrunity.

4. What is the author's attitude towards Chinese M&As in western developed countries?

   A. Slightly optimistic. B. Slightly pessimistic.

   C. Neutral. D. Indifferent.

Exercise 2 Fill in each of the blanks with the appropriate words given. Change the form of the word when necessary.

incentive hotbed drum up on a par with foothold moderate

1. Tax ________ paid by the government to exporters rose by more than 20 percent in the first two months of 2009 from the same period last year as new trade-boosting measures kicked in.
2. The Qingdao Tax-free Zone has become a ________ for overseas investment.
3. It can help ________ more business if you have someone to look at your business from an outsider's perspective.
4. Their products are ________ with the best foreign makes.

5. China's auto industry is expected to grow at a ________ pace this year amid concerns about oversupply and fierce market competition, according to a new report.
6. It may be many years before the new company can gain a secure ________ in the market.

Exercise 3 Translate the following sentences into English.

1. 中国对外投资的大好前景得到了许多专家的认同。
2. 中国公司考虑国际并购的两个主要动机是提高海外市场份额和获取专有技术。

Text 40 From Tiny Workshop to Shining Light of a Dynamic Sector

中国私企海外竞购——“蛇吞象”

导读 一个是世界上鲜为人知的中国私企，另一个是大名鼎鼎的全球汽车零部件供应商巨头，但不是前者为后者代加工，而是前者要“蛇吞象”收购后者。这家中国公司名叫万向集团，创始人是鲁冠球。1969年，鲁冠球以一间修车铺起家，如今已成为一家年收入超过400亿元的中国汽配领域龙头企业，而且还是一家真正意义上的跨国公司。近10年来万向公司海外收购马不停蹄，自2000年收购一家美国公司以来，通过一系列嵌入式并购，万向目前在海外已经并购或控股了31家公司。继去年收购了福特旗下的部分零部件业务后，万向如今又把目光盯上了曾是世界汽车零部件第一供应商——德尔福公司，有意收购其部分资产。

The heads of many large private companies in China had a tough patch in their early years, as they battled to become established in an often hostile environment.

Yet few had to struggle quite as much as Lu Guanqiu, the founder of auto-parts maker Wanxiang.

In 1969, Mr Lu opened a workshop to repair old agricultural machinery. The timing could not have been worse. Private business was illegal and profits outlawed at that time. At times, his repair shop was shut down. On other occasions, Mr Lu had to appear at "struggle" sessions, where he would be denounced for his capitalist tendencies.

"We just had to bear the humiliation and carry on," says the 61-year old Mr Lu, who now sports a neat, dark suit and a tie-pin with the company logo.

Things have moved on a little since then. Last year, Wanxiang notched up revenues of *renminbi* 25.2bn ($3.3bn) from its sales of water pumps, bearings and axles and exported $818m of goods. This year Mr Lu believes that exports will break through the $1bn mark.

In the process, Mr Lu has become to shining light of China's dynamic new private sector. He is currently placed 11th on the list of China's richest people, with personal assets estimated at $1.1bn.

The market for auto parts is growing rapidly, but there are still considerable risks for companies such as Wanxiang.

Multinational companies such as Bosch[1] and Visteon[2] have invested heavily in China, taking a large part of the top end of the market, which requires a higher technological level.

At the same time, Chinese companies are facing ever-fiercer competition for lower value-added products from manufacturers in countries such as India.

With raw material prices rising and wages on China's east coast also surging, the cost advantages that companies such as Wanxiang enjoyed a decade ago are quickly being eroded. Mr Lu says the average wage in China is still only one-20th of what employers in the US pay. "But we will not be able to rely on low labor costs for much longer," he adds.

To avoid being squeezed in the middle, Wanxiang is trying to adopt three approaches.

The first is greater scale. By expanding production to achieve economies of scale, the group hopes to remain competitive in some product lines. The rapid expansion in the Chinese car market has facilitated such an approach. Car sales have risen from 700,000 in 2001 to nearly 3.5m this year and every carmaker in the world has sunk investment into China—all of which has raised demand for parts.

Secondly, the arrival of the multinational car-makers has pushed the group in another direction—improving the technological sophistication of its products. In order to win business from the likes of General Motors and Ford, Wanxiang has had to invest in new machinery and revamp its manufacturing processes.

Mr Lu says that foreign carmakers will pay 50 percent more for an important component than their Chinese competitors. "But the requirements are much higher in terms of accuracy and technology," he says.

The third approach is the most radical—making acquisitions in the US and Europe. Even now, it is rare to hear of Chinese companies trying to do cross-border takeovers, but it was very new when Wanxiang first ventured abroad in the late 1990s.

Mr Lu says the company has learnt from experience how to manage acquisitions in the US. With some of its earlier deals, Wanxiang tried to move most of the operations and technology back to China and in the process generated enormous resistance.

A proposed takeover of an engine-parts maker in Michigan in 1998 fell apart when the company's union rejected the reduced employment benefits offered to its US workers.

Now, Mr Lu says, the group takes time to find the right balance between preserving some jobs in the US and taking advantage of lower costs in China. He boasts that a joint-venture with Rockwell Driveline[3], an axle-maker that was undergoing bankruptcy proceedings when Wanxiang invested in 2002, has not lost any jobs in the US. "The key question to get right is how much activity to leave in the US and how much to bring to

---

① 博世有限公司是德国最大的工业企业之一,从事汽车技术、工业技术和消费品的产业。

② 威斯顿是福特公司下属的汽车零件厂商。

③ 这是总部在美国威斯康星州密尔沃基的一家主营动力、控制和信息系统与服务的跨国公司,年销售收入达50亿美元。

China," says Mr Lu.

All that experience with US negotiators and trade unions will come in handy, as Wanxiang is now trying to play in a different league. Over the past year, the company has been involved in negotiations with Delphi, the bankrupt parts supplier that used to be a GM subsidiary, and with the components business of Ford, as the financial problems of both families of companies have become the most sensitive issue in US corporate politics.

Words and Expressions

outlawed [ˈaʊtlɔːd] *adj.* 违反法律的;法外的

denounce [dɪˈnaʊns] *v.* 受到谴责,公然抨击,告发

sport [spɔːt] *v.* 〈口〉惹人注目的穿戴

bearing [ˈbeərɪŋ] *n.* 轴承

axle [ˈæksl] *n.* 车轴;轮轴

erode [ɪˈrəʊd] *v.* 侵蚀,腐蚀

revamp [riːˈvæmp] *v.* 改良,翻新,修补

hone [həʊn] *v.* 用磨刀石磨,磨练

a tough patch 〈英〉倒霉,不走运;艰苦的经历

get into its swing 适应情况

notch up 创下,赢得

in a different league 另一类型的人(物)

Exercises

Exercise 1 Choose the best answer for each of the following questions.

1. Which of the following statements is not true?
   A. Despite the growing auto part market, there are still considerable risks for companies such as Wanxiang.
   B. Multinational companies have taken a large part of the top end of the market in China.
   C. Wanxiang's cost advantages enjoyed a decade ago have disappeared.
   D. Wanxiang's proposed takeover of an engine-parts maker in Michigan in 1998 aborted.
2. To avoid being squeezed in the middle, Wanxiang is trying to adopt the following approaches except ________.
   A. achieving greater scale
   B. improving the technological sophistication of its products
   C. making acquisitions in the US and Europe
   D. playing in a different league
3. For Mr Lu Guanqiu, the key to keeping the acquired foreign companies on the right

track lies in ________.

A. wisely coping with their resistance

B. knowing how to play in a different league

C. deciding know much activity to leave in the country and how much to bring to China

D. improving the technological sophistication

Exercise 2 Fill in each of the blanks with the appropriate words given. Change the form of the word when necessary.

squeeze denounce erode revamp notch up

1. Union officials ________ the action as a breach of the agreement.
2. With this performance, she has ________ her third championship title.
3. The rights of the individual are being steadily ________.
4. More and more college graduates are being ________ out of the job market
5. We want someone not just to cheerlead but to help us ________ our organization.

Exercise 3 Translate the following sentences into English.

1. 今年的出口将突破10亿美元大关。
2. 为了赢得来自通用汽车和福特汽车等公司的业务,万向集团必须投资增加新的机器,并改善其制造流程。
3. 在过去的一年中,万向集团一直在与德尔福进行谈判,这家已破产的零部件供应商曾是GM的子公司,也曾为福特提供零部件。

Text 41　We Must Prepare for the March of China's Giants

不可小觑中国大公司的异军突起

导读　虽然中国已成为世界第二经济大国，但其直接海外投资还属小字辈，其2005年的海外投资总额仅是美国的五十分之一。可是在未来的数年中，变数不小，万万不可小觑正在崛起的中国大公司。一些公司已经在世界舞台崭露头角，如联想(Lenovo)、海尔(Haier)和中海油(CNOOC)等，与世界跨国公司巨头一比高低，有朝一日它们将成为中国的通用电气、埃克森、飞利浦、丰田或三星等世界级跨国公司。

China is the world's second biggest economy, but when it comes to business investment in other countries it is still a very small player. The stock of China's direct investment abroad in 2005 was only one 50th that of the US.

In coming years these relative positions will dramatically change. Though official policy favours outward investment, China's companies are constrained by restricted access to foreign exchange. As the financial system is gradually deregulated, China will become the headquarters of Chinese versions of General Electric, Exxon, Philips, Toyota and Samsung. Already Chinese companies such as Lenovo, Haier[①] and CNOOC are beginning to compete with leading multinationals. It will not be many decades before Chinese businesses own more assets abroad than those of any other nation.

One spur is China's foreign exchange reserves, which at more than $1,000bn are equal to nearly a third of total US direct investment abroad. As it did for Japan in the 1980s, the accumulation of vast reserves stimulates outward direct investment. Reserves now held as US dollar securities pay low returns, are subject to considerable foreign exchange risk, require sterilization and are a highly visible symbol of a manipulated, cheap exchange rate. Recycled as foreign direct investment, by contrast, the underlying trade and financial account surpluses have no impact on the money supply, the long-term earnings rate is higher, the exchange rate risk is mitigated by the variety of revenue sources, while the capital outflow takes the upward pressure off the exchange rate. Chinese companies gain new markets, technologies and control over resources.

It is not only the problem of reserves management that will drive higher foreign direct investment flows from China. In the Central Intelligence Agency's purchasing power

---

① 海尔集团，它是世界第四大白色家电制造商、中国最具价值品牌。海尔在全球建立了29个制造基地，8个综合研发中心，19个海外贸易公司，全球员工总数超过5万人，已发展成为大规模的跨国企业集团。

parity rankings, China's economy is nearly three-quarters of the size of the US economy. It is growing at about three times the rate of the US economy and may continue to do so for decades.

China's saving exceeds its domestic investment and the gap is predicted to persist. China should, therefore, continue to run current account surpluses, while the US runs deficits. We should also expect that, over the long term, the US dollar will depreciate and China's *renminbi* (RMB) will appreciate. That trend will make business assets in the rest of the world cheaper for Chinese companies and more expensive for US ones. China will be investing in foreign business assets a rising share of increasing current account surpluses, using a currency increasing in value.

The inevitable result of China's path of gradual deregulation and integration into the global economy is that Chinese multinationals will, within a decade or two, be as pervasive and dominant as US, European, Japanese and Korean multinationals are today. The global economy is unprepared for this transformation. Unlike trade in goods and services, there is no agreed multinational framework of rules for foreign investments, no forum in which rules are made and disputes settled. Instead, over 5,500 bilateral and regional agreements attempt in various ways to set the rules for foreign direct investment.

China's fast-increasing importance in outward FDI makes the current negotiation of a free trade agreement between China and Australia an interesting marker for one of the great trends in the global economy in coming decades. It will be the first FTA China has negotiated with an Organization for Economic Co-operation and Development economy (other than the companion talks with New Zealand).

Australia has things Chinese companies want to own. Under current investment rules, however, Chinese investment in Australia encounters considerably more obstacles than US investment. Australia demands that every investment proposal from a government-controlled entity undergo inspection by its Foreign Investment Review Board[①]. Since many Chinese businesses have government ownership stakes, the requirement is onerous. Even where the business is not government-owned, Australia requires a FIRB notification for all investment proposals of more than $50m. Effectively, all Chinese investment proposals must be reviewed. For US investment, only takeovers worth more than $800m need be notified and a greenfield development needs no FIRB approval at all.

Australia will change its rules for China. How it changes them, and what China is prepared to concede in return, will hint at the shape of bigger and broader agreements to accommodate the new giant in multinational business.

---

① 外国投资人审查委员会，简称 FIRB

Words and Expressions

deregulate [ˌdiːˈregjuleɪt] *v.* 解除管制
sterilization [ˌsterɪlaɪˈzeɪʃn] *n.* 本外币对冲
manipulate [məˈnɪpjuleɪt] *vt.* 操作,控制,手持
mitigate [ˈmɪtɪgeɪt] *v.* 镇静减轻,缓和缓和下来,减轻
pervasive [pəˈveɪsɪv] *adj.* 遍布的,弥漫的,渗透的
entity [ˈentɪtɪ] *n.* 实体;存在;统一性
onerous [ˈɒnərəs] *adj.* 繁重的,费力的;负有法律责任的
greenfield *adj.* 未开发地区的,农村地区的
be constrained by 受到……的制约
subject to 在……影响之下,使服从,从属于

Exercises

Exercise 1 Choose the best answer for each of the following questions.

1. China is the world's ________ biggest economy, but when it comes to business investment in other countries it is a ________ player.
   A. first; big B. second; small C. third; small D. fourth; big
2. What will be conducive to the higher foreign direct investment flow from China?
   A. Gradually deregulated financial system.
   B. The accumulation of vast reserves.
   C. China's current account surpluses.
   D. All the above.
3. Which of the following is true according to the text?
   A. The stock of China's direct investment abroad in 2005 was one fifth that of the US.
   B. It will be many decades before Chinese businesses own more assets abroad than those of any other nation.
   C. Chinese investment in Australia encounters considerably less obstacles than US investment.
   D. China's saving exceeds its domestic investment and the gap is predicted to persist.
4. Chinese multinationals can consult ________ in the course of their foreign direct investment.
   A. multinational framework of rules
   B. some forums in which rules are made and disputes settled
   C. previous bilateral and regional agreements
   D. nothing

Exercise 2　Fill in each of the blanks with the appropriate words given. Change the form of the word when necessary.

spur　accumulate　transform　bilateral　inspect　persistent

1. He is much careful of the ________ of knowledge.
2. We will continue to cement our friendly ties with our neighbors and ________ in building a good-neighborly relationship and partnership with them.
3. Economically, the two countries have carried out pragmatic cooperation and witnessed ________ trade volume increasing year by year.
4. The scope includes the capability to perform the required ________, test or calibration.
5. Governments cut interest rates to ________ demand.
6. Socialist ________ is a twofold task, one is to transform the system and the other to transform man.

Exercise 3　Translate the following sentences into English.

1. 他在股票交易中买卖精明，赚了很多钱。(manipulate)
2. 2008年，中国投资者的非金融领域对外直接投资额达407亿美元，比上年增长63.6%。(foreign direct investment)
3. 个人和企业是依法存在的对等的独立实体。(entity)

Text 42 Things Are Looking Lovelier for Lenovo

联想:柳暗花明又一村

导读 联想2005年以总值12.5亿美元的现金和股票收购IBM的PC部门,成为继戴尔和惠普之后全球第三大PC供应商。并购后,来自对手公司Dell的联想新CEO威廉·阿梅里奥走马上任,新官上任三把火,通过裁员、重新定位、降低成本等一系列措施,顺利度过艰难险阻的"后悔"期,在短短的一年多时间内,联想的毛利润由14%上升到14.3%,股票上升3.6%,在美国的市场份额由3.9%上升到4.2%,柳暗花明又一村,联想又进入了平稳发展阶段。

Acquisition of IBM's PC division hasn't been smooth for the Chinese computer maker, but a new product mix and big box sales have helped.

It has been a wild year for Lenovo, the Chinese computer maker that last year made a splash by taking over IBM's PC division. The acquisition made Lenovo a global leader among Chinese companies and catapulted China's No. 1 computer brand into contention for the top spot among global PC makers, trailing only Dell and Hewlett Packard. ①

But digesting the former IBM unit hasn't been easy. After only a few months with an IBMer at the helm, the company brought in a new chief executive, William Amelio, from Dell. He came in focused on cutting costs and repositioning Lenovo to compete against his old company. Even as Lenovo had to contend with aggressive price cuts from Dell, Amelio and his team had to look over their shoulders at Acer, the No. 4 in the global ranks.

Lenovo also lost market share in the US and other non-Chinese markets. Even before the Lenovo takeover, the IBM business had been struggling, and the transition seemed to accelerate the slide. Investors weren't happy: Lenovo's Hong Kong-listed shares dropped 40 percent from December to June. "There was talk that Lenovo was experienc-ing serious buyer's remorse," says Martin Kariithi, an analyst with Technology Business Research, a market watcher based in New Hampshire.

STREAMLINING. Then on Aug. 3, Lenovo announced its second-quarter results, which appear to show that the heartburn from IBM is abating. Lenovo reported sales were up 11 percent, to $3.46 billion. Net profit was $5 million—not great, but more than double the previous quarter. Restructuring costs were lower than expected, and Lenovo is regaining market share in the US, China, and elsewhere. The company's stock price

---

① 这次并购使联想成为中国电脑行业的领头羊,并且跻身于世界私人电脑行业季军,仅次于戴尔和惠普。

jumped 3.6 percent in Thursday trading in Hong Kong following the announcement, a reflection of the good feeling many now have about the company.

What's behind the turnaround? For starters, Amelio has lowered costs by eliminating 5 percent of Lenovo's workforce, or some 1,000 positions. More important, that's 10 percent of the company's non-China workforce, says Ho, a sign that Lenovo is dumping high-cost employees it inherited from IBM and instead focusing on lower-cost China.

All of those job cuts hurt the bottom line[①] in the short term, with Lenovo reporting $147 million in restructuring costs for the quarter. But in an Aug. 4 report, Deutsche Bank analyst William Bao Bean writes that the number is better than what he had expected. According to Bean, "Lenovo is on the right track."

PRODUCT MIX. Another good sign for Lenovo is that it's starting to see the results of a move to diversify its US lineup. Early this year, the company launched a new range of PCs, using the Lenovo name rather than IBM's Think brand, targeted at small- and mid-sized businesses in the US, a market IBM had largely ignored.

To better reach that segment, Lenovo has expanded sales to big box retailers such as Best Buy and Office Depot. That has helped Lenovo reverse its slide in US market share, moving from 3.9 percent in the first quarter to 4.2 percent in the second. The product mix is improving, too, with growing sales of more profitable notebooks leading to gross margins of 14.3 percent, up from 14 percent in the previous quarter.

There's still a long way to go. Even with the rebound in market share, Lenovo faces a rough road in the US, where rivals are fighting hard for old IBM customers who might have reservations about switching to a PC maker from China. And Lenovo is particularly vulnerable to a Dell-inspired price war, says Kirk Yang, a managing director with Citigroup in Hong Kong.

MATCHING PRICE CUTS. Dell is slashing prices by as much as 22 percent, with buyers saving an average of $100 per machine. Lenovo's US customer base is similar to Dell's (both are strong with corporations and consumers) while HP and Acer focus more on small- and mid-size businesses.

So "Lenovo has to match Dell's price cuts," says Yang, who says he's uncertain whether the Chinese company will be able to make the old IBM unit a success. "So far, Lenovo management hasn't shown that they can consistently make money from the business, particularly in the US."

LOOKING UP. To compensate, Lenovo is probably going to be pushing even harder in its Asian backyard. The company is well-positioned to use its experience in China to grow in the other emerging giant, India, says Joseph Ho, an analyst with Daiwa Institute of Research in Hong Kong. "Lenovo is going to hit the Indian market," he predicts.

Lenovo's sales there are still tiny, but that will change, he says, adding that Lenovo

---

① 最终赢利,损益表底线

has an advantage over Dell, because Indians are not used to buying PCs online. When people aren't accustomed to e-commerce, "the Dell online purchasing model doesn't work," he says. "India is a big positive for Lenovo." That's down the road, though. For now, the key markets are China and the US And after a year of difficulty, they're starting to look better for Lenovo.

Words and Expressions

catapult [ˈkætəpʌlt] *v.* 弹升;迅速成名
remorse [rɪˈmɔːs] *n.* 懊恼,遗憾
streamline [ˈstriːmlaɪn] *v.* 精简机构
heartburn [ˈhɑːtbəːn] *n.* 烧心,消化不良
abate [əˈbeɪt] *v.* 减少
turnaround [ˈtəːnəˌraund] *n.* 彻底的转变
lineup [ˈlaɪnʌp] *n.* 产品阵容;节目安排
reservation [rezəˈveiʃən] *n.* 保留意见
vulnerable [ˈvʌlnərəbəl] *adj.* 易受伤的,无防御能力的
make a splash 引起轰动
at the helm 掌权
look over one's shoulders at 小心提防

Exercises

Exercise 1 Choose the best answer for each of the following questions.

1. Which of the following statements is not true concerning Lenovo's acquisition of IBM's PC?
   A. The acquisition of IBM's PC hasn't been smooth for Lenovo.
   B. Levono lost market share in the US markets after this acquisition.
   C. After the acquisition, Lenovo still targets at the strong corporations and ignores the SMEs.
   D. After the acquisition, Lenovo has become the world's third largest PC makers.
2. What made Lenovo gain the turnaround?
   A. Job cuts.
   B. The launch of a new range of PCs.
   C. Cooperations with big box retailers.
   D. All of the above.
3. Lenovo is going to attach more importance to the markets in ________.
   A. Asia B. Africa C. Europe D. South America

Exercise 2 Fill in each of the blanks with the appropriate words given. Change the form of the word when necessary.

abate dump at the helm buyer's remorse turnaround

1. All the group members believe that with Mrs Smith ________, they will certainly make great margins.
2. Due to the New Policy by Roosevelt in 1933, the social suffering from the Great Depression had ________ a lot.
3. The change of leader led to a ________ in the fortunes of the Labor Party.
4. The ________ of goods to foreign countries is prohibited by law, because it can severely affect the sales of home manufacturers.
5. As to some corporations, if they are blindly crazy at acquisition of other companies regardless of the efficiency, they may probably encounter the ________.

Exercise 3 Translate the following sentences into English.

1. 虽然海尔企图收购美泰以失败告终,但不可否认的是,这一事件在美国已经引起轰动。(make a splash)
2. 考虑到可持续发展战略对整个国民经济有极大地促进作用,我们毫无保留地支持这些措施。(without reservation)
3. 当下,有很多公司都采用精简机构的方案来减少自己的开支。(streamline)

Text 43 Haier Withdraws from Maytag Bid

海尔退出竞购美泰克

导读 近几年来，有关中国并购海外企业的新闻逐渐多了起来：联想收购IBM全球个人电脑业务、TCL集团合并了法国老牌家电厂商汤姆逊的彩电业务，组建了全球最大的彩电帝国。这一连串的动作，使得美国《商业周刊》都不禁惊呼：中国正在走向并购时代。在这一轮中国公司全球并购浪潮中，海尔集团也不甘落后：美国时间2005年6月21日，经过长时间的酝酿和考虑后海尔终于亮出了自己的初步收购美国第三大家电巨头美泰克公司的计划。然而一个月后美泰克就宣布：海尔及其合作伙伴贝思资本和黑石集团正式退出了对美泰克的竞购。全球第一白色家电巨头惠而普最终以每股17美元总价13.7亿美元击败海尔每股16美元的竞购。事后，专家分析海尔竞购失败原因之一是过于谨慎、出手缓慢，美泰克公司是一家价值47亿美元的美国家电巨头，旗下具有美泰克，Hoover，Jenn-Air与Amana等白色家电与小家电世界著名品牌。

Haier Group, China's largest home appliance manufacturer, has withdrawn from the contest to acquire US firm Maytag Corp.[①], according to the latter's website on Tuesday. Maytag, the third largest appliance maker in the US, said it had received a letter from Haier America Trading[②] and its partners, Bain Capital Partners LLC and Blackstone Management Associates[③], saying "they have determined not to further pursue the transaction to acquire the outstanding shares of Maytag." The $16 per share bid from the Haier-led consortium on June 21 was topped earlier this week by Whirlpool's $17 offer, totaling $1.37 billion. Maytag's board will meet later this week to decide if it wants to pursue Whirlpool's offer, according to sources. In May, an investor group led by Ripplewood, a New York-based private equity firm, submitted a bid to buy Maytag for $1.1 billion, or $14 a share. A month later, Haier, Bain and Blackstone offered a $1.28-billion bid, which Maytag immediately said it would consider. Haier, based in east China's Shandong Province declined to comment on the withdrawal, saying the firm "cannot provide any

---

① 美泰克，美国家电市场的第三大企业。以生产真空吸尘器著称，但该公司近年来经营情况每况愈下。

② 海尔美国公司，它由海尔与美国当地经验丰富的家电经销商Mike Jemal在2001年合作成立，专门在美国销售海尔冰箱、空调和其他家电。还在南卡罗来纳州建立了制造工厂，保证产品的零售供应。

③ 贝恩资本以及黑石集团美国两家知名私募基金。海尔当时是联合这两大集团向美泰提出收购计划的。

information at the current stage" and neither Blackstone nor Bain could be reached. Wei Huawei, a senior consultant with Beijing Fore-sight Innovation Consulting Co. Ltd., said it was a pity and a big loss for Haier to lose the deal. He said the successful purchase of Maytag would have given Haier—already a household name in its home market—instant brand recognition in overseas markets where it has been trying to expand. Wei thought Haier's acquisition attempt was "too cautious and too slow." Maytag is a $4.7 billion home and commercial appliance company focused on North America and certain international markets. Its brands include Maytag, Hoover, Jenn-Air and Amana. It is the third-largest US appliance maker behind Whirlpool and General Electric. With an increasing number of Chinese enterprises going abroad, more and more of them are participating in global acquisition campaigns. Successful cases include computer maker Lenovo's purchase of IBM's PC business and TCL Multimedia's purchase of the TV-making assets of France's Thomson①.

Words and Expressions

consortium [kən'sɔːtɪəm] *n.* 联营企业,财团

Exercises

Exercise 1 Choose the best answer for each of the following questions.

1. According to the passage who won this bid for Maytag?
   A. Haier. B. Ripplewood.
   C. Whirlpool. D. Blackstone.
2. Which of the following statement is not true, according to the passage?
   A. Maytag is a home and commercial appliance company in America.
   B. It was a pity and a big loss for Haier to lose Maytag bid.
   C. Maytag, Hoover, Jenn-Air and Amana are all appliance companies in America.
   D. Today more and more Chinese enterprises participate in global acquisition campaigns.

Exercise 2 Fill in each of the blanks with the appropriate words given. Change the form of the word when necessary.

consortium submit cautious pursue purchase decline

1. The government has been ________ in its response to the report.
2. It is the Anglo-French ________ that built the Channel Tunnel.

---

① 2004年1月28日,TCL与汤姆逊签订了正式的合作合同;同年7月29日,TCL与法国汤姆逊合资组建的全球最大彩电企业TCL——汤姆逊电子有限公司。

3. We intend to ________ this policy with determination.

4. Completed projects must be ________ by 10 March.

5. There has been a sharp ________ in the interest in buying the houses.

6. ________ refers to an organization intending to acquire goods or services to meet the needs of business.

Exercise 3 Translate the following sentences into English.

1. 报纸第二天发表了撤销声明。

2. 他们在几个欧盟国家购买了一些产业。

Text 44 3Com Deal Check over Security Concerns
华为入股 3Com 美国政府忧心忡忡

导读 华为科技联手美国私募股权公司贝恩资本斥资22亿美元全面收购3Com公司；贝恩资本将持股83.5%，华为将持股16.5%。3Com公司董事会已批准此宗交易，但此交易还须经过美国"外国投资委员会"的国家安全审查。阻碍此交易的障碍是3Com的Tipping Point网络入侵防御系统产品，该产品可以检测网络传输的数据包是合法的还是恶意的，以防止遭受攻击。美国政府对此交易忧心忡忡，因为包括美国国防部在内的很多政府机构都是Tipping Point的客户。

Washington is expected to scrutinize on national security grounds yesterday's joint acquisition of 3Com, the US networking group, by Huawei Technologies, a Chinese telecoms equipment maker, and Bain Capital, the US private equity[①] firm.

The deal is worth \$2.2bn in cash. Bain will take a stake of more than 80 percent, while Huawei's ownership will remain below 20 percent, insiders said.

Among 3Com's products is an "intrusion prevention" technology[②] that helps clients, including the US defence department, defend themselves against hackers.

Bryan Whitman, a Pentagon spokesman, said he was "not aware of any concern" over Huawei taking a stake in 3Com.

But Sami Saydjari, a former Pentagon cybersecurity expert and currently chief executive of Cyber Defense Agency, said Huawei's ownership of hardware and important network components would be "really worrisome."

"Any Chinese-related deal that touches on government IT systems, even in a minority capacity, is going to be something that the Committee on Foreign Investment[③] looks at closely," said Christopher Simkins, an attorney at Covington & Burling[④] and former US Justice Department official.

---

① 私募股权，私人股权，它是股权或权益(Equity)的一种，既能发挥融资功能，又能代表投资权益。

② 入侵防御技术，一种比防火墙之类的现有的网络安全解决方案更全面、更智能的检测方法，使用户的网络免受多种类型的网络入侵与攻击。

③ 美国外国投资委员会，它是由财务部主管的内部代理的委员会。

④ 科温顿·柏灵律师事务所

Words and Expressions

scrutinize [ˈskruːtɪnaɪz] *v.* 严密审查;检查或观察以重要关注;

insider [ɪnˈsaɪdə] *n.* 内部的人,知道内情的人,权威人士

take a stake 入股

Exercises

Exercise 1 Choose the best answer for each of the following questions.

1. Washington is expected to scrutinize the joint acquisition of 3Com by Huawei Technology and Bain Capital on grounds of ________.

   A. high return on investment B. national security

   C. business scandals D. a massive cyberattack

2. Sami Saydjari, a former Pentagon cybersecurity expert and currently chief executive of Cyber Defense Agency, regarded Huawei's deal as ________.

   A. a great success

   B. of no concern

   C. really worrisome

   D. meaningless since it was only in a minority capacity

3. The deal will be worth ________ in cash for Huawei.

   A. about $440mn B. about $1.76bn

   C. $2.2bn D. about $2bn

Exercise 2 Fill in each of the blanks with the appropriate words given. Change the form when necessary.

take a stake of acquisition private equity in cash aware of

1. For that world leading corporation, a deal worth $2mn ________ is just nothing particular.
2. In today's competitive marketplace, ________ firms, consultants and mezzanine providers are under unprecedented pressure to structure deals and develop exit strategies that meet or exceed investor expectations.
3. The Ministry of Railways is expected to ________ around 35 percent in a new investment group to finance the Beijing-Shanghai high-speed railway, sources said.
4. For the purpose of the Provisions, mergers and ________ of a domestic enterprise by foreign investors shall mean that foreign investors, by agreement, purchase equity interest from shareholders of domestic enterprise with no foreign investment.
5. The aim of such a match is to make people ________ the problem of poverty.

Exercise 3　Translate the following sentences into English.

1. 据国外媒体报道，微软、AT&T等公司呼吁美国反垄断监管部门严密审查Google收购DoubleClick案。
2. 在恶劣的大环境下，惠普公司宣布，以股权收购方式，收购康柏计算机公司，这一收购案的市值总计250亿美元。
3. 总部设在日本的一家保险公司，于1991年在北京设立代表处，并在去年12月份得到了中国人寿保险公司29%的股份。

Text 45 New Actors Play a Vital Role in the Global Economy
全球化经济中新角色闪亮登场

导读 日前中国工商银行宣布斥资55亿美元收购南非标准银行20%的股权，这无论对非洲和中国而言都是一个里程碑，因为这既是中国公司迄今最大的一笔海外投资，也是非洲最大的一笔外国直接投资。世界资本市场巨资交易通常发生在发达国家之间，偶尔也发生在发达与一些发展中国家之间。此次交易乃是两家新兴市场金融机构之间的一宗重大交易，折射出一个国际经济新趋势正在悄然发生：新角色闪亮登场，他们的新资金、新合作关系终将变革传统的世界资本市场交易模式。

The recent announcement of the Industrial and Commercial Bank of China's $5.5bn investment in 20 percent of Standard Bank of South Africa was a milestone for Africa, and for China. The largest-ever overseas investment by a Chinese company, it is also the largest foreign direct investment in Africa.

Just as remarkable is the fact that this was a major transaction between two emerging markets institutions, reflecting a broader trend in new flows, new actors and new partnerships that is transforming capital markets.

For the past five years we have seen a strong period of global growth and wealth creation driven by the opening of new markets, financial innovation, favorable credit conditions and disciplined corporate management. Perhaps more striking has been the breadth of this growth—across geographies, asset classes and industries. We have one global economy, but it is increasingly powered by multiple engines, with multiple sources of demand and liquidity.

The new flows go beyond the increased investment in emerging markets to include investments from those markets into mature economies, and cross-border investments between emerging economies. Since 1990, cross-border capital flows have grown more than 10 percent annually. Over that period, capital inflows to emerging markets have grown twice as fast as inflows to developed countries. Investment flowing to developing countries now accounts for nearly half of world total FDI inflows, compared with only 20 percent in 1990. Even excluding China, the share doubled to 32 percent.

New actors—be they private equity, hedge funds, sovereign wealth funds, or state-controlled entities—are playing a critical role in driving these new flows. While there is a broad understanding of the role and practices of private equity and hedge funds, there is more uncertainty about the intentions and capabilities of the state-linked funds and companies.

One concern is whether the sovereign wealth funds will want to take controlling stakes in some of these large companies, rather than remain passive minority investors. Another surrounds the transparency of their strategies, practices and investments. Still another is whether political considerations will affect investment decisions—whether, in other words, they will act as a sovereign or as a fund.

While I am confident these concerns can be addressed through increased openness and transparency, sound practices and risk management, it is not evident that there will be a convergence in the character of these funds along a western model, as some are calling for. If anything, there is growing evidence of an emerging plurality of market models around the world, reflected in part by the variety of investment vehicles. Russians, Chinese and certain Gulf states—to mention a few examples—are each practising capitalism in their own distinct way, none of which is identical to the way it is practised in the west. As those models appear to deliver growth and stability, they are less likely to be adapted to a purely western model.

A protectionist response that seeks to restrict investments by these new actors in the global economy, or subject their activities to cumbersome vetting processes, is clearly not the right response. Given the common interest on all sides in maintaining open investment regimes and free trade to sustain global growth, a dialogue involving both governments and the new actors could go a long way towards dispelling myths and creating real transparency.

This emergence of new flows and new actors from new models of capitalism reflects a natural diversity of social and economic practices that is in no way incompatible with the process of globalization. This new ecosystem of global capital is not only generating great opportunities for established investors from both developed and developing countries; it is also, in the case of Africa's attraction for Chinese and Russian investors, presenting an opportunity for the continent to share in the benefits of globalization.

This is not to say that the risks or challenges of investing in emerging markets have disappeared. Nor is it to diminish the importance of maintaining reciprocity of access to markets, and a sound regulatory and legal framework to provide confidence in the rule of law. It is to suggest that the next stage of globalization will likely require the global economy to accommodate a greater diversity of market models if we are to take full advantage of the new flows, new actors and new partnerships that will drive global growth in the future.

Words and Expressions

convergence [kən'vɜːdʒəns] *n.* 汇集，集中

incompatible [ˌɪnkəm'pætəbl] *adj.* 互斥的，相悖的

reciprocity [ˌresɪ'prɒsɪtɪ] *n.* 互惠，互助

the Gulf states 海湾国家

subject to 遭受,经受

Exercises

Exercise 1 Choose the best answer for each of the following questions.

1. Which of the following can not be of use in getting rid of the concern that whether political considerations will affect investment decisions?
   A. Increase of openness and transparency.
   B. Implement of sound practices.
   C. Operation of effective risk management.
   D. Enforcing more restrictions on these investment decisions.
2. What's the right attitude towards the emergence of new flows, new actors and new partnerships?
   A. Restricting these investment by the new actors.
   B. Subjecting their activities to cumbersome vetting processes.
   C. Adapt ourselves to diverse market model.
   D. Setting up more obstacles for these activities.

Exercise 2 Fill in each of the blanks with the appropriate words given. Change the form of the word when necessary.

protect liquid critical sovereign convergence address require reciprocal

1. Financial institution must maintain sufficient ________ to meet the demands of depositors.
2. Reducing levels of carbon dioxide in the atmosphere is of ________ importance.
3. The declaration proclaimed the full ________ of the republic.
4. We must ________ ourselves to the problem of traffic pollution.
5. Thousands of supporters ________ on London for the rally.
6. He has filled all ________ for promotion.
7. The two colleges have a ________ arrangement whereby students from one college can attend classes at the other.
8. The country has a high level of industrial ________.

Exercise 3 Translate the following sentences into English.

1. 世界经济的多元化趋势日益明显。
2. 新经济、新参与者、新合作关系的出现反映出社会和经济行为的自然多样性。

Text 46 Chinese Firms "Not Ready" for Overseas M&As

中国公司海外并购时代尚未到来

导读 Michael Thorneman 就职于一家瑞典并购咨询公司，在过去的 5 年中，平均每年帮助 10 家中国内地企业进行海外收购业务。而令人吃惊的是他竟建议中国公司目前不该走出国门进行海外并购，理由是：全球并购业务每 3 起中就有 2 起是失败的；中国公司因匮乏经验往往准备工作马虎，仓促决策。他提出四大海外并购准则：瞄准正确的目标，知道何时该放弃交易，如需要应联手他人共同出手，应有预防不测的心理准备。

Having spent the last five years in China working on an average of 10 merger and acquisition (M&A) deals every year, Swedish M&A consultant Michael Thorneman, surprisingly, is advising against mergers and acquisitions for mainland companies looking to expand overseas.

Thorneman noted that most Chinese companies are not ready to expand overseas through acquisitions as they have limited experiences of international M&A.

"We should all keep in mind that two out of every three mergers and acquisitions in any geography fail. It is very difficult to successfully acquire and integrate companies," he said.

"This is the big paradox of mergers and acquisitions they are difficult to execute successfully, yet empirical evidence shows that it's extremely hard to keep on growing over a longer period of time if you don't acquire at some point," he said.

The implication is, he noted, that companies have to be fully aware of the challenges posed by acquiring and integrating with other enterprises, as well as of the skills they can bring to bear on the M&A process.

The answer is to be disciplined in decision making and follow four principles: Pick the right target, know when to walk away from a deal, integrate the two companies where it matters and be ready for the unexpected, Thorneman advised.

For Chinese companies that want to venture abroad yet lack experience in international M&A, growing organically may be a better option than to acquire.

"For Chinese companies, one of the most dangerous strategies to pursue is to go global just because of increased competition in your home market or that you are jumping onto a trend.

"The best strategy to pursue is to ensure that they first build a strong position in their core business in the home market before going abroad," he said.

Since Chinese authorities started advocating the "Chinese companies go global" strategy in 2000, a flurry of high-profile global M&A deals made by Chinese companies such as Lenovo, TCL, Haier, CNOOC and CNPC[1] have been sending shockwaves through the worlds of business and politics.

"Generally speaking, the jury is still out on which ones will be successful," said Thorneman, "Lenovo is an example of a Chinese company that has many of the right attributes for succeeding internationally."

Yet even post-merger Lenovo has to face a dizzying array of integration challenges such as limited cost reductions and synergies, according to analysts. The cost reduction possibilities through downsizing seem limited and synergies in integration of procurement between the ex-IBM PCD and the old Lenovo may not be feasible in the near future.

Though the number and size of outbound M&As by Chinese companies is still very small in a global context, it has been growing at a rapid rate in recent years from $600 million in 2000 to more than $8 billion in 2005, according to a recent Bain study quoting the *Asian Venture Capital Journal*.

More outbound M&As by Chinese companies are forecasted in the years ahead as macroeconomic imperatives push China beyond its export-driven model.

Foreign assets in the energy and branded goods sectors are expected to become particularly attractive to Chinese companies.

"Successful acquirers have a clear acquisition strategy, avoid overpaying and build up certain core skills in M&As," Thorneman said.

The same thing can be said for foreign acquirers embarking on inbound investments in China.

Foreign acquirers of Chinese assets fall under two broad categories, Thorneman noted. The first comprises strategic investors or called "corporate buyers" which are operating companies buying other businesses to expand or defend their market share and build a sustainable market position.

The second comprises private-equity buyers[2], also called "financial buyers," who buy minority or majority stakes in companies to improve their performance with the aim of eventually selling them at a profit.

With 15 years of consulting experience serving private-equity firms, Thorneman is ready to defend the role of private equity firms, which Chinese authorities maintain a cautious stance on. "It is in the best interests of both China and the overall economy to allow both corporate as well as financial investors to have a role in developing the market economy by increasing the competitiveness of Chinese companies," he said.

---

① 中国石油天然气集团公司，它是一家集油气勘探开发、炼油化工、油品销售、油气储运、石油贸易、工程技术服务和石油装备制造于一体的综合性能源公司。

② 私人股权投资指称任何一种股权资产不能在股票市场自由交易的投资。

Foreign corporate investors making acquisitions in China are primarily doing this by having a long-term perspective on the market, said Thorneman.

The corporate transactions in almost all situations are very long-term oriented. As for private equity buyers, "it is a misperception" to regard them as purely "cruel and barbaric" profit takers, said Thorneman.

"Many of the PE firms today are very growth-oriented," he said, "they work both on growing revenue and improving the cost position of the acquired company. When they do sell it, in many instances they sell it to corporate buyers which generally means that the company they bought is now a stronger and better-performing company than it was a few years back."

Words and Expressions

empirical [ɪm'pɪrɪkəl] *adj.*	实证的,以经验为依据的
synergy ['sɪnədʒɪ] *n.*	协同，配合，企业合并后的协力优势
misperception [mɪspə'sepʃən] *n.*	错误知觉
barbaric [bɑː'bærɪk] *adj.*	野蛮的，粗野的，毫无约束的

Exercises

Exercise 1 Choose the best answer for each of the following questions.

1. All of the following statements are false except that ________.
   A. it's estimated that two out of every five mergers and acquisitions in any geography fail
   B. growing organically may be a worse choice than to acquire for Chinese companies that want to venture abroad yet lack experience
   C. Chinese companies' strategy of going global is only for avoiding competition domestically
   D. it's better for companies to set up a strong position in their core business inside before going abroad
2. What did Michael Thorneman advise Chinese company to do well in the M&A process?
   A. To be disciplined in decision making.
   B. To know when to walk away from a deal.
   C. To be ready for the unexpected.
   D. All the above.
3. We can know from the passage that Thorneman's attitude towards present M&As is ________.
   A. positive B. negative C. neutral D. not known

Exercise 2 Fill in each of the blanks with the appropriate words given. Change the form of the word when necessary.

downsizing embark sustainable a flurry of synergy

1. That success was capped by ________ honors, most notably a Billboard award for Top Female Country Artist of 1994 and an Academy of Country Music Award for Favorite New Female.
2. Grove, the president of Intel, producer of the Pentium micro-processors, feels that the new ________ between computers and Net technology will have multiple implications for industry of the future.
3. With the vigorous push and backing of local governments, the enterprises stepped up ________ to improve efficiency.
4. The first Chinese Olympics in history is expected to prompt the country to ________ on a huge infrastructure spending spree.
5. There is also a consensus on the importance of promoting and facilitating ________ economic growth.

Exercise 3 Translate the following sentences into English.

1. 在跨国银行纷纷在中国展开业务的同时,中国本土银行也开始了他们的海外扩张。
2. 在来势汹汹的外资银行面前,中资行需要变被动防守成主动进攻,通过海外扩张发展壮大自己以应对挑战。海外扩张并把外币进行投资,无疑是降低风险的有效途径。
3. 而当下,投资海外以获取资源、能源、品牌以及销售渠道已经成为中国国内企业突破发展瓶颈,解决经济外部失衡的必由之路,中国的银行业也不例外。

Key to the Exercises

Chapter One Stronger China

Text 1 A Less Fiery Dragon

Exercise 1

1. B 2. D 3. D

Exercise 2

1. revision 2. extrapolate 3. accounting for
4. slash 5. has been swung

Exercise 3

1. PPP, rather than market exchange rates, is regarded as a better measure of the relative cost of living, since it is based on goods and services households can buy with their domestic currency.
2. China's share in world's exports reached 8.8 percent by 2007, making it the world's second largest exporter, said the National Statistics Bureau.
3. The European Central Bank have slashed interest rates to 3.25 percent over the past month to prevent deflation from taking hold.

Text 2 Unstoppable yet Unsustainable

Exercise 1

1. D 2. A

Exercise 2

1. be reluctant to 2. leaving out of 3. mete out
4. was conferred to 5. makes for

Exercise 3

1. We sincerely hope that your company can show extraordinary resilience in the face of waves of difficulties and challenges in the future.
2. All multinational companies make expanding the local markets a priority of their development plan.
3. It is effective to stem the corruption through ameliorating an enterprise's internal environment.

Text 3 As China Grows, So Do America's Woes

Exercise 1

1. D 2. A 3. C

Exercise 2

1. stuff 2. tacked on 3. fraction
4. to the forefront 5. fluctuate 6. reversal
7. spiral

Exercise 3

1. The fast development of economy sends China into an upward spiral in the world.
2. His several years' assiduous study in the university and rich work experience helped him accomplish the financial committee's work.
3. As investors digested the layoffs in the financial sector as signs of economic weakness, Wall Street fluctuated today.

Text 4 Get Ready for the Next Big China Effect

Exercise 1

1. A 2. B 3. D

Exercise 2

1. capitalize 2. overhanging 3. hefty
4. sloshing 5. written off

Exercise 3

1. Traditional values have been reasserted.
2. Needless to say, with the copyright law properly implemented and software market properly managed, the piracy problem is bound to be settled.
3. In recent years, more liquidity has been imported into China via huge trade surpluses (running at $20bn a month), plus foreign investment and "hot" money inflows.

Text 5 China Economy: Breathing Fire

Exercise 1

1. D 2. C 3. A

Exercise 2

1. dampen ... down 2. trade surplus with
3. get runaway 4. bullish

Exercise 3

1. Due to the growing flow of cheap Chinese goods into the American market, the Sino-US relation has been increasingly tense.
2. China's foreign exchange reserves, the biggest in the world, have tripled in size from 609.932 bn dollars in 2004 to 1905.5bn dollars in September, 2008.

Text 6 The Rural Roots of China's Economic Miracle

Exercise 1

1. D 2. B

Exercise 2

1. tout 2. privatized 3. be deviated
4. intuitive 5. endorsed 6. counsel

Exercise 3

1. China will succeed or fail not because how many skyscrapers Beijing and Shanghai have but as a result of the economic fortunes of its vast countryside.
2. Grassroots democracy is an effective measure to the village governance.
3. The success of low-tech businesses in rural China will force urban companies to innovate in their production and technology to maintain their competitive edge.

Text 7 Chinese Market Economy Puzzle

Exercise 1

1. B 2. D 3. B

Exercise 2

1. liberalize 2. electronic gadget
3. economic reforms 4. qualify ... for
5. obliged

Exercise 3

1. China's economic status is far better than the academic expectation.
2. Moscow's economic reforms is supposed to get rewarded.
3. China meets all the criteria of a fully-fledged market economy.

Text 8 Bringing Best Practice to China

Exercise 1

1. A 2. D 3. C 4. D 5. C

Exercise 2

1. incur 2. procurement 3. endemic
4. inventory 5. impeded

Exercise 3

1. An enterprise has to incur certain costs and expenses in order to stay in business.
2. The inflexibility of the country's labor market seriously impede its economic recovery.
3. They hit upon another idea to augment their income.
4. Hedge can help them offset inventory loss when commodity price fall.

Text 9 Spending Time

Exercise 1

1. C 2. A 3. D

Exercise 2

1. spill over 2. sharp drop 3. market slump
4. implement 5. pessimistic outlook

Exercise 3

1. What sort of slowdown China experiences during the next few years remains unclear.
2. The sector of the economy that will inevitably suffer is exports, which have been one of the principal drivers of economic growth in recent years.
3. Chinese government has more room for maneuver than most others responding to a slowing economy.

Chapter Two China, Inc.

Text 10 China's Firms Set Sights on World

Exercise 1

1. D 2. C 3. C 4. D 5. D

Exercise 2

1. bankrolling 2. sharp jump 3. shortage
4. backdrop 5. wholesaling

Exercise 3

1. The number of US visas issued to Chinese executives and managers who transfer to US posts within their companies nearly doubled.
2. Chinese leaders worry about the political impact in a society where families spend up to half their incomes on food.
3. Chinese firms are still learning the kinds of data-driven market analysis.

Text 11 Chinese Firms Make "Startling Progress" in Productivity

Exercise 1

1. D 2. C 3. D 4. A

Exercise 2

1. startling 2. outpace 3. adopt 4. lumber
5. pose 6. restructure

Exercise 3

1. The principle of the cooperation of P&G and Wal-Mart is collaboration, planning, forecasting and replenishment.
2. Domestic private Chinese firms and joint ventures exhibit productivity growth that outpaces foreign firms.
3. Toyota is a famous enterprise with strong international competitiveness. His sale scale and profit ability take a leadership in the world auto manufacturers.

Text 12 China's Champions "Run Risks Overseas"

Exercise 1

1. D 2. B 3. A

Exercise 2

1. margins 2. singled out 3. acquired
4. recommendations

Exercise 3

1. This year, the revenues of this country's tourism only amounts to $15bn, while the US has more than 10 times the number.
2. China's outward investment is only a small fraction of its inward foreign direct investment.
3. Many colleges underinvest in the research of science and technology, failing to take advantage of opportunities to develop into world-class universities.

Text 13 Companies: Cultural Confusion What Goes Around Comes Around. It's China's Turn.

Exercise 1

1. C 2. D

Exercise 2

1. nuance 2. plummeted 3. hands-off
4. haggled ... with 5. gobbled up

Exercise 3

1. Lenovo's acquisition of IBM's PC division turns out to be a lucrative investment.
2. The Chinese companies going global can know the ropes of local market in foreign land through market research.
3. This state-owned enterprise faced insolvency as a result of their improper management.

Text 14 The Chinese Are Coming; Expanding Chinese Companies Have Finally Discovered the Old World.

Exercise 1

1. D 2. C 3. D

Exercise 2

1. grabbed 2. foray 3. snap up
4. Dignitaries 5. flagging

Exercise 3

1. Chinese government has been prodding its enterprises to look overseas, build global brands and tap into foreign know-how.
2. Since opening to the outside world, Chinese private-owned enterprises have sprung up.

3. In the past few years, the city's Chinese population has surged from just a few hundred to some 10,000 and more than 2,000 Chinese-owned enterprises have helped revive Prato's flagging textile industry.

Text 15 Don't Know Li-Ning? Ask Shaq!

Exercise 1

1. C 2. D 3. D

Exercise 2

1. concession 2. Accessories 3. run-up
4. rolled out 5. rounded out 6. lower-end

Exercise 3

1. He rounded out the tour with a concert at his hometown.
2. Considering the different income brackets of their customers, they put a style of low-end product on the market this year.
3. All of the sportswear companies count on entering Chinese market in the wake of the country's successfully bid to hold the 2008 Beijing Olympic Games.

Text 16 Chinese Bank Knocks Citigroup off Top Spot

Exercise 1

1. C 2. B

Exercise 2

1. hits record high 2. overtake 3. steep rise
4. shortage of

Exercise 3

1. Some analysts pointed out that the annual report of OECD was not quite satisfactory and sparked fears among people.
2. The turnover of Wal-Marts' overtook other supermarkets, ranking No. 1 in the world.
3. Undeniably, misallocation of resources will greatly affect the process of economic development.

Text 17 ALIBABA.COM IPO: Magic-Carpet Ride

Exercise 1

1. A 2. D 3. D

Exercise 2

1. tap 2. shoestring 3. secure 4. eponymous
5. add-on 6. stampede 7. storefront 8. yarns

Exercise 3

1. The company was floated on the stock market in 1995 and has been working very well since then.
2. The study is the cornerstone of the whole research program. So we have to do lots of initial work to ensure its proper working.
3. We need to tap the expertise and skill of the people we already have. Only in this way can we secure a place in the market in the fierce competition.

Text 18 Lenovo Says It Proves China's Products Are Among World's Best

Exercise 1

1. D 2. D 3. A

Exercise 2

1. language proficiency 2. credited to
3. high-profile 4. impressed by 5. boom
6. layoffs

Exercise 3

1. Worldsourcing is mainly identified as finding the most talented and innovative people.
2. Lenovo has expanded its industrial scale all over the world with centers of innovation in Beijing, Japan and North Carolina in America.
3. Integrated Microelectronic Inc. is looking to increase its facilities in China and to expand its market share in Vietnam although there hasn't been any given timetable.

Text 19 How Corporate China Is Evolving

Exercise 1

1. D 2. D 3. C

Exercise 2

1. straddle 2. vestige 3. spectrum 4. stark
5. shuffle

Exercise 3

1. Businesses vied with each other to attract customers.
2. The firm's payroll has one field for gross pay and one for net pay.
3. My wife spent money without stint.

Chapter Three Made in China

Text 20 A Year Without "Made in China"

Exercise 1

1. A 2. C 3. B

Exercise 2

1. trumped 2. erupted 3. meet his match
4. chaos 5. coated

Exercise 3

1. He knows where he stands on the matter.
2. We hit the first rut in the road when we found all matches already wet.
3. We didn't fool ourselves into thinking we'd bring back a single job to unplugged company towns in Ohio and Georgia.

Text 21 Made-in-China Christmas for Americans

Exercise 1

1. B 2. A 3. D

Exercise 2

1. live it up 2. toil 3. were adorned
4. churned out 5. collectively

Exercise 3

1. Even the White House now celebrates a made-in-China Christmas.
2. Two-thirds of the farmers in the surrounding countryside have left the land to become part of Yiwu's mega-export machine.
3. More than 7,000 farmers from that village collectively manufactured some 100 million Christmas decorations for exports in 2004, earning close to $48.3 million.

Text 22 Made by America in China

Exercise 1

1. B 2. A

Exercise 2

1. transformations 2. sizzling 3. the bulk of
4. excel at 5. lopsided

Exercise 3

1. The Chinese-American economic relationship is becoming as complex as the two countries security relationship.
2. China has to buy more products from abroad to feed its skyrocketing economy.
3. The United States should recognize that it has a trade deficit because it spends beyond its means.

Text 23 China's New Model Army

Exercise 1

1. C 2. C 3. B

Exercise 2

1. boasting of 2. head-on 3. debut
4. burgeoning 5. sets the bar high

Exercise 3

1. Europe's crowded mid-size car segment will get an exotic new entrant.
2. China's burgeoning car industry seeks to follow Japanese and Korean producers into the rich but saturated markets of the developed world.
3. HSO is deliberately setting the bar high by launching this new car in Germany, Europe's largest car market.

Text 24 Made in China Labels Don't Tell the Whole Story

Exercise 1

1. C 2. D 3. D

Exercise 2

1. distortion 2. out of step 3. render
4. assembly

Exercise 3

1. In fact, China is the world's biggest final as-

sembly shop with minimal local added value.

2. The rate of unemployment in US manufacturing has been increasing year by year, which is because of impressive productivity gains.

Text 25 Nations Dust off Their Antidumping Duties in Response to Chinese Pricing

Exercise 1

1. B 2. A 3. D 4. C

Exercise 2

1. designate 2. antidumping duties 3. reverse
4. levy 5. energy-saving

Exercise 3

1. Countries official blocks on imports have fallen to record lows, although that trend seems to be reversing as complaints against unfair competition from China increase.
2. With rising complaints from its companies against China, the US has opened a new front that the EU may follow.
3. So far the EU, although it is watching the US case closely and reviewing its own use of trade defense instruments, has not followed suit with a countervailing duty case.

Text 26 Mattel Apologizes to the Chinese People

Exercise 1

1. D 2. C 3. D 4. A

Exercise 3

1. flaws 2. shoddy 3. testimonies
4. volte-face 5. humiliating

Exercise 4

1. Mattel was forced to deliver a humiliating public apology to the Chinese people on Friday.
2. Mattel's volte-face had been driven by a need to build bridges with Beijing.
3. Mattel, which has been making toys in Asia for several decades, has been considered a model for how to outsource manufacturing.

Text 27 From "Made in China" to "Invented by China"

Exercise 1

1. C 2. D 3. B

Exercise 2

1. drive down 2. deep-seated 3. inhibit
4. striking out

Exercise 3

1. In university circles there is common agreement that the greatest barrier to academic development is the improper interference of the government.
2. With its Confucian heritage, China places great emphasis on education, but there is also a heavy deference towards authority.
3. On top of these obstacles, Chinese innovation faces the further threat of intellectual property theft.

Text 28 The Future of Chinese Global Brands

Exercise 1

1. C 2. B 3. C 4. A 5. D

Exercise 2

1. overwhelming 2. sponsor 3. propelled
4. merger

Exercise 3

1. China remains the world's second-largest economy, but in terms of per capita gross domestic product, it is only 9.8 percent of the size of the US, according to the research.
2. PPP is regarded as a better measure of the relative cost of living, since it is based on goods and services households can buy with their domestic currency.
3. US consumers were shying away from the shops.

Chapter Four China's Buying

Text 29 China Digs for Raw Materials to Sustain Fast Growth

Exercise 1

1. B 2. A 3. B 4. D

Exercise 2

1. foray 2. unleashed 3. havoc 4. kick-start 5. elusive

Exercise 3

1. Last year's profits were swelled by a fall in production cost.
2. Electricity, gas and water were considered to be natural monopolies.
3. The case continues to reverberate throughout the financial world.

Text 30 Ramping up Investment All Round

Exercise 1

1. B 2. B 3. D 4. C

Exercise 2

1. on top of 2. in turn 3. is blessed with 4. laid the ground 5. been given a degree of

Exercise 3

1. The new bonds have been oversubscribed.
2. Annual pay increases will be in line with inflation.
3. In some respects, the most powerful operators in the energy are the energy companies themselves.

Text 31 Airbus in $ 17.4b Deal with China

Exercise 1

1. C 2. B

Exercise 2

1. negotiated 2. security 3. separatist 4. forged 5. deterioration 6. boosts

Exercise 3

1. The candidate addressed the audience in an eloquent speech on the meeting.
2. Ultimately, the two parties signed the contract after their negotiation.
3. After one-year period of research and development, the new machine has gone into service since last October.

Text 32 Ultra-luxury Cars Enjoy Fast Sales Growth in China

Exercise 1

1. A 2. B 3. D

Exercise 2

1. boost 2. lure 3. staggering 4. immense 5. debut

Exercise 3

1. A partner of Chrysler and Fiat, Chery is widely seen to have the strongest research and development capability, with the biggest lineup among Chinese carmakers.
2. Most Chinese car brands have been making rapid progress in recent years as a result of rising prosperity and the consequent increase in vehicle demand in the world's most populous countries.
3. Commenting on such pompous boasts, an analyst of US auto consultancy CSM says, "They are only trying to grab publicity."

Text 33 China's Hunger for Luxury Goods Grows

Exercise 1

1. B 2. A 3. D 4. B

Exercise 2

1. escalated 2. prestige 3. sprung up 4. extravagance 5. rumpled

Exercise 3

1. Chinese consumers are increasingly willing to buy big-ticket items like houses or cars on installment.
2. Another result of China's comparative lack of knowledge about luxury brands is that foreign brands not considered luxury brands in their home markets may be considered luxury in China.

Text 34 China Border Town: Gateway to Cheap Vietnam Resources

Exercise 1

1. C 2. C

Exercise 2

1. tiny 2. heralds 3. autonomous 4. rumble
5. boosts

Exercise 3

1. China enjoys every advantage for closer economic cooperation and trade ties with ASEAN countries.
2. With an economy roaring ahead at more than 10 percent a year, China needs more and more raw materials.
3. Many trucks chock-a-block with Chinese-made machinery and automobile parts rumble across Puzhai, a tiny border town, which takes on a busy scene.

Text 35 Coffee Sales Booming in China

Exercise 1

1. B 2. D 3. B

Exercise 2

1. instant coffee 2. consumption
3. First-mover advantage

Exercise 3

1. As the rock rolled down, it gathered momentum.
2. These measures can spur the consumption as well as the local economy.

Text 36 Formidable China Effect Keeps the Commodity Bulls Running

Exercise 1

1. C 2. B

Exercise 2

1. pops up 2. correlation 3. compelling
4. expires 5. come on stream

Exercise 3

1. More and more investors intend to apply hedge against inflation.
2. After the steepest development of economy, then levels off and tilts to the service.
3. The formidable China effect has become a compelling power in the world's economy.

Text 37 China's Surging Coal Demand Leaves Costly Queues at Australian Port

Exercise 1

1. D 2. A 3. D

Exercise 2

1. recriminate 2. constraint 3. veteran
4. flummox

Exercise 3

1. The rail system and the coal loading capacity have not got to work in harmony, which has been one of the reasons of bottleneck problem.
2. Quotas do have helped reduce queues, but some people hold the idea that they basically subsidise inefficient production.
3. Unlike many state-controlled ports in emerging markets such as India, Newcastle runs as a private operation.

Chapter Five China's M&A

Text 38 China Goes Shopping

Exercise 1

1. D 2. A 3. D 4. C

Exercise 2

1. assets 2. forego 3. was itching to
4. bid/bidden for 5. Equity

Exercise 3

1. With deep-pocketed Chinese crowding the auction rooms, sellers have less to fear from retreating private equity firms.
2. Haier Group had raised its bidding price for US Maytag Corp. to $2.25 billion from the previous $1.28 billion.
3. You must be happy. You've been itching to go on a business trip for months.

Text 39 Hey, Big Spender

Exercise 1

1. A 2. C 3. B 4. B

Exercise 2

1. incentives 2. hotbed 3. drum up
4. on a par with 5. moderate 6. foothold

Exercise 3

1. The bright outlook of China's outward investment was hailed by many pundits.
2. The two primary motivations for Chinese companies considering foreign mergers and acquisitions (M&As) are to expand overseas market share and to acquire technology expertise.

Text 40 From Tiny Workshop to Shining Light of a Dynamic Sector

Exercise 1

1. C 2. D 3. C

Exercise 2

1. denounced 2. notched up 3. eroded
4. squeezed 5. revamp

Exercise 3

1. Exports in this year will break through the $1bn mark.
2. In order to win business from the likes of General Motors(GM) and Ford, Wanxiang has to invest in new machinery and revamp its manufacturing processes.
3. Over the past year, Wanxiang has been involved in negotiations with Delphi, the bankrupt parts supplier that used to be a GM subsidiary, and provide components for Ford.

Text 41 We Must Prepare for the March of China's Giants

Exercise 1

1. B 2. D 3. D 4. C

Exercise 2

1. accumulation 2. persist 3. bilateral
4. inspection 5. spur 6. transformation

Exercise 3

1. His clever manipulation of the stock markets makes him lots of money.
2. In 2008, the overseas direct investment (non-financial sectors) by Chinese investors was $40.7 billion, up by 63.6 percent over the previous year.
3. Persons and corporations are equivalent entities under the law.

Text 42 Things Are Looking Lovelier for Lenovo

Exercise 1

1. C 2. D 3. A

Exercise 2

1. at the helm 2. abated 3. turnaround
4. dumping 5. buyer's remorse

Exercise 3

1. Although Haier has failed to acquire Meitai, yet undoubtedly, this has made a splash throughout the US.
2. Concerning that the sustainable development strategy can greatly accelerate the national economy, we're in favor of it without reservation.
3. Nowadays, many corporations cut their operating cost by streamlining.

Text 43 Haier Withdraws from Maytag Bid

Exercise 1

1. C 2. C

Exercise 2

1. cautious 2. consortium 3. pursue
4. submitted 5. decline 6. Purchasing

Exercise 3

1. The newspaper published a withdrawal the next day.
2. They have made acquisition in several EU countries.

Text 44 3Com Deal Check over Security Concerns

Exercise 1

1. B 2. C 3. A

Exercise 2

1. in cash 2. private equity
3. take a stake of 4. acquisition 5. aware of

Exercise 3

1. It was reported by overseas media that companies such as Microsoft and AT&T appealed to US Anti-monopoly Supervision Department to scrutinize Google's acquisition of DoubleClick.
2. In the depressed condition, HP Company proclaimed to acquire Compaq Computer Company, which totally cost $25bn.
3. The Japan-based insurer, which set up its Beijing representative office in 1991, took a 29 percent stake in PICC Life Insurance Company last December.

Text 45 New Actors Play a Vital Role in the Global Economy

Exercise 1

1. D 2. C

Exercise 2

1. liquidity 2. critical 3. sovereignty
4. address 5. converged 6. requirements
7. reciprocal 8. protectionism

Exercise 3

1. World economic diversification has become an increasingly obvious trend.
2. The emergence of new flows, new actors and new partnerships reflect a natural diversity of social and economic practices.

Text 46 Chinese Firms "Not Ready" for Overseas M&As

Exercise 1

1. D 2. D 3. B

Exercise 2

1. a flurry of 2. synergy 3. downsizing
4. embarking 5. sustainable

Exercise 3

1. China's banks are launching overseas expansion projects while multinational banks vie to start operations in China.
2. Confronted with foreign banks keen on securing larger stakes in the Chinese market, Chinese banks have to get stronger through investing overseas, and it's undoubtedly an effective way to lower risks.
3. It has been a must choice for Chinese enterprises eager to overcome their development bottleneck to invest overseas in order to obtain resources, energies, brand influence and sales channels, and the banking sector is no exception.